SECRET AT THE WATER'S
Edge

E.W. BRENT

Dedication

This book is dedicated to my Best Friend.
To Gypsy, my very first inspiration for writing. Her divine
guidance helped me through every step of the way. I love
and miss you Mom, RIP.
With special thanks to my friends and family for all their
wonderful support! I could not have done it without you.
To all my readers who took a chance on me and my debut
novel. I hope you enjoy it. I poured my heart and soul into
it, just for you!

Prologue

Some say life is like that of the ocean. One minute all is seemingly calm, gently rolling along, as do the waves on a clear day.

Suddenly, without warning, the waves fiercely start to build. They splash uncontrollably against the shore, bringing about change, wanted or not. Much like TC's emotions every time he thinks of her, the woman of his dreams.

So many questions crossed his mind. Was she imaginary? Was she an angel or a devil woman? Why couldn't they have met decades ago and why has fate brought them together now? What is her magic, the magic that possesses his soul? Questions for which he had no answer. He realized that you can't help who you fall in love with.

It was complicated, not unlike that of the deepest depths of the ever changing sea, hiding its own secrets and lies. Never knowing what lies at the water's edge.

Chapter 1

Terrance Chadworth Martin, a name he never liked, was distracted by his thoughts as he looked at his poker hand. He remembered coming home from first grade, telling his mother he would no longer answer to Terrance. That from now on he was to be called TC, because the kids at school made fun of him all day. As she knelt down to wipe his tears she had replied "But, Terrance it is an old family name and my maiden name, you should be proud of it!" Being the loving mother that she was, she gave in to TC. He sure missed her, God rest her soul.

As he focused on the cards in his hand, TC became disgusted by his unusually bad luck for the night. He looked at his watch. It was just half past midnight. He reached for his beer and takes a quick assessment of the amount of liquid inside the bottle. Enough for one last sip, he thought, as he raises the bottle to his lips. With one gulp, the cool liquid is fully consumed to his satisfaction. TC tosses the bottle into the nearly overflowing container of empties. Looking at his cohorts, he smiles wryly.

"That's all of my money you cheating assholes are getting from me tonight! I'm going for a walk on the beach before hitting the sack."

Pushing his chair back as he stands, he tosses his cards on the table. They land face up showing only a six of hearts high. Hardly a hand worth betting on. It was just a friendly game of poker between old military buddies, something to pass the time. They were on one of their men-only retreats. Something they tried to do at least once a year. Most times there were four of them, Gunny Sergeant, Dalton, Andy and TC. This year however, there was only Gunny, Andy and TC. Dalton was not able to go this year due to "unforeseen circumstances" as he put it to TC; however, the guys all knew the translation meant his wife Tabitha didn't want him to go. Truth be told, she didn't like him going at all.

"Too many BB's," (babes in bikinis) she had often said any time a beach location was involved. Panama City, Florida certainly fit that bill.

"Aww hell man! Come on! That's no damn way to be! Don't be a damn sore loser, TC!"

Gunny shouted after him as TC made his way down the hall to the back door. TC steps onto the wooden deck. It was only ten or so steps down to the sandy beach. He could still hear Gunny's bellowing as he reached the last step. Impishly smiling and shaking his head at the thought of how easy it was to still get a rise out of his old Gunnery Sergeant, even after all these years. Gunny was the only one of them that was fully retired military. He was a good ten years older than the rest of them. A little gruff on the exterior, but a man with a big heart. A secret that he kept well hidden from most. He was of small stature standing only about 5'5 and perhaps weighing about 150 pounds soaking wet. But don't let his size fool you; he more than made up for that with his attitude. He was a man you could count on that was for sure. He had been there many a time to save TC's ass in more ways than one. And if you crossed him, you'd have hell to pay. With his lifelong career in the Marines he was a tough old bird, there was no doubt about that. His grey hair and multitude of deep lines that crossed his face was a manifestation of the years gone by. He was TC's training sergeant and his first taste of the Marines, many years ago. TC would never forget the first day they met.

"By damn I said stand up straight! You are a damn Marine! Get it? A proud Marine! Gunner Sergeant shouted at them from under the brim of his camouflage hat. A hat that was of little use in blocking the bright afternoon sun from his deep brown eyes.

With both hands folded behind his back he walked up and down the line of men, shouting instructions as he went. A very large and bulging vein in his neck pulsated with each angry word that left his lips. A vein that the men all swore would burst one day in a fit of anger. Pacing back and forth, he stopped in front of each of them, as though to scrutinize them individually. The young recruits avoided eye contact, all except one. Gunny knew from that moment that TC might be trouble. He couldn't have been more wrong. TC was an exemplary Marine. Their bond and friendship would turn out to be a lifelong adventure. Gunner Sergeant didn't skip a beat looking into TC's steel blue eyes as they boldly stared back at his own.

"Son! Do you comprehend what stand up straight means?" TC abruptly straightens his back and shoulders "Yes! Yes sir Sergeant Sir!"

"That will be Gunny to you, boy! Gunny Sir!"

"Yes sir! Gunny Sir!" TC yelled back.

Turning to point a finger at the rest of the men, Gunny continued.

"And that goes for all of you assholes! For the next six weeks I will be your first and only thought! You will probably hate me before it is all over, but I don't give a damn! My job is to make you or break you and the choice on the outcome is yours!"

TC would never forget that day as long as he lived. Gunny and he had been through some tough times that was for sure. Lots of good memories and some horrific ones too.

Having reached the last step, TC felt the sand quickly cover his bare toes, as it gave way to his weight. He stood there for a moment relishing the feel of the cool sand beneath him. The smell of the salt water filled the air, giving a slight tickle to his nostrils. TC could hear the waves beating against the shore. It was such a familiar sound, such a familiar feeling.

Damn! The sea sure has a beckoning call to me. Nothing quite like the sight and sound of the ocean. Surely, I must have been a pirate or a sailor in a former life! Chuckling at his thoughts, he takes a long and much needed stretch before his walk. I sat too long giving those jerks my money and my body is sure letting me know.

As TC made his way down to the water's edge, he heard a very distant rumble of thunder. He tilted his head upward toward the sky, his eyes combed the darkness. There were a few very tiny flashes of lightening off in the distance. I should have time for a quick walk, it looks like the storm is a ways off.

As he walked the shore, a sense of nostalgia filled his mind and he couldn't help but reminisce on some of the great times he had on this very beach. Some of them with the guys and some with his family. The years have certainly gone by quickly, he thought. Much more quickly than he had anticipated. Sadness and anger filled his mind. He kicked at the sand as though it were a football and he the player trying a futile attempt to save the game in the last minute of play.

"Damn it! Where did all the time go anyway?"

Guess all the issues with a career, the military stints and a marriage, not to mention five kids has really made the time fly by. Not that it hadn't been a good life. Not that at all. There were good times and bad times and the so, so times. Damn the past! Time to live for the future! And myself for a change! With that thought came a loud clap of thunder, forcing him back to the here and now. Taking a quick look at the sky he realized that a dangerous storm was definitely approaching. The moon was slowly being masked by some dark and ominous clouds. He could see lightening more frequently lighting up the sky. I'd better turn back, don't want to get caught in a lightning storm on the beach that is for damn sure. He turned to make his way back to the beach house, realizing he had walked much farther than he thought. I sure hope I make it back before that storm catches up to me! Quickening his steps to a slight jog he was nearly back to the house when he noticed an image just ahead of him at the water's edge. Stopping, he realized it is that of a woman. An unexpected sight, given the time of night and the pending storm.

TC is lost in the sight of her. Something about her captivates him, not to mention she is a beauty. She is walking toward him, looking down and stopping every few minutes to pick up what he assumed to be seashells, gently placing them in the basket she was carrying. She is as oblivious to his presence as she seemed to be of the upcoming storm. With the light from the houses and each lightening flash, TC was able to see her quite well. She was wearing a long flowing white dress, or gown, maybe even a swimsuit cover up as it appeared to be spilt all the way up one side, he wasn't really sure which. He was more interested in what was in it, rather than the piece of clothing itself. The top had scalloped shoulders with a very low neckline that only begged to show more of her very well-endowed breasts. The white gown seemed to glisten like the moon with each movement that she made. The silky material rippled smoothly across her bare skin, not unlike that of the waves along the shore. A sudden gust of wind whips the gown loosely between her legs forcing TC's attention to her lower body. The side slit in the material gave way to the image of a very shapely leg. She leaned over to pick up what he was now sure was indeed a seashell. Her abundant breasts do their best to spill over the edge of her dress, only to suddenly retreat back to the safety of the garment when she rose. She had long curly hair that flowed well past her shoulders. With each flash of light TC could see it was a deep brown with glistening hints of auburn. A wisp or two of bangs gently caressed her brow. A section of her thick curls were tied loosely to one side with what appeared to be a shiny purple ribbon. The length of the ribbon, as well as, the loose strands of hair seemed to be dancing to their own tune. It was as if the wind was the maestro in some grand concert hall directing each strand as it darted wildly. As she rose from retrieving yet another shell from the sand, a series of lightning flashes began, lighting up what seemed like the entire shoreline. A giant clap of thunder immediately followed. TC saw her body flinch with fright, the basket of shells she was carrying fell silently onto the sand at her feet. Her attention is now focused on the oncoming storm. She raised her head to look at the sky above her. By this time TC has walked close enough to see her furrowed brow and the obvious fright in her eyes. Eyes that looked so huge and beautiful in the night. They were a beautiful Caribbean green. Strangely, they seemed to have an internal light all their own.

Just as she started to bend to retrieve her basket, she suddenly stopped in mid-movement. She obviously realized that she was not alone. She had been totally unaware of his presence until that very moment. She stood there motionless. Her eyes met his. It felt as if time had stopped, no thunder, no lightening, no waves noisily slapped at the water's edge. TC's heart was racing, he could tell by the movement of her chest that she was breathing heavily. Of course, even in this moment his RTP (Random Thought Process) took over and he was off on an immediate fantasy of her being breathless over him and not the impeding storm. Not to mention, the fact that she had just been startled by a stranger, on the beach, all alone in the middle of the night. Frustrating as it was, that's how his RTP worked, most of the time anyway. Cursed with it, more so than the average person.

With their eyes fixed on each other and TC back from his fantasy, he was sure she was pretty shaken by his presence. He was exceptional at reading facial and body language, thanks to all those years of military training. TC was about to speak but before he realized what was happening, there was a flash of light from the sky. A giant streak of lightening made its way to the beach between the two of them. A light so bright it was blinding. The hair on the back of TC's neck stood up. He immediately threw his arms up and over his head as if to shield himself from the threat, as he attempted to take a step toward the woman. A natural instinct to protect her from harm; an automatic reflex obtained in the military. A deafeningly loud clap of earth shaking thunder followed.

Then there was total darkness.

TC attempted to open his eyes, it felt as though they had been glued shut. Try as he might he is unable to keep them open for more than a second or two. After a few moments with them squeezed tightly shut, he tried to calmly re-coop his thoughts, telling himself they were not glued shut, that was ridiculous, and he could get them to stay open if he tried hard enough. He opened them again only to see darkness and feel nauseated. His head was spinning like a bird in a downward spiral with only one wing to guide it. After a few moments, the dizziness and nausea subsided only to be replaced by an aching head.

He felt as though he had been knocked senseless. He reached up to rub his forehead, his eyes still closed. It was raining and he could feel each raindrop as it fell onto his shirtless body with a slow but definite tap, tap, and tap. Blinking through the rain and trying hard to get his eyes to focus was taking every bit of strength within him. The rain came more frequently, hitting him with a much harder force, it awoke his senses. As he again blinked through the raindrops, he realized an image appeared to be leaning over him. His eyes filled with a foggy blur and gave way to darkness yet again.

"TC! Look out!" He heard Gunny yell. "Incoming!' came another voice. TC felt a force against his back that felt like he'd been hit by a tank. He could feel his body falling forward and his face sinking into the wet soil. Flashes of bright light, one after another, along with unbearable screams of terror.

"STOP! No! Stop! Enough!" TC shouted back. "I am not in Saudi!" He struggled to open his eyes and get up, but the best he could accomplish was to open his eyes to the blurry night. He was awake, or so he thought. Was he having a flashback? Another PTSD episode? Or was his imagination on overload, as there appeared to be an image kneeling over him. Blinking a few times, he was finally able to determine the image; it was that of a woman. She was on her hands and knees leaning over him, barely inches from his face. She seemed to be saying something but TC was unable to hear a word she was saying. Her lips were moving but no sound was heard, at least not by him. Blinking through the raindrops he could see that she had the most beautiful eyes he'd ever seen. He fought hard to stay conscious, and to keep a clear vision, TC was desperately trying not to drift back into another PTSD episode.

TC laid there looking into her eyes, his thoughts erratic. Her eyes! They were so very gorgeous. One moment blue and the next a vivid green, changing like the sea before and after a storm.

He noticed they were encased by long feathery lashes. Raindrops appearing atop them resembled tiny sparkling diamonds. Her long dark locks of hair coiled in wet ringlets around her angelic face. Longer strands of hair dangling over him, expunging their own droplets of tiny dancing diamonds. Diamonds that searched for the perfect spot to lie upon his naked chest, each dropped as though in slow motion, one by one.

TC raised his arm and attempted to touch her face. Is she an angel? Just as his hand reached her hair, darkness overcame him yet again. His hand fell limply to his side, taking along with it the purple ribbon neatly entwined between his fingers. Total darkness prevailed.

Opening his eyes, TC was not sure where the hell he was. A few seconds later he realized he was lying flat of his back on the sandy beach. Man, what the hell happened? He rubbed his head as though that would clear his thoughts enough to ascertain what had transpired. Still a bit dazed, he starred up at the night sky. Well, at least the rain has stopped. At least I think, I remember it raining.

He saw the twinkling stars above him, which added to his confused state of mind. Had the storm had been real or perhaps imagined? He rolled over to his side, laying there for a moment he still felt a bit weak. What the hell happened? Did I pass out? Last I remember I was walking on the beach or was I playing cards with the guys? Shit! Too much beer maybe? Damn, this feels worse than the last hangover I had at Andy's last wedding. Maybe I simply passed out? Even though he was unsure of what happened, he knew he had to get up. Finally feeling like he was able, he placed his right hand in the sand to push himself up, but in doing so he felt something strange between his fingers. He looked at his hand, there appeared to be a shiny purple ribbon clenched in his fist. "What the hell is this?" Still not thinking clearly, he shoved the ribbon into the pocket of his shorts. As he stood, he still felt a little light headed. He managed to make his way to the steps of the beach house. He grabbed the railing to steady himself.

His head was still aching. Suddenly he could hear the sound of guns and the screams that followed. He yelled. "Stop, stop!" As he reached his hands up to his temples.

"I will not have another flashback! Please dear God! I have had enough of them!"

His hands tightly pressed against his head, as though to stamp out the evil thoughts. As quickly as they had come, they dissipated. Leaving him with a slight ache in his head.

TC reached the top of the deck, he turned back to look at the beach before he proceeded toward the door. As he gazed off into the distance, he could have sworn he saw something white flash by for just an instant. A chill ran up his spine.

"What was that?" he murmured. "Was there something on the beach or was it just my imagination?"

A tiny flicker of lightening way off in the distance indicated the end of the storm. As he reached for the handle of the screen door, a sudden strange feeling came over him. Something seemed to be calling to him. He turned back toward the ocean. TC saw the waves were now gently kissing the shore. All was seemingly very empty. His eyes scanned the shoreline in hopes of what he was not sure. Not another soul appeared to be in sight. What was it that was beckoning him to the water's edge?

Chapter 2

"Eleven A.M.!" TC heard the shout. "Get your lazy ass up man! We have a full day ahead of us, TC!   Do you think you can sleep all damn day?"

"Okay, OKAY Gunny! Damn it I'm getting up!" TC responded. He wasn't normally a late riser like this, but the events of the night before had not allowed for much sleep. Not to mention the fact that he felt the twinge of a slight headache. Damn, didn't think I drank that much beer last night.

He rose up in bed and swung his lean tanned legs over the edge. TC was about to plant his feet on the floor, when suddenly a flash of white and purple clouded his head, followed by a case of vertigo. He leaned back against the headboard to steady himself. The colorful flashes quickly came and went, followed by what looked like diamonds falling from the sky.

Damn! What is going on? Flashback? Dreaming? A possible memory? What the hell am I trying to remember? Purple! White! Falling diamonds! None of that makes any sense! Sometimes I do think I am just damn crazy.

It was true, TC's mind had been pretty messed up when he first returned from active duty. It had taken a while to digest all the pain and destruction war had bestowed upon him. If not for a few good doctors, his wife and his fellow Marines, who knows how bad it could have really been, not that it hadn't been bad enough anyway.

"Enough of that thought." He said to himself as he moved to the edge of the bed, forcing better thoughts to emerge from the previous day.

It had been their usual first day procedure. Check into the beach house, unload the truck, and fill the fridge with beer. They didn't want to forget the important things, after all. He snickered.

Then, of course, all that was followed by their poker night. He smiled at the thought of how his wife, Jan, would perceive the importance of the beer in the fridge. Oh well, that was Jan for you, their priorities were definitely different. And seemingly more so as of late.

Jan was a few years younger than TC. She stood about 5'8 and had a very slender build. TC was always telling her that he felt she needed to put some meat on those bones, but she was extremely paranoid about being overweight. She was a pretty woman with light blue eyes and blonde hair which she now kept in a very short boyish bob, unlike when they first met. TC missed her long locks but she refused to grow them back. When he would bring it up she would comment, "Five kids, no time for hair fixing, besides I like it short." TC finally gave up mentioning it. She was his first and only wife of twenty plus years. They met through a mutual friend just after Jan had graduated from college. He was home on leave from the Marines. His friends all tried to tell him not to get involved so fast after *the* breakup. TC didn't think Jan was a rebound girlfriend, as most of his buddies did, he always scoffed at their warnings.

Needless to say they were all shocked when he informed them they were getting married. They had been dating less than a year and only got to see each other when he had R & R. He remembered Andy's comment like it was yesterday.

"What the hell man? You get her knocked up?"

"No Andy, nothing like that, it is just time that's all, just time."

Knowing TC's stubborn streak they all knew it was useless to try to talk him out of it.

If she was a rebound girlfriend, it sure had been one hell of a rebound after this many years. They were not immune to their share of marital woes, even had a short separation a few years back. TC's stint in the Marines along with many years as a reservist, let alone the trials and tribulations of nearly raising five kids had not torn them apart.

The breakup the guys referred to was his relationship with Heather. She abruptly ended their affiliation his senior year of college, the day of graduation to be exact. TC never understood what went wrong. She could never give him a real reason either. Heather was the love of his life, or so he thought at the time. She was a gorgeous tall redhead with a set of the fullest lips he'd ever seen. They had been pretty much inseparable the last three years of college. They shared the same classes; the same sets of friends and pretty much enjoyed the same tastes in everything. He remembered Heather jokingly saying that they had so much in common it was like they were a brother and sister by another mother and father. They would often laugh about that, but looking back years later, he realized maybe that had been their true connection instead of the romantic one they sought. The last year they were together, there was more fighting and less laughter. The breakup was hard on TC.

Some said it was why he joined the Marines; he himself admitted it probably had a lot to do with it. A change of scenery was definitely needed. Every once in a while, an old memory would creep into his thoughts. He had heard years after their breakup that she was killed in an automobile accident. The news haunted him for a long time. It took a while, but he was finally able to make peace with it, knowing that God has a plan, of some sort, for everyone. He was thankful for the time that they had spent together.

Another shout came roaring out from Gunny, interrupting his thoughts. "Yes Gunny! I hear you! I'll be there in a minute!" As he stood up, the white sheet from his bed fell to the floor. He reached down to pick it up, a shiver ran up his spine, causing him to physically shake. Something haunted him about it, but he wasn't sure why. It made him think of Jan, who always complained about his kicking the covers off her at night. She accused him of having fitful dreams, which he always denied. She said she felt a distance from him and it was due to his refusal to share his tormented dreams with her. He tossed the sheet back on the bed and frowned at the thought. He reached for a pair of shorts, as he slipped them over his lean naked body he caught his own reflection in the mirror.

He was a handsome middle-aged man, he stood about 6'4 with short black curly hair that showed a slight greying at the temples. His moustache and neatly trimmed beard were quite the opposite. They were both mostly all grey with just a little black here and there. The color combination really set off his deep blue eyes. He looked again, at his reflection in the mirror, he slapped himself on his flat stomach.

Heck, still looking pretty good, not bad at all. Those three days a week at the gym seem to be paying off. Yep, don't want that proverbial beer belly like old Gunny's. Smiling at the thought, he made his way down the hall toward the kitchen. The smell of bacon was overwhelming, suddenly he realizes he could probably eat his weight in Andy's special bacon and egg omelet. Damn, I sure hope he made it this morning!

As usual, Andy was at the stove frying up some bacon. He was always their designated cook, since that was what he did for a living. It was just easier to give in to him and let him do the cooking, in lieu of listening to his complaining over how they didn't do it correctly. Besides which, it gave them ample opportunity to aggravate the hell out of him with their childish pranks. The usual, salt for sugar, loosened tops and so on, they had indeed ruined a few good meals, always making it up to Andy with a paid steak dinner and plenty of beer to boot. And of course, the usual promise that they would quit screwing with his kitchen. Andy always knew it was a promise they would not keep.

TC pulls a nice big cup from the cabinet and reaches for the coffee pot only to find it empty.

"Damn! You wake a man up and then there is no coffee! What the hell is wrong with this picture?"

He directed his comments at Andy since Gunny seemed to be nowhere in sight.

"Hey! Don't look at me. I'd have left your ass in the bed all damn day. Gunny was the one yanking your chain this morning!"

Andy stood a few inches shorter than TC, but his stature was much thinner, to the point of being somewhat lanky. He was always the brunt of the 'don't trust a skinny cook' jokes. But a damn good cook he was. With dark hair and glasses he was not the most handsome man, but he must have something going for him as he certainly attracted the women. The only problem was keeping them. Maybe he just picked the wrong ones.

TC filled the water for the coffee and started the pot brewing. He took a seat at the kitchen table just as Gunny walked into the room, his usual morning paper tucked neatly under his left arm. He pulled out the chair next to TC, a giddy look upon his face.

"Well hot damn! Sleeping beauty is finally up!" He slapped the newspaper open without looking at TC, causing it to make a loud pop.

"To hell with you Gunny." TC quickly replies.

Andy turned to them both and shook his spatula as though in a warning. "Can't you two carry on a civilized conversation?" He turns his attention back to the eggs without waiting on an answer.

TC and Gunny look at each other innocently, shrugging their shoulders. Gunny winks at TC and they both chuckle under their breath. Poor Andy, they were always doing something to get under his skin.

Gunny pretends to look at his morning paper, with one eyebrow cocked. "What Andy? This is us being civil to each other. You should damn well know that by now."

With spatula and skillet in hand Andy walks over to the table and scoops the omelet into each of their plates, he then takes his own seat next to Gunny. "Yeah, well, I keep hoping for change Gunny! But, I forgot you can't teach an old dog new tricks! Now let's eat!"

Having finished his meal and with a last sip of coffee, TC puts his dishes in the sink.

"Well time for a shower if we are going to make that bike show. Give me twenty minutes and I'll be ready." Gunny and Andy both nod their heads in agreement.

Back in his room, TC is glad they chose the beach house this year and not a condo, as it afforded each of them to have their own private shower. "I share that enough at home." He murmurs to himself. As he turns on the water, he hears Gunny bellowing for him to hurry up. TC yells back in the same manner. "I'll be out in fifteen!"

Knowing Gunny's impatience, a quick shower was all he had time for. Stepping out of the shower with the water still dripping from his body, he reaches for the towel hanging by the door. As he places his hand on the white towel, another flash of white rippling in the wind fills his head. It is gone just as quickly as it came. Confused, he looks at the thick terry cloth towel in his hand. His fingers gently caress the material as he frowns.

"Damn it! There it is again! White! White! White! What the hell does it mean?" He grumbles, angrily to himself.

After he sufficiently dries off, he tosses the towel over the shower door. Methodically reaching over to pick up his shorts he'd worn the night before. Emptying the back pocket first, he removes his wallet, then his keys from the right pocket. Although, his left pocket is usually empty, except for maybe a coin or two, he figures he may as well check it to be sure.

He reaches his hand in his pocket, to his surprise he feels something soft and silky. Frowning he pulls his hand out and with it comes a purple ribbon whirling around like a Texas twister. What the hell? Where did this come from? Puzzled by the find, he stands there for a moment, holding the ribbon in his hand. Again, he is visited by a flash of light and a set of gorgeous eyes; just as before, they are gone too quickly, and he is unable to focus on them.

TC's forehead breaks out into a cold sweat. He tries closing his

24

eyes again, as though to recall the image, but nothing was forthcoming. He shakes his head in dismay.

"It must have been some crazy dream I had last night!" he affirms. Knowing Gunny would be shouting again in a minute, he hurries to shove the ribbon into the pocket of his clean khaki shorts. Quickly sliding on the shorts, sure enough, he hears Gunny's impatient yell.

"TC! Did you drown?"

Rolling his eyes at Gunny's humor and slipping into a pair of blue deck shoes, he yells back. "I'm coming! I'm coming!"

He grabs a comb, giving his hair a quick run through, then tosses the comb on the dresser before grabbing a t-shirt as he scrambles to meet the guys. He struggles to put on the t-shirt and walk down the hall at the same time.

Quickly stepping out the front door, clothing intact, he reaches the sidewalk and turns toward town. In only a few long strides he easily caught up with Gunny and Andy.

Chapter 3

Even though it is early spring, there is quite a crowd, due to the motorcycle rally that is being held in town. The annual event is a big money maker for the locals. TC is excited to be there. Attending the motorcycle rally was one of the items on his bucket list. He loved all things automotive, be it cars or bikes. There was plenty of each to see. All makes, models, years, colors you name it. The biggest contributor was, of course, Harley Davidson, his own personal favorite. He had longed for a Fat Boy Harley for quite some time, but Jan didn't approve, so that purchase was never made. Every time he would mention it, she would go off on a tirade of how one day someone would knock on her door to tell her he had been killed on the stupid bike. She went on and on that she would be left to raise the kids without a father. At some point, he had just decided it wasn't worth all the headache, but a man could still dream about it.

As the three of them walked down the sidewalk, it wasn't only the bikes that caught their attention.

"Alert! Alert! BB's!!! TC shouted and they all chuckled. Gunny added his own thoughts.

"Yeah, too damn bad Dalton didn't have balls enough to tell

Tabitha he was coming."

"Now Gunny you know sometimes you just have to give in to keep the peace!"

"Andy what the hell do you know about giving in to keep the peace? How many women have you gone through now? Hell, you change women like you do socks!" Gunny winks at TC.

"Yeah, well variety is the spice of life Gunny. At least that is what they say."

Andy quickens his stride and gets a bit ahead of TC and Gunny who are stopped to check out a particular bike. A few minutes later Andy hears TC's signal whistle and he turns back to look for them. TC is pointing at some hot babe walking just a few steps behind Andy. She is wearing a bikini that barley covers anything. Andy, as if on cue, falls in stride right beside her. Gunny looks at TC.

"One of these days Jan is going to kick your ass or shoot out those wandering blue eyes of yours!"

"Hell Gunny, I'm married not dead! Doesn't hurt to admire a little beauty. Jan knows I don't mean a thing by it. I'd never jeopardize my marriage, Gunny. Told myself a long time ago I'd behave, even if Jan and I aren't perfect."

Gunny nods his head in agreement, slapping TC on the back in fatherly manner. "Don't I know it boy? Don't I know it?"

Thirty minutes or so later they finally catch up with Andy who has stopped to look at a 1973 Chopper. He hears Gunny behind him. "Well, would you look at that?'

"I know! Right Gunny?" The excitement in Andy's voice is obvious, as he turns to look at TC and Gunny.

"Is this an awesome specimen or what? I love this paint job, the American flag looks cool as shit!"

"Well, hell I wasn't talking about the bike, I was referring to the way you were caressing that motor with your hands, boy. Might say, I'm a little disappointed though, I thought sure you'd be caressing the bikini babe we last saw you with by now." Gunny turns to wink at TC, as Andy turns a little red faced.

"Women! Who needs them?' The last three put me through hell. I'm just here for beer, poker and bikes!" TC and Gunny look at each other and in unison exclaim. "She turned him down!"

They hug each other and pretend to sob, then burst out laughing. Andy's face contorted.

"You two assholes will never grow up!" I'm starving, let's grab some lunch." He points over to a hot dog vendor just ahead.

"Sounds like a good idea. TC replies.

Meandering their way through the crowd Gunny snags an empty table for them while TC and Andy stand in line to purchase their dogs and beer. After a couple of hotdogs each, and more than a few beers, they head out again. A couple more hours left to explore the rally. The crowd of people had grown much larger by late in the afternoon. There were all kinds of people, in all kinds of attire. People watching was another favorite pastime of TC's. Jan never understood that either, she was much too impatient. TC attributed a lot of that to his military years, where there were days you had to be patient. He learned to read people and their actions as well. Just as they turn a corner he catches a glimpse of someone he thinks he recognizes. A woman with long auburn hair. He pauses for just a moment, unsure of where he knows her from, but pretty sure he has seen her somewhere before. It was just a quick sighting, and before he could focus on her again through the crowd, she was gone,

28

nowhere to be seen. Gunny and Andy, aware that TC had stopped dead in his tracks, turn back to see what the matter is now.

"TC, you alright boy? Not having another flashback, are you?" Worried, Gunny places his hand on TC's arm.

"No. Um, no Gunny" TC replies clearing his throat. "No, I'm ok just thought I saw someone I knew."

TC did not realize he had put his hand in his left pocket and was tightly holding the purple ribbon.

"Well good TC, let's head back to the house and get ready for the bonfire tonight, maybe a little afternoon siesta is in order." Gunny turns to look at Andy, who is nodding his head in agreement.

"Hey you sissies! Time to get up! We got a bonfire to attend and need to get there early to claim a good spot." Gunny is spry and feeling good after his late afternoon nap. As he enters the kitchen TC is standing there with a bit of a smirk across his face.

"Well, Gunny, we sissies didn't take a nap! Instead we went to the market and purchased the steaks and potatoes, and stocked the ice chest with beer. Not to mention that the truck is loaded and ready to go. So, get your lazy ass in gear, we are ready and waiting! Andy is putting the beach chairs in now."

"Well about time you two did something constructive." Reaching into the fridge to grab a cola. "Let's hit the road boys!"

Driving down the beach road, Andy points out the perfect area. "Here TC, this should be the best spot to see all the bikes as they cruise by, a good spot to build the bonfire too."

TC pulls into the designated parking area. Before unloading the truck, they all take a walk down to the water's edge with beach chairs and a beer in tow. TC stands there gazing at the ocean. He is mesmerized by the sound of the waves rushing up to meet the shore. A cool, gentle breeze stirs the evening air; he loves the smell of it. It is close to sunset and the sky is ablaze with colors of yellow, blue and pink scattered beautifully along the horizon. The sun looks like a majestic orange ball about to touch the emerald green water, or so it seemed.

Something is haunting at TC. He just can't quite put his finger on what it is. His right hand holding his beer and the left hand in the pocket of his jeans. Unconsciously TC caresses the purple ribbon between his thumb and forefinger. He is so absorbed in his own thoughts he didn't even realize that Gunny had walked up right beside him.

"Sure makes a man seem really small in the scheme of things, doesn't it TC?'

TC keeps looking at the water. "Yes, Gunny Sir, It sure does and it sure is a sight to behold. I never tire of looking at it." Gunny agrees, cutting his eyes to the side to look at TC. "Looks like they are starting to white cap a little bit."

"Yep, white capping." TC replies, still looking out at the sea.

Taking another drink of his beer, he thought, Damn, white! What is it about that color? Something is tugging at his memory; shaking his head he sloughs it off to that crazy dream he had a few nights ago. Crazy indeed, emerald eyes with diamond eyelashes, what nonsense is that? His thoughts are interrupted by Andy's yells. "Are you two going to give me a hand or you going to stand there all damn day? Didn't know I was going to have to cook and unload the damn truck!" Gunny looks directly at TC.

"Whoa! Hot damn! What has that boy's feathers in a ruffle, TC?"

"I think he got a call from his ex, or soon to be ex, I should say, and he has been in a pretty foul mood ever since."

"Well, hell let's go give him a hand. Don't want the night to be ruined with any belly aching. Maybe the rally will put him in a better mood."

TC and Gunny arrive at the truck as Andy is struggling to remove the ice chest. TC reaches over and grabs the ice chest and proceeds to carry it to their spot. Andy stands there looking a bit dumbfounded. TC turns back to look at Andy. "Get the portable grill and charcoal."

Gunny grabs the bag with the cooking utensils and food and helps Andy set up the cooking area. Once done, Andy readily takes over in order to prepare their steaks and spuds. Gunny and TC each wander off in different directions. Walking along the shore, they gather any stray pieces of drift wood to build their bonfire in front of the beach chairs. Knowing as the evening progresses, they would appreciate not only the sight, but the warmth of it as well.

It wasn't long before they had a good little bonfire crackling, both men standing there gazing at their accomplishment like two proud parents.

"Damn good fire!" They both chimed simultaneously, touching their beer bottles together in a toast to themselves, chuckling before taking a drink.

The smell of Andy's steaks fills the night air causing their stomachs to begin to rumble. It wasn't a minute later and Andy shouts.

"Soups on!"

He didn't have to make a second call. TC and Gunny are by his side with plates and fork in hand. Their chairs are turned toward the road to watch the procession of bikes and cars as they enjoy their meal. The area is well lit along the road, with the vehicle lights, allowing them to admire the cars and bikes in all their glory. There must have been hundreds of the most awesome rides you could imagine, and all in one place. Some had extreme paint jobs while others were just average. There were Vintage choppers and the like. A 1966 Harley that came streaming by, was TC's favorite. It had a blue and white motor with the Harley Davidson emblem in chrome. Each fender was also blue and white; the seat was black leather with studded trim. Behind the driver's seat was a pillion seat, also trimmed in shiny silver studs. The dual mufflers were shiny chrome. It really made TC salivate for one of his own. Gunny agreed with TC on the 66 model, however, he preferred the one with the American eagle painted on the motor. Andy liked that one as well, but admits there were too many he liked to be able pick a favorite.

"Much like his women." Gunny whispered to TC and they both chuckled.

Taking the last bite of his steak, TC lays his fork down and picks up his beer, as if in a toast in Andy's direction.

"Damn Andy! If it is one thing you do to perfection, it is knowing how to cook a great steak! Best damn steak I've had in a long time."

"Oh hell, TC! You are just saying that because you were starving and didn't have to lift a finger to cook!" Andy downs his seventh or eighth beer for the night.

"Now wait a minute Andy, I have to agree with TC here. Those were some damn good steaks.'

"Yeah, well Gunny you are just happy you weren't choking down one of TC's overcooked, dry ass steaks. You two aren't fooling me with all these compliments. You are both just too lazy to cook your own!" Andy laughs and reaches for another beer.

TC, holding his beer, points one finger at Andy. "Look here asshole, my steaks are." He pauses for a moment. "Are usually pretty damn good, most of the time." His turn to smirk and slug another drink of his own beer. Gunny looks at both of them in disbelief.

"You are both full of shit. Everyone knows I am famous for my steak grilling. Why, hell fire, I taught Andy every damn thing he knows. I was his best teacher, critic and consumer all rolled into one! Hell fire! I ate anything he put in front of me. I just didn't want to put you two to shame, that's all." Raising his own beer for another drink. TC and Andy look at each other and without a word they yell.

"Incoming!"

They toss their beers and charge at Gunny, flipping his chair over in the sand with him in tow, falling over themselves in hysterical laughter.

Rolling over to his knees, Gunny looks at them both.

"Damn you two! What the hell? You made me spill a perfectly good beer! I just opened it too!"

As he wipes the sand from his chest.

"You two are assholes and paybacks are hell!"

TC and Andy are trying to control their laughter as they upright Gunny's chair. Each offering a hand to help him up.

Andy reaches in the ice chest for fresh beers, offering one to Gunny and then to TC as he opens his own.

They sit another hour or so watching the parade of vehicles. Eventually the vehicles became less and less in numbers, along with the beer in the ice chest. They all seem too content to move or maybe, each was just in their own little world, absorbed by their own private thoughts.

TC turns his chair to face the ocean. It is a beautiful moonlit night. He could see the rippling waves as the flames of their bonfire flicker in the wind, sending tiny little sparks dancing toward the midnight blue sky. The sound of a waves crashing in to shore, brought TC's attention back to the water's edge. That nagging thought of something. He places his hand in his pocket and pulls out the purple ribbon. Feeling the soft satin material in his hand, he closed his eyes.

A few moments pass and then, there it was! The image that had been haunting him! It was a little more vivid now. It was a woman in a white gown, her dark brunette hair tied with a purple ribbon. She had green eyes bright enough to light the world. His heart began to race, his fists tightly clench in his lap. The white gown was rippling wildly in the wind. Her beautiful eyes....

Abrupt darkness overcame him. TC opens his eyes. He has broken out in a cold sweat, again. His body flinches, as he suddenly feels hand on his shoulder.

"You okay son?" He hears Gunny ask. "TC! You having another flashback."

TC realizes he is slumped down in his chair and rights himself as he replies to Gunny.

"I'm fine Gunny, no flashback. Just lost in thought I guess, maybe dozed off for a minute." He manages a fake enough smile, in hopes of reassuring Gunny.

"I must have been dreaming of a hot babe in a bikini, that's all Gunny." Mustering up a slight smile for Gunny's benefit.

Gunny gives TC another worried look, as he takes his own seat again.

"Well TC, you seemed kind of in a trance of sorts. I thought your PTSD was much better these days. You might want to pay a little visit to the doc when we get home."

"Damn Gunny. What are you, my wife? You worry as much as she does. Shit, I just dozed off that's all."

Gunny not buying it as he looks at TC and replies.

"Um hum. Guess that would explain the sweat streaming down your face on such a cool night."

Feeling a little guilty at having snapped at Gunny, TC changes his tone.

"Ah, hell Gunny, you worry too much. I am fine, just fine."

The road activity had pretty much ceased, with just an occasional diehard driving by every now and then, and their fire barely a glowing ember.

TC rises from his chair and starts kicking sand into the fire, watching the smoke disperse into the night air.

"Well guess we best be packing it in, we'll have a long drive back to Nashville in the morning. "You got that right TC." Gunny rises and folds his beach chair.

"Hell fire you guys, I'll be okay, I'll get a home." Andy slurs out, as he tries to rise from his own chair, only to fall tumbling to the sand.

Gunny looks at TC.

"Yep, time to pack it up. Looks like we will have to carry his sorry ass again! Damn Andy. He never knows his limit."

It wasn't that Andy had a drinking problem, he just never knew when to quit having a good time. Pretty much the same reason he was now on his fourth ex-wife.

Gunny and TC managed to get the truck and Andy loaded

without too much trouble. Arriving back at the beach house, they each have Andy by the arm trying to get him up the stairs and into the house. He is pretty much a limp noodle and only semi conscience. As they reach his bedroom door Andy looks at Gunny.

"Gunny man, I love you Gunny!" he slurs and distorts his speech as he turns his head to the opposite side to look at TC.

"TC, you are the best friend I never had. You, Gunny and Dalton, you all got me at my side. Not like those bitches I married, who left me dried and high, err higher and dried up, you know, right." His speech pretty incoherent through uncontrollable hick-ups, he looks back at Gunny.

"I love ya man, you know right baby?'

TC and Gunny roll their eyes at each other.

"Oh shit!" they both exclaim as they feel Andy go limp within their hold.

TC is looking at Gunny.

"Ready Gunny? On a count of three. One! Two! Three!"

They toss Andy onto his bed sprawled out like an upside down turtle. They remove his shoes and TC covers him lightly with a sheet.

"Yep, one hell of a hangover for him in the morning. Long drive home for sure."

Gunny nods as he turns out the light to Andy's room.

Making their way down the hall to their respective rooms, Gunny stops before entering his. TC stops beside him. He saw Gunny giving him a worried look. TC has seen that look before from Gunny, many a time and he remembers it all too well.

On a MAGTF (Mag-Taf, Marine Air Ground Task Force)

mission it was their last night in Iraq. They had taken refuge in what was left of an abandoned building. It had been a long day and they were all past the point of total exhaustion, consequently not at the top of their game. Gunny had laid his gun to the side, a little out of reach and was in the process of removing his boots. His feet were aching and he was beyond tired.

Suddenly, a small girl appeared from out of nowhere. She had an AK47 pointed right at Gunny, her finger on the trigger about to release it. Gunny froze. She had a death stare in her eyes, one they were all way to familiar with. TC reacted the only way his military training would allow. One shot through the heart and she fell to the floor. Blood was splattered everywhere, including all over Gunny. TC walked over to her and knelt down beside her. His big hands trembling. He reached down to remove her hair from over her little face.

Hell, she couldn't have been twelve or so. TC began to sob fervently. Gunny came over to him and held him in his arms, both men bawled like babies. Just one of the many flashback TC had to deal with due to his PTSD.

TC looks at Gunny as he walks past him giving him a little slap on the back.

"Goodnight Gunny, sleep well, I'll see you in the morning." Looking back just in time to see Gunny's half grin and hear a goodnight in return. TC shuts his bedroom door behind him, laying his truck keys on the night stand; he walks past his bed and slips quietly out the door onto the deck. He stands there a moment looking at the ocean. He closes his eyes and thought of the vision of the mystery woman he had seen earlier. How he had almost made a fool of himself with a complete stranger at the rally, thinking she was the woman he had obviously conjured up in his mind! Wondering what it all meant and where the hell it was coming from. He had no idea. Releasing a heavy sigh, he reaches his hand in his pocket, taking out the ribbon. He looks at it as though it would unlock the answers he needed. Sighing again, he shoves the ribbon back into his pocket. Taking in a deep breath of the cool night air, he looks at the ocean. What am I trying so hard to remember? Who is this woman? Is she imagined? Dreamt up in my imagination? But, how would that explain the purple ribbon? Unless, it was just some trash on the beach that had found its way into my hand and perhaps I just tied it in to my dream. Hell fire with my RTP, imagination and PTSD all going, on no telling what the hell I might come up with.

Getting angry with his thoughts he takes one last look at the ocean, before calling it a night.

"What is compelling me to come to the water's edge?"

Chapter 4

A loud clap of thunder abruptly wakes TC, shattering his deep sleep, causing him to immediately sit upright in bed, sweat pouring from his forehead. Looking around, he realizes he is at home in his own bedroom and obviously dreaming again.

Damn it! You'd think after two years I would not still be having dreams of an imaginary mystery woman with green eyes!

The rain he thought he heard was only his wife Jan in the shower of their master bath. He flops his head back on the pillow, thankful that he is home.

He had just returned from two weeks of seminars and meetings in Dallas and as usual he had a lot on his mind. He lay there for a moment, relishing in the comfort of his own bed.

"Those hotel beds are never as comfortable as they are supposed to be." He grumbles as he rolls over onto his side.

He hears the bathroom door open and looks over to see Jan. She is exiting the bathroom with nothing but a towel around her body and one loosely piled on top of her head; her long lean legs still wet from the shower. TC couldn't help but notice how they glistened like the morning dew on a cool spring morning. He raises up on one elbow and pulls back the sheet showing Jan his bare legs stopping short of his bulging privates. Giving her his best suggestive look, he grins and motions for her to come back to bed.

"Really, TC! You know I have to leave for work soon. And that I detest morning sex!"

She retrieves her robe from the edge of the bed, giving him a look of distaste and returns to the bath. TC hears the familiar hum of her hair dryer. Frowning, he throws back the covers and reaches for his shorts draped across the chair. Pulling them on, he starts downstairs to make coffee. Shit, wonder what the hell has her ass all riled up this morning? Okay, so I have been gone a couple of weeks, no reason to be such a grouch. Angrily he fills the water in the coffee maker and starts the coffee brewing. Going upstairs to the bedroom, he meets Jan coming down.

"See you after work. I've got an early meeting this morning. The kids are all gone too."

With a quick kiss on his cheek she is out the door. TC heads for the shower himself. As he turns on all the jets, he steps into the oversized shower. The one that Jan insisted they install when building the house, so they would be able to shower together.

"Yeah well, that doesn't seem to be happening much lately." He grumbles again. He closes his eyes leaning his head back to let the warm water beat against his body for a few moments before reaching for the soap, lathering himself completely. While the shower is doing its job sending the soapy bubbles trickling down his body, he vigorously shampoos his hair. Satisfied he is clean, he places a hand on the cool tiled wall to rest his weight against it, letting the water rinse the shampoo and soap from his skin. The sound and feel of the water brought back memories of his mystery lady. If only he could recall it all. It haunts him on most days.

A drive in the country should would feel good today. He thought. He turns off the water and exits the shower onto the soft fluffy white mat that lay on the tiled floor. White, hum? He realized Jan must have been shopping while he was in Dallas, he was pretty sure that mat had been blue when he had left. Reaching for his towel he dries his hair, face, and then body. He hangs the towel neatly back onto the rack. Standing there, looking at it for a moment. At least she won't be able to complain that I threw it on the damn floor again. What's up with that woman anyway? He remembers she had not been that excited when he came home. Not like in the old days when she would meet him at the door with a long embrace and even longer kiss, possibly pulling him straight to the bedroom. Things have definitely changed between them. He wasn't sure why, but things were indeed different. He'd been thinking about it a lot lately, not because there was anyone else in either of their lives, at least he didn't think so. Was it his fault or Jan's that things seemed to be off kilter? Hell, maybe it was both of them. He couldn't put his finger on a definite cause, just the effect. Could it be it was as simple as boredom? Twenty some odd years is a hell of long time if you think about it. Or, could it be the day to day stress of life and raising five kids? That sure had not been an easy one. The child rearing itself was something that caused them conflict. He felt Jan was always too lenient. She felt he was too strict. They especially had conflict with their first born, Joshua, who was now 22 and on his second year of college. He had sloughed off his first two years after high school until TC put his foot down and told him to either go to college or move out on his own and be a responsible adult. Yeah, that went over like a ton of bricks with Jan. TC felt it had to be done, otherwise

41

Josh would be 30 and still trying to 'figure it out', as Josh had liked to put it during so many of their family discussions. Yes, Jan certainly played favorites with Josh.

Audra who was 20 pretty much had her act together. She graduated from dental assistant school and had just moved into her own apartment not far from her job. She landed a lucrative position, with a young dentist who seemed a little more interested in her personally, than just professionally, but Audra denied it. TC and Jan weren't buying it, not from listening to Audra when she would fill them in on her day on their weekly Thursday evening dinners together. Joseph, their third born was 19. He joined the Navy just a few months after graduation last fall and TC could not have been more proud. Jan, on the other hand was not a happy camper. Even though he only planned a four year stint in order to obtain the education and training he wanted in the aviation field, Jan didn't approve. Annalisa, their 17 year old daughter would be graduating this May and marrying her childhood sweetheart, Davis, in September. The two of them have been inseparable since the first grade. TC chuckled at the memory of coming home one day from a military training weekend still dressed in his uniform to find the two of them on the back porch swing. Annalisa jumped to her feet when she saw him. The excitement in her voice told him how much she had missed him.

'Daddy! Daddy, Davis needs to talk to you Daddy it is real important." Her blue eyes wide with anticipation. She was the spitting image of her mother, with blonde hair and blue eyes. And she sure knew how to tug at TC's heartstrings. He knelt down to give her a big hug while looking over at Davis, who was sitting there in the swing, his little legs dangling off the edge. He was gingerly holding a jar filled with grass, holding it up to look inside it. Once he saw TC was looking at him he immediately jumped off the swing and came toward them.

TC being the ornery soul that he was sometimes, decided to have a little fun at poor Davis' expense. In his gruffest authoritative voice he asked "Well son, what is it?" TC saw Davis' little neck juggle up and down as he swallowed hard. He stood there with his little freckled face and big blue eyes staring back at TC. TC stood up releasing his hold on Annalisa. He knew his towering height over the little fella might just do him in. It was all TC could do to keep from laughing.

"Well, Davis what is you have to say to me?" TC's hands now on his hips. Surprisingly, Davis suddenly stood as straight as possible, throwing up his little hand for a salute to TC.

"Well sir, I err, I just wanted to let you know that Annie and I are engarraged. And we just want you to know 'cause Annie said that is the way it goes." Pausing a moment to catch his breath, he quickly continues very excitedly. "She saw it in a movie!" all the while scuffling his feet back and forth.

"Hum, engarraged you say?' Still not quite sure what Davis was trying to say. "Yes! Sir engarraged!" Nodding his little red head in agreement with TC's reply.

"Look Daddy, he even gave me a ring!" Annalisa shoves her little hand up to TC sporting a fine specimen of a four- leaf clover tied around her pointer finger.

"AH! Yes, I see what a nice ring too! Should bring you lots of good luck! Engarraged huh."

"Yes sir, that means we are gonna get married, like our mommies and daddy's "

TC stood there a moment with a plethora of mischievous comments streaming through his head, but he decide they would all be wasted on a five year old. So instead he looks at the two of them and replies.

"Well Davis, I think that is a great idea and I believe you will make my daughter very happy, therefore I give you my blessing under one condition."

Annalisa and Davis are beside themselves with excitement. "Yes sir, what is that sir?"

"Well" choosing his words carefully. "Both of you must brush your teeth every night and keep your rooms clean."

Davis' little face lights up like the sun itself. "Yes sir!" he turns to Annalisa.

"Ok Annie let's go hunt lizards now." Annalisa smiled, grabbing her grass and stick filled Mason jar from under the porch swing and off the two of them went. Hand in hand on a lizard hunting adventure.

That had only seemed like yesterday and a wonderful memory TC would never forget. Davis was to join the Marine Corps after graduation and Annalisa was happy to be a trailing spouse. "Whatever makes Davis happy, she had said.

Then there was Jacob, last but not least. He had just turned 14 and at that awkward age. Always had his nose in a book or a computer, which TC never understood. Couldn't get that boy interested in sports of any kind, unlike his brothers. The jury was still out on him, not that TC didn't love him. He positively loved all his children. However, Jacob was a surprise child. Not one that was planned. TC had tried to get Jan to fix that issue after Annalisa was born; figuring two boys and two girls was perfect. But no, Jan said they would just have to be careful. Hell, with four kids already, the odds would say that Jan was not the best at remembering to take that little pink pill. Yes, TC had some resentment. By this time in his life he had expected to have all his kids out of the house. Instead he had one still in college and two not even out of high school yet. His plans for travel would have to wait a while longer. He had hoped to take Jan to some of his favorite places, places he had been during his military stints. He also wanted to be the center of someone's attention again. Yes, he knew he resented finding out she was pregnant again. But, he did love Jacob all the same. He was sure Jan sensed it, but neither of them ever voiced it. It had however, been the beginning of a wedge that, albeit subconsciously, had done its damage to drive them farther apart.

Having dressed, TC grabs his keys from the foyer table, and is out the door in a flash. Just as he is backing out of the garage, his cell phone rings.

"You have an incoming call from Gunny" comes the voice over his audio. TC smiles and accepts the call. "Hello Gunny!"

"TC! Welcome back man!" Gunny's rough voice is a welcome sound to TC's ears.

"How the hell are you Gunny? Got any good news to share?"

"Hell yeah! I'm still alive and hungry! I was calling to see if you wanted to grab some grub with me today?"

"Well, Gunny that might be a tough one on my first day back at the office. Can I let you know after I get there and see what kind of fires I have to put out?"

"Sure, sure no problem. You sound a little off TC, everything ok?"

"Yeah Gunny, just the Monday dulls I guess. Could have used some R & R after the Dallas deal but duty calls. So back to work it is. Would have been nice to come back home and load up for one of our annual trips, especially since the last one we took was year before last."

"Yeah, well I fear if you take off again without Jan, you will be looking for a good divorce lawyer!"

TC could hear Gunny's slight chuckle, if only he knew how true that might very well be. His thoughts took off on their multiple arguments and lack of affection of late.

"TC, did I lose you?"

"No, sorry Gunny you know that RTP of mine and yes you are correct about Jan; she has been in a pretty foul mood lately."

"Well, all the more reason for a nice long lunch, TC, to let off some steam."

"Okay, okay Gunny let me get to the office and see; I'll call you about 11:00."

"Sounds fair enough."

TC hears a click on the other end. Shaking his head at how Gunny ends a call almost all the time. Never a goodbye as it were, just a final statement of fact.

The drive in to work was not long enough for TC. A drive was the best way for him to collect his thoughts, clear his mind, and go from a bad mood to a good mood again, depending upon traffic, of course. This was the reason he didn't mind the 45 minute or so commute into the main city of Nashville. Jan, on the other hand, complained about it daily. Pulling into his parking spot, he sits for

46

a moment, just to get into the right mindset before going in and maybe because one of his favorite songs was playing. Garth Brooks, "Shameless" yeah, he liked that song. He had a very wide range of musical likes. It drove Jan crazy, along with most of his buddies. Smiling halfheartedly at the thought he exits toward his vehicle and goes inside.

Entering his office, he tosses his briefcase on his desk, and starts shifting through the stack of mail that Susan has left for him. Just as he takes his seat he hears a verbal "Knock, knock", looking up at Justin standing at his door. Justin is one of his Realtor's. He's been with the firm about fifteen years and a top producer. Although slightly high strung and somewhat of a know it all ass sometimes, he was a likeable enough kind of guy. Short and stocky built with bright red hair and freckles covering his face and arms, he definitely made you take notice of him.

"Hey Boss Man, how was Dallas?" Without waiting for an answer, he continues. "Yeah, yeah I know it was a bore right, well I hate to bust you the first day back, but listen, I got this deal that needs to close on Thursday or it's going to walk TC! It's a big commission and I've been working on it for months and..."

"Hold up a minute Justin." TC stops his rambling. "What the hell is it you actually want me to do? Cut to the chase, Justin."

"Ok, TC okay, well we can't seem to get in at River House Title for closing! Man, everything is ready I promise, we just need that date. That bitch Sarah who was there quit on them. They have a new person; they gave me some grief about catching up or some bullshit. I just need you to work your magic and make it happen for Thursday." He sits the file on top of the briefcase, shoves his hands into his pockets, and waits for TC to reply. TC looks at the overstuffed file; giving Justin that you'd better not be bullshitting me look.

"Okay, I'll call John Rivers and see what I can do."

"Thanks boss!" he turns on his heal and takes off down the hall, whistling a tune as he goes, assuming all life's problems had just been solved.

If only it were that simple, TC thought as he picked up the file. Better at least skim through it before I make that visit. Even though he knew Justin spoke the truth and the file would be in perfect order. After glancing through the file, he finished going through his mail and messages. Nothing else of urgency. Susie, as always took good care of the place while he was gone. Susan or Susie as she liked to be called had been with him almost since day one. She was eight years older than TC and exceptional in her job. TC depended upon her heavily and paid her accordingly. He was never one to take people for granted. Pressing Susie's intercom button on his phone he hears "Yes sir?"

Replying he states. "I'm going over to River House, should be back in a couple of hours."

With her usual cheerful reply she acknowledges. Stuffing the file in his now empty briefcase he exits the building through the back door that leads out to the parking lot. Opening the back door of his truck, he tosses the briefcase on the seat. Once on the road he picks up his cell phone to call Gunny.

"Hello TC! Hungry yet?"

"Sorry, gunny looks like it will have to be tomorrow, got a few fires to put out over here, but tomorrow for sure."

Gunny, being his usual sarcastically funny self, replies "Well, let's see TC being that I am retired, um, I suppose I can pencil you in for tomorrow. Want to meet at Bobo's at 1:00?"

"That sounds great Gunny, haven't had any good ole' Bobo's BBQ in months!"

"Perfect TC, don't out do yourself today, whatever you don't get to, will be there waiting on you the next day, son."

"Yes, sir Gunny sir!" He hears the usual buzz on the other end of the phone.

TC pulls in a parking spot at River House. He couldn't help but feel a little guilty at having to disappoint Gunny, even though he knew Gunny understood. Retrieving the briefcase from the backseat he enters the front lobby of River House Title.

"Good morning Deidra! Is Mr. Rivers available?" Before Deidra could answer, TC hears John's voice behind him; he turns to greet Mr. Rivers.

"TC! TC how are you" Extending his hand to TC for a manly handshake with a big broad smile on his face. John Rivers and TC go back a very long time. They have a great friendship and the same went for their working relationship. TC gave lots of business to River House and John was the type of man that appreciated that and his friendship as well. He was a very intelligent man and very successful in his business dealings. John was a man of his word and all of Nashville knew it. He was fairly tall, of slender build and in his early 70's but still very active and at the top of his game. He had a full head of silver hair, which you would swear glistened in the sunlight, accompanied by pale blue eyes that would often twinkle when he was up to a little mischief. Without fail, he would greet you with a genuine smile and a strong handshake. He had a special way with people, which TC knew contributed to a big part of his success.

Extending his hand to John, reciprocating with a big smile of his own.

"Hello John, how are you? How is Mrs. Rivers doing? Is she keeping you in line?"

John chuckled covering TC's hand with his other hand in a gesture to show how genuinely pleased he was to see TC.

"You know she is right on top of that! Keeps her busy! And me too!" As he winks at TC and releases his hand. "Your family is doing well I suppose?"

"Yes Sir, John, thank you for asking, we are all doing great."

"Good! Good! Come on in my office TC and have a seat. What brings you to see me today TC?"

" Well John, Sorry to drop in without an appointment, I just got back in town and Justin has a closing that needs to happen this Thursday and he mentioned you had a new closer..."

Before TC could finish John is back on his feet

"Oh my goodness! I forgot you haven't had an opportunity to meet my new closer and partner. You will really like Sam!"

TC noticed a seemingly new twinkle to John's eyes. "I was lucky to find someone with so much experience and a great, great asset to the firm. I am sure you and Sam will get along incredibly!" He is motioning TC down the hall to the office at the end of the corridor. TC was thinking it used to be an oversized board room. With a slight knock on the door John opens the door to reveal a very newly decorated room, in which no one else was present. There was a very large and ornate mahogany desk sitting in the center of the room; two nicely padded red leather chairs in front of it and a very nice black one sitting behind it. Directly behind it, between the two windows, was a massive painting that immediately grabbed his attention. It was an oil painting of the ocean at sunset, beautiful bright yellows, blues, and pinks adorning the sky and white capping waves rushing to the sandy shore. He noticed a little metal tag at the bottom of the center of the frame that read "The Water's Edge", no artist signature, however.

Visions of a purple ribbon suddenly went through his mind, but before it went any further, he hears John's voice.

"TC, TC! I'd like you to meet Sam." TC had been so engrossed in the painting that he had not heard Sam enter the room. He turns around with an outstretched hand, expecting to meet Sam and to his surprise, is greeted with a sweet feminine voice saying "Samantha". As she extends her hand to TC, she has a beautiful smile on her face. TC is beside himself at the site of Sam.

A Samantha after all, was not what he was expecting; he just assumed that Sam was a he and not a she. Smiling to himself, he suspected John Rivers did that on purpose, just to get a little chuckle at TC's expense, that sly old dog! He thought as he shook Samantha's hand.

She was a beautiful woman. Only standing a little over 5 foot he guessed, if you removed those 4 inch red high heels. Probably a few years younger than himself. Her dark auburn hair was swirled nicely on top of her head with a little curly strand slipping down to one side. She had gorgeous blue green eyes. Very striking eyes indeed, and the first thing that caught his attention. Okay, being a man, maybe it was her very voluptuous figure that had caught his attention first.

Once their hands touched and eyes met, Samantha and TC stood there frozen in mid shake, as though in a hypnotic state. John cleared his throat in an attempt to gain their attention but neither of them noticed. He waited a moment, glancing from Sam to TC and back again. Finally, a little nervously he said.

"Shall we take a seat?"

TC and Sam suddenly released their hands and a few of the papers from the files in Sam's left hand went spilling to the floor. Both men reached down to retrieve them giving them back to her.

"Oh my goodness, thank you both so much. I seem to be very clumsy these days. Please, gentlemen have a seat. I will have Deidra bring some coffee if you would like?"

John unsure of what just transpired between Sam and TC spoke first.

"Yes Sam that would be a great idea, I'm sure TC would enjoy some."

Turning for an acknowledgement from TC, who still seemed to be mesmerized by Sam.

"TC, Coffee okay with you?" John has to ask a second time before getting a response from TC. For a moment. John thought TC might be slipping into a flashback and was relieved when TC finally replied.

"Yes, that would be great."

Samantha walks over to her desk and buzzes Deidra.

"Yes Ms. Samantha?' "Deidra, would you please bring in some coffee, three cups please and cream and sugar."

"Of course! I will have it to you in a moment; I actually just made a fresh pot."

TC hadn't moved from the spot, he was standing there looking at Samantha. He had not noticed to the left of the door was a large square coffee table with four large cushioned leather chairs surrounding it. John had taken a seat at the one to the far left. TC, suddenly feeling like a gapping fool, joined Mr. Rivers, sitting across from him. Sam walked over and took the seat next to John. TC was having a difficult time paying attention, as John proceeded to narrate on Sam's credentials and how lucky he was to have her come on board. TC's RTP kicked in when he heard John say that although Samantha grew up in Nashville, she had just recently moved back home, from Florida. Florida conjures the beach in TC's mind. He is abruptly brought back to the conversation at hand when Deidra knocks on the door and enters with the coffee.

"Shall I pour, Ms. Samantha?"

"No. Thank you Deidra I will take care of it, thank you for bringing it."

Deidra was a good employee and very loyal to John. She was Samantha's personal assistant. In her early forties, she was medium height, a tad bit over weight, with long blonde hair she always kept pulled back at the nap of her neck. She was very personable; always seemed to know ahead of time what anyone wanted, which was kind of freaky at times. A little too nosey to suit Sam's taste, but extremely efficient; therefore Sam tolerated her overly inquisitive nature, on most days anyway. Being divorced, she said she didn't need a man herself; however Deidra was forever trying to fix up everyone else. Spending most of her free time reading those cheap romance novels, Sam never understand the reasoning behind that.

Samantha reaches for one of the cups and pours the first one handing it to John, knowing he prefers his black. As she pours a second cup, extending the cup to TC, her hand begins to shake slightly, causing the cup to rattle a bit against the saucer. Somewhat embarrassed, she blushes. Looking up at TC she manages a confident look.

"Would you care for cream or sugar?"

TC is shaken as well, but manages a reply.

"Yes, both please."

Having taking a sip of coffee, John sits his cup on the table and looks at TC.

"I am so sorry, TC I got so involved in filling you in on Samantha, that I totally forgot you had your own purpose for stopping by today."

TC himself, had forgotten all about the reason for his visit until John brought it up.

"Oh, yes the um, Brandywine closing. Justin needs that to happen this Thursday."

Glancing at Sam he explains. "Justin, is my top Realtor"

TC then looks back at John.

"Well, he insists this must close on Thursday, so I was stopping by to see if we could possibly make that happen?"

Again glancing back toward Sam, he sits his coffee cup down. TC picks up his briefcase that has been sitting on the floor beside him. John looks as Sam for her approval; Sam looks at them both.

"Well, of course I will do my best to oblige, after all John speaks so highly of you and your staff, I am sure it will be a simple closing. I will have Deidra set a time and give Justin a call this afternoon to confirm."

"That would be perfect and greatly appreciated. I believe that would make me obligated to return the favor sometime."

TC gives Sam a big smile. She couldn't help noticing what a nice smile it was. Their eyes locked on each other for a lingering moment before John clears his throat again. About that time, Deidra appears again, as she so often does without warning. Mr. John, that conference call you were expecting is on line three.

"Oh my goodness, I must get that one! Thank you Deidra, I will be right there."

As John turned his attention back to TC, he remarked.

"It was so nice to see you again TC, we will do lunch soon, yes?"

He shakes TC's hand and out the door he goes, leaving Sam and TC alone.

Sam stands. "If you will excuse me for just a moment, I will give this file to Deidra to make that appointment call.

TC stands when she does, smiling handsomely at her. "Of course Sam and thank you."

She returns to her office to find TC standing in front of her painting, gently running his finger across the metal tag. The sight of him there, touching it, was a little unsettling to her, she waits a moment. Finally TC acknowledges her presence.

"Beautiful painting." He says as he looks at her and smiles. "Thank you, yes I do love it."

"Are you the artist?'

Blushing she replies. "Well, not that I admit that to everyone, but yes I am." Looking at TC through her lashes, then back at the painting if embarrassed.

"Wow! I can't imagine why on earth you would not! It is a gorgeous painting. You must be a woman of many talents. Have you painted professionally?"

Laughingly she replies "Oh my goodness no! I am hardly that good! Just dabble a little in my spare time. Very relaxing for me, my artwork."

"Well, I must admit the Water's Edge," He refers to the name on the tag, "is my favorite escape. I love the ocean, it seems to always cast a spell upon me as does this painting, you have captured it very well Samantha.' TC turns to look at her. "As I said you must be a woman of many talents."

He noticed how her huge gorgeous green eyes, now seemed to be a light blue almost matching the blue in her painting. Becoming a little nervous with his gaze upon her, Sam asks. "Would you care for another cup of coffee TC?"

"Oh, no thank you Sam, or do you prefer Samantha?' Sam detects a mischievous gleam in TC's deep steel blue eyes.

"Actually I do prefer Sam and on certain occasions, Samantha." Smiling back at him with her own mischievous look. All signs of any nervousness have dissipated from them both. TC was surprised and amused by Sam's quick flirtatious humor. She's going to be an interesting one, this Sam, of that he was sure.

About that time Sam's intercom sounds, she answers to hear Deidra.

"Sorry to interrupt Sam but Mr. Martindale is here about to have a hissy fit and insists on seeing you now. What shall I tell him?' "Tell him I will be with him in just a moment, thank you Deidra."

Looking back at TC "I am sorry to cut our visit short; it was certainly a pleasure to meet you. John speaks so very highly of you."

"My pleasure I assure you, perhaps we can get together one day next week?" He replies as he picks up his briefcase.

"Yes, that would be great; I will look forward to hearing from you."

Sam notices Deidra poking her head around the door so she leaves the conversation at that. "Deidra, please send Mr. Martindale in." Smiling at TC as he makes his way out the door.

He nods a goodbye to Deidra as he goes by her. Once to his

truck, he breaks out in a nervous sweat. A chill runs up his spine and all is black for just a split second. His hand still on the door handle, he hears a loud clap of thunder, opening his eyes he realizes his hand is soaking wet! "Damn it!' He yells, quickly opening the door and jumps into his truck before he is totally soaked.

"Shit! Thought I was having another flashback and it really is raining!" Half laughing at himself and happy knowing he did indeed escape another dreadful flashback of some sort.

Drying his hands off with a napkin, he starts his vehicle. Watching the droplets of water hitting his windshield, something was haunting him, he shivers, from the cold rain he assumed.

He sees bright green eyes staring through the raindrops, another clap of thunder. Brunette hair with a hint of Auburn tied with a …. Purple ribbon! He immediately starts frantically searching through his console. There it was! After two years of dreams and nightmares about a woman on a beach at the water's edge. The painting flashes through his mind. This is too weird. Just too weird indeed. He shakes his head in disbelief. Could it be? There was something about those eyes! Unable to wrap his mind around the possibility, he gently placed the purple ribbon back into the console. His heart still pounding. Although the purple ribbon had sort of solidified the fact that the mystery woman was real, he never really believed it. He thought he had conjured it all up in his mind, with a little mixture of truth, the ribbon, and his wild imagination.

Why would she have left him on the beach if she had been real? Could it possibly be? Could she be the mystery woman from the water's edge?

Chapter **5**

Samantha is alone if her office, having smoothed the ruffled feathers of Mr. Martindale, she turns in her chair to look at her painting. Her mind though, is seeing TC's face instead of the ocean. Seeing him, definitely rattled her, it had been all she could do to retain her composure. Sam remembered him all too well from that night on the beach, how could she not! He had been embedded in her brain ever since. Something about his deep blue soul searching eyes haunted her. From the first moment she saw him, she knew he saw straight to the core of her being and it more than frightened her.

Did he remember her? Of course not, why would he? She becomes agitated with herself at the thought. Suddenly her intercom sounds again with Deidra's voice.

"Sam your hubby called and asked that you give him a call back when you were free. Oh and I'm taking off for lunch. Wanted to let you know before I left."

Sam sighs before answering. "Ok Deidra, thank you. Have a good lunch."

"Sure thing." Replies Deidra leaving Sam with welcomed silence again. She sat there looking at the phone as though in a trance finally picking it up to call Ash.

"Hey Ash, Deidra said you called".

"Hey honey, yes, I just wanted to let you know I was going to be a little late again and not to wait supper on me. As a matter of fact why don't I just pick us up some Chinese on the way home? You won't be starved, will you?"

Sam could hear the smile in his voice. "No, I won't be starved. You know I do not like Chinese." Giving way to his funny little gesture. She hears Ash chuckle as he replies.

"Okay, okay how about I stop and pick up one of those chicken salads you like?"

"That would be much better, Ash. I will see you when you get home then." Samantha places the receiver back in its holder not giving the conversation another thought. Trying to focus on her work at hand, her mind wonders back to when she first met Ash, short for Ashley. She was at a New Year's Eve party with Tony, just as friends, not that they were dating or anything like that. He was the brother of her best friend, Dakota. Tony was nice, very proper and very much a gentlemen. He was a handsome enough man of average build, although quite tall, right at 6 foot. He had a full head of dark sandy brown hair that showed just a tiny bit of balding, toward the back but you really didn't notice. His much darker brown and slightly graying beard and moustache seemed to be more of the focal point to his face, along with his bright green eyes that lit up with each smile. She had introduced Ash and Tony when Ash needed some car repair. Tony was an auto mechanic by trade. He and Ash just seemed to hit it off and had been best friends ever since. He was even Ash's best man at their wedding.

Tony would often stop by Sam's office just to say hello or drop her by a sandwich or one of her favorite drinks from a local drive through. She never really thought much about it, they were all friends after all. Dakota would often tease Samantha that Tony had a crush on her. She said he never married because he was waiting around for her. Sam just scoffed it off to Dakota being Dakota.

Tony did like to tease her. She remembered him walking up behind her at the party and slightly poking her in the ribs, almost causing her to drop her drink. He definitely was a lot of fun that was true enough. She did secretly agree with Dakota, that Tony might have a bit of a crush, but she would never admit it to her. She also didn't understand how Ash and Tony got along; they had nothing in common aside from golf games and a beer every now and then. She would sometimes mention to Tony that she didn't see his connection to Ash, and he would always reply.

"Yeah, kind of like you and Ash, eh Sam?'

With a wry look on his face, followed by a knowing smile. Tony was a mess for sure, but she did enjoy his friendship and Ash didn't seem to mind it either. Tony was correct, Sam and Ash had about as much in common as he and Ash. Not just personality traits but physical traits as well. She was only 5'1, Ash was 5'11. He was a blue eyed blonde and she was a green eyed brunette. They couldn't agree on movies or TV shows. She liked romantic comedies; he liked the ones that either scared her to death or made her nauseous. They did not agree on food or music venues, although she did like most all kinds of music, she was not a fan of the harder rock that Ash preferred. Ash was an English professor at Vanderbilt. They both had prior marriages and neither of which had produced any children. That being one of the few things they did have in common. She really wasn't sure what had brought them together ten years ago.

60

Maybe it was loneliness or just being comfortable with each other. They had their good days that was true enough, but of late, they were very few and far between. They had not even been intimate in a couple of years. She had tried talking to Ash about it but he just scoffed it off to being tired or not in the mood. She even mentioned that little blue pill that so many middle aged men seemed to be crazy about, but Ash showed no interest. Of late, she felt more like he was her brother instead of her husband. Their distance had definitely grown larger the last three or so years. But they were still together. She was not sure why.

Chapter 6

Spring and summer were some of the busiest months for the real estate industry, and with interest rates being at an all-time low, it had kept TC pretty busy. People were buying, selling or refinancing and in turn he had kept River House Title just as busy. He had decided this morning that he best be paying them a visit with some appreciative gestures, as it had definitely been a profitable year for them both. Just this week alone, he had twelve closings scheduled there, very profitable indeed. Any thought of River House always brought up thoughts of Samantha; his RTP went wild and crazy at the thought of her. They had seen each other quite often over the last few months. Their friendship and admiration for each other had indeed grown. The bond between them was strangely immediate, as though they had been old friends from the start. The months from that first meeting to now had definitely been interesting to say the least. Their conversations would fluctuate from discussing stressful business situations to comical events in their personal lives, or happenings with their respective families. Their friendship was growing stronger and stronger with each encounter. He always looked forward to seeing Sam and she always had a big smile for him without fail.

Sitting at the red light waiting for traffic to clear he then made a quick right turn going down another block and then pulling into the parking lot of his favorite florist, Kelsey's. They knew him well there. As he entered the establishment, the sweet floral smell was a pleasant welcoming. It was a quaint little shop well known for the best service in town. TC was barely inside the door before he was met by the owner herself, Ms. Kelsey. She was a very short chubby little lady of Scottish decent, still with a heavy accent. She was the sweetest little old lady you'd ever meet, and always ready to be of help.

"TC! How good to see you!" She calls out in her heavy accent. A big smile across her face, her cheeks slightly blushing.

"How in the world have you been TC, busy I am sure! Yes?" as she hugs him tightly.

"Well, I am much better now that I have a hug from you! And a pleasure to see your beautiful face Ms. Kelsey"

"Ah! TC! I see you still enjoy flirting and making us old women feeling like we are 20 again! That flirting is going to get you into trouble one of these days TC!"

He noticed the twinkle in her eyes. "Well, a guy can only keep hoping Ms. Kelsey, only keep hoping!' Giving her a winning smile and a wink and he walks over to smell the beautiful bouquet of bright yellow roses.

She blushes even more. "Oh goodness TC! You are a mess I don't know how Ms. Jan puts up with the likes of you!"

Following closely behind him as he checks out a few more displays, she frowns as though she suddenly remembers business. She reaches for her tattered brown leather address book, the one that contains all her business contacts information. As she rattles on. "Oh my! Did I forget Jan's birthday? You know I always remind you! Or let's see, it's June, anniversary? Oh TC I am so sorry I must have lost my mind, to not call you." A worried frown upon her face. Before she can continue her tirade TC stops her.

"Now, now Ms. Kelsey you know good and well that you have never let me down, never missed a phone call yet! No, I am here to get some good cheer for River House Title. I've been working them pretty hard this summer and figured I needed something to brighten their day! So, of course I thought of you!"

He gently releases the flower he was holding, watching it glide back to its rightful place, as he turns to smile at her.

Kelsey smiles back at TC. "So what are you thinking? Roses?"

"Yes, I think so Ms. Kelsey! You always make the best choices for me! These are gorgeous and so very fragrant." He had a special knack for making people think things were their ideas.

"Give me two dozen in your prettiest large crystal vase and make it look extra special with all the other stuff you throw in there." "Yes, yes the baby's breath and the green leaf fillers. Of course! I will make it the best for you TC! And I have the perfect round crystal vase that, well, it looks like a big crystal ball! It is gorgeous! Who knows maybe it will even tell you your future TC, if you stoke it just right!" Giving him a little wink herself.

TC responds with a big laugh, hugging her again.

"You! Are the best Ms. Kelsey."

He makes his way toward the door and turns to look back at her. "Oh and I need one of those potted plants for Deidra. You know her likes, so just fix me up something for her, please. I have another errand to run and I should be back in about an hour. Will that give you enough time to have it ready?"

"Of course! Of course!' She replies smiling broadly as she is shooing him out the door.

TC drives across town to the liquor store, picking up John Rivers favorite bottle of brandy and a bottle of wine for Mrs. Rivers. He lingers at the wine wondering should he purchase a bottle for Sam.

"Hum I just don't see Samantha as a wine drinker, for some reason, so I best do some investigating before going that route. He picks up a couple of bottles for Jan, though, and a couple of six packs of his favorite beer and a few more for the upcoming BBQ at his house. It was the Fourth of July weekend and they always had some sort of celebration.

Arriving back at Kelsey's, he is stunned to see how beautifully Kelsey has made the arrangement. "Honey, you are the best! These are fantastic!" He exclaimed as he gave her a warm hug.

Ms. Kelsey beams with pride. "I made it extra special, just for you TC, just for you!"

Thanking her again and paying with a nice tip to boot, he loads them in the back seat of his truck. The aroma immediately fills the cab. Slowly making his trip over to River House he arrives with everything safely intact. Pulling in he notices the lot is almost empty and immediately looks at his watch. "Well, no wonder, it is almost six o'clock." He quickly parks retrieving the brandy and wine for John. Taking note that Sam's car is still in her usual parking spot, he enters the door. Deidra greets him with a smile. "Hello TC!"

"Hello to you Deidra. Is John still here?" Before Deidra has a chance to answer he hears John's voice behind.

"I believe you caught me just in time TC."

TC turns around placing the liquor package under one arm and shakes John's extended hand. Smiling he replies.

"I knew I had good timing. I brought a little token of appreciation for you and a little something for Mrs. Rivers." He hands the brown paper bag to John.

John smiles, taking the bag from TC without any hesitation. "Now you know that is not necessary." Winking he adds. "But it is greatly appreciated and will go perfectly with the dinner Estelle is preparing tonight."

Holding the door open for John, TC pats him on the shoulder as he passes. Don't want to make you late for dinner with the Mrs. Please give her a kiss for me, John, will you?"

"Thank you TC, I will surely do just that. She will be appreciative of the surprise as well, you have a good evening now TC." He watches as John Rivers gets in his car.

Love that old man. He and Gunny have been really good to me. He thought as he watched John exit the lot. Turning his attention back to Deidra, who has as usual, been intently watching everything going on. It felt as though she was reading his mind. How does she do that? he wondered.

"Got something else in my truck. Would you mind holding the door for me Deidra?"

"I certainly will TC, certainly will." She smiles and gets up to wait by the door. In just a moment TC is back with the bouquet and the potted plant. Handing the potted plant to Deidra he smiles. "A little thank you for you too Deidra, I know you are a very important part of the team around here."

Taking the plant Deidra smiles. "Thanks TC I will put them

66

with my others, you are too good to me! And yes, you can go on into Ms. Sam's office; she doesn't have anyone with her."

As TC thanks her and takes a step down the hall Deidra calls after him.

"TC, how did you know yellow roses were her favorite?" Looking back at Deidra over his shoulder he replies.

"Just a lucky guess, I suppose."

Wondering to himself why she even asked? So inquisitive that one.

Arriving at Sam's door, he sees she has not noticed him yet. He places the large vase of roses in front of his face and loudly clears his throat. Sam, somewhat startled, looks up and sees flowers, and a mystery person holding them. Getting up from her desk and walking over to the doorway she attempts to take the flowers but feels a resistance. She releases her grasp on the vase, taking a step back she asks, "May I help you?" TC lowers the vase.

"Why yes you can! I was looking for the gorgeous brunette that runs this place, ah, but I see I have found her!" Smiling he walks over and sits the oversized vase on the corner of her desk. Sam follows, leaning over to smell the bouquet as her hand gently caress one of the roses.

"Oh my goodness, these are beautiful! They smell so wonderful! Yellow, my favorite rose color. TC! This is so sweet of you, thank you so much! Please have a seat. Do you have time for a visit? Or just playing delivery boy today?" Giving him a flirtatious smile.

TC is beside himself thinking how beautiful she is and almost gasps out loud. He recovers quickly, hoping she hadn't noticed as he takes his seat.

"Just a little token of appreciation Sam, for all of your hard work the past few months. It has been a mad house for us and I know it has been the same for you."

"Well, that is what makes for a good work day I always say. Better to be busy than bored. And you certainly make sure that doesn't happen around here TC." Smiling sweetly back at him.

"John and I do appreciate your business that is for sure. It has been a pleasure working with you and getting to know you better."

Her face slightly flushes as she lowers her lashes to lean over to smell the flowers again. Just as TC is about to speak, the intercom chimes in with Deidra's voice.

"Sorry to interrupt Ms. Sam, but Mr. Zimmerman is on the phone and insists talking to you. I wouldn't have answered it this late but I thought it was a call I was expecting, sorry."

Sam gives TC a questioning look.

"I am sorry. Do you mind?"

"Of course not Sam, by all means." He starts to rise from his chair, but Sam motions him to sit.

"Please put Mr. Zimmerman through Deidra".

"Yes ma'am." Deidra responds.

As Sam is talking to her client, TC is soon oblivious to her words as he takes assessment of her beauty. Her dark hair was pulled back a little on each side of her face revealing a pair of long delicate earrings adorning each earlobe. With each movement she made, the silver would flash a little twinkle, as though it were winking at him. His RTP whisked him away in a daydream. Wondering what it would feel like to walk up behind her and move that little strand of hair that was so teasingly embracing her shoulder at the edge of her neck. It was swirled around in a little curl pointing toward her

68

breasts. Which led him to notice how nice she looked in the red blouse. Definitely her color. It was a scoop neck top that let a little bare skin show just below the collarbone. Bare skin that looked so sweetly soft. Skin that he longed to touch. His pulse began to quicken.

"Sorry about that, TC." He abruptly hears Samantha say, bringing him back from his daydream. He looks up just in time to see her warm smile. His face turned a little pink at the thoughts he had just had. He was thankful that Sam appeared totally unaware.

"Well, hard work must agree with you because you look very beautiful today, not that you don't look beautiful every time I see you." Nervously clearing his throat as he had not actually meant to say that out loud.

"Why thank you kind sir!" She flutters her eyelashes at him in a jokingly flirtatious manor. TC smiles back knowingly.

"Well Sam, I actually had another reason for coming to see you today. A special request of sorts."

"Really? Well I could hardly refuse such a handsome man who comes bearing gifts. What can I assist you with TC?"

"We are celebrating Independence Day with a BBQ pool party at the house. With just a few close friends and some Marine buddies of mine, we would love it if you could come and of course bring your husband. John and his wife will be there.

Samantha hesitates for only a moment.

"Um, oh sure, I will check with Ash and see if he has anything going on, I never know with him." She smiles and quickly adds. "Thank you for the invitation. Should I bring anything?"

"Just your pretty smile!" Then he adds without thinking. "Also a swimsuit unless you plan to skinny dip!" He manages to recover nicely before she can reply by adding.

"Oh and invite your friend, Dakota, is it? And her husband too, of course. The more the merrier!"

"Well, that is very nice of you TC, I will certainly ask Dakota and Ron if they can join us."

TC reluctantly rises from his chair. "Well I best be heading home and let you do the same. You have my cell number; just call me and let me know if you can make it."

"I surely will TC." She glances at the small stack of files on the corner of her desk. "Oh, and would you mind taking these files with you to give back to Justin?"

"Sure, be happy to." He takes the folders from Sam and they both enter the hallway just outside her office door. Pausing for a moment still talking business, Sam leans up against the wall that has a bulletin board with various papers attached with push pens and the like. She inadvertently loosens a piece of paper causing it to slip from its hold on the board. It gently floats to the floor at Sam's feet. TC, being the gentlemen that he is, bends down to retrieve the rogue piece of paper. All the while taking note of the sexy red shoes she is wearing and the nicely tanned legs they are supporting. Raising up, he reaches beside her head to reattach the paper, putting his hand at a very close proximity to her face, right at eye level. They were only inches apart, face to face. How easy it would be to lean down and give her a kiss. TC's hand began to tremble ever so slightly. They were so close, less than an arm's length from each other. The animal magnetism between the two of them seemed to fill the air. Sam felt it. TC felt it. Anyone in the room surely would have felt it. Both of their pulses quickened. TC felt as if his heart were going to pop out of his chest. He could feel the temperature rise in his face. Being so close to her at that moment really rattled him. Sam noticed the slight shake of his hand and turned to reach up and hold the paper as TC attached it back to the board. Putting their hands within inches of each other, so close she could feel the heat between them. Causing her own RTP fantasy. Thoughts of how close his hand was to her face. Of what if might feel like to have it touch her. She could almost feel the warmth of his hand on her body. Suddenly jarred back to reality by the ringing of TC's cell phone attached to his belt loop. He didn't bother to answer the call. Still looking at Sam; her looking at him. The continual ring of the phone was enough to bring them back to the here and now. TC takes a step back from Sam. As they both turn to continue toward the exit, they see Deidra sitting at her desk. Her body was stiff and rigid looking, almost as though she were frozen. She had been intently watching them. Deidra realizing that TC and Sam were both looking at her suddenly felt like a voyeur, her own face turning a little pink. A very rare feeling for her inquisitive self, to say the least. Deidra nervously starts to fidget with the papers in her hands and tries to pretend she didn't notice TC and Sam. But notice them she did. No one could have missed what just transpired between them. It was so intense; how could anyone not have noticed. The obvious strong attraction between them filled the entire room. TC, feeling the sudden urgent need to exit immediately, took a step toward the door.

"Well, err got to go, thanks Sam, see you soon." He was out the door in a flash before Sam could even respond.

As TC unlocks his truck door, his hands are trembling. Yes, he felt it and his body was certainly letting him know. His face turned red at the thought of anyone noticing that slight bulge that had begun to grow in his slacks. He couldn't get out that door fast enough. Thank goodness no one seemed to notice. How embarrassing that would have been, he thought, as he sat there for a moment trying to regain his composure. But his mind still had other ideas. He was so close to Sam, he just wanted to press her against that wall with his own body. He wanted to take his hand and touch her face, to trace her lips ever so lightly with his fingers. He really wanted to kiss those sexy full lips. At that moment when she looked into his eyes, he felt as though she was touching his soul. Frustrated, he adjusted himself in his seat before starting his truck and headed for home.

Sam, feeling somewhat overwhelmed, returned to her office. After straightening her desk and putting things in order for the next morning, she picks up her purse taking a last smell of the roses. She turns out the light and shuts her office door. She walks by Deidra without looking at her.

"Deidra, lock up and go home for heaven's sake. I'll see you in the morning."

"Yes ma'am." She hears, as she exits the door making her way to her own car and heading toward home as well.

Chapter 7

It was a perfect day in Nashville. Mother Nature was obviously in a good mood and had blessed them with a perfect July Fourth weekend. Perfect for a BBQ and a cool dip in the pool.

"TC! Did you remember to get the ice and enough charcoal?" Jan yells as TC is unloading his vehicle in the driveway. "Yes! For the fourth time! I got the charcoal, I got the ice, and I remembered the meat!"

TC makes his way past her to the kitchen counter. She is preparing one to those nasty cold noodle salad things with green peas that he detests. He takes one look and his face contorts to disgust.

"Really? TC! No one said you had to eat any of it. There will be other guests here that might actually enjoy it and appreciate my effort. And I was simply asking if you remembered everything, no need for you to be so curt about it!"

"Well, if it hadn't been the hundredth time you asked me, then maybe I wouldn't have been."

Jan angrily opens the fridge door shoving the salad onto the shelf, slamming the door back closed. "Well, just a minute ago it had only been the fourth time!" She turns and heads for upstairs. "I'm going to take a quick shower before everyone starts showing up; maybe you need a shower TC! A cold one!' As she reaches the top of the landing she hears TC yelling after her.

"Is that an offer to join you? Cause if it is, I am not in the mood!" "Hardly' comes her tart reply followed by the slamming of their bedroom door.

"Damn! What the hell!" He grumbles as he grabs a beer from the fridge slamming the door back himself.

Opening the sliding glass doors, TC goes outside. "Maybe a cold beer and some fresh air will help." He thinks as he slides the door closed. As he downs a few drinks of his beer, his eyes scan the area to be sure he has set everything up for the BBQ. Satisfied that he had, he glances up at their bedroom window. What's up with that woman these days anyway? Before his thoughts go any further, his cell phone rings. He looks at it seeing it is Samantha. Instantly his mood changes for the better.

"Hello! Samantha! I hope you are not calling me to tell me you have changed your mind?" "Au contraire, TC, not at all. I was just calling to double check to see if there was anything I could bring and to thank you again for including Dakota and her husband."

"I appreciate the offer Sam, but I believe we will have more than enough food and drinks for that matter. I am looking forward to meeting your friend and her husband." And as an afterthought he added "And of course, Ash too!"

"Great TC, we are looking forward to meeting Jan as well. We will see you about three then."

TC hangs up the phone putting it back into his belt holder and then takes the last few drinks of his beer, checking his watch for the time.

"Well, I guess I'd better get that charcoal going." Mumbling as he rose from his chair. Andy had left TC with explicit instructions on when to start the coals in order that he may cook the meats to perfection. "Such a perfectionist." TC thought as he shook his head and lit the fires. It wasn't long before he heard the side entry gate opening; it was Andy and his cute little blonde date. They greeted TC on the deck.

"TC, how the hell are you man?" Andy extends his hand to TC.

TC shoves a spatula in Andy's hand while grabbing him on the shoulder with the other hand, smiling all the while.

"Doing great Andy, who is this lovely woman by your side?" TC wondering how the hell Andy could get the most gorgeous women! She was cute, with silky black hair and brown eyes and an olive complexion.

"TC this is Marlena. Marlena meet TC" Andy points back and forth at the both of them.

"Nice to meet you Marlena, welcome to our home."

She smiled kindly. "Thank you TC, it is a pleasure to be here." About that time TC sees Jan coming from the house with a drink tray and Gunny in tow, a beer in his left hand.

"Hey Gunny! Where is Martha?"

Before Gunny can reply Jan chimes in. "Oh she is inside, TC, taste testing my pea salad; she said it was perfect by the way." Giving her husband that I am right smirk. TC rolled his eyes.

Jan offers Andy and Marlena a drink and introduces herself to Marlena.

"Oh, and Dalton called said he and Tabitha would be pulling in the driveway in about ten minutes, if you could lend them a hand with the ice chest. That was about five minutes ago." With the smirk still on her face.

TC goes around front to help Dalton with his oversized ice chest. They were just starting to unload the truck. Dalton looks at TC and nods.

"Hey TC, thanks for helping man. I see Andy's jeep is here. Did he bring his latest blonde chick?"

"Blonde? Guess I missed that one; he has a different one today, and yep, she is really cute." TC lifts one side of the chest and Dalton the other. Dalton grunted at the weight. "Yeah, well how much you want to bet she will be gone by Thanksgiving?"

"Damn man, how the hell did you and Tabitha load this heavy thing?"

Dalton smiled. "We loaded it after we put it in the truck." He turns to wink at Tabitha as though it were a private joke of some sort.

Tabitha looks at them both as if in distaste. "Really! You two are so incorrigible! Give the poor girl a chance for heaven's sake!" TC and Dalton laughed. They all go around back. TC introduces them to Marlena as they join the others.

It is not long before the girls retreat to the house to finish preparing the food. The guys are all gathered around the grills with beers in hand. Soon the house and yard are filled with guests. The smell of the meat cooking on the grills, the splashing and laughter coming from the pool, all indicative of a good start to a perfect 4th of July celebration.

Promptly at three p.m. Ash and Samantha arrive in the driveway. Just as they are getting out of their car, John and Estelle pull in behind them.

"Good afternoon Sam. Ash good to see you too." John extends

a hand to Ash smiling at them both.

"Good to see you too John, and Mrs. Rivers you are looking good this sunny afternoon, can I assist you with that pie?"

Estelle takes Ash's outreached hand as he helps her from the car.

"Well, thank you Ash that would be great. I have two more pecan pies in the back. Hello Samantha dear." Giving Sam a hug. Sam reciprocates and offers to carry a pie, as well as. Estelle reaches in the back seat for her wine bottle tote.

As they enter the back yard, Sam is surprise to see so many people. She had no idea it would be such a large crowd. Ash seemed surprised too but it didn't matter to him; he never met a stranger anyway. Ash sits the mini cooler and pies on the table and turns to look at Samantha.

"I'm ready for a beer. How about you Sam? Want one of your frozen daiquiri pouches?"

"Sure, yeah." Half paying attention to what he is saying as she scans the crowd looking for TC.

Ash hands her drink to her and gets his beer. He glances over at a table where he sees fresh glasses stacked beside a big chest filled with ice. Another ice chest was stacked with a large quantity of beers and wine coolers protruding through the ice. A sign in front read. "Help yourself!"

"Would you like a glass for that Sam?

"Yes, Ash, that would be great." He is back in a flash with a glass of ice for her and another beer for him. He was never one to miss out on anything that was free for the taking. This trait, if you will, had never set well with Samantha. It wasn't like he needed the money after all. Most days she was able to just ignore it. She pours her daiquiri into the glass and takes a sip of the drink. As she looked up, she saw TC across the yard on the other side of the pool. He had spotted her as well and their eyes meet. He smiles, and heads her way, his eyes never leaving her. Sam touches Ash on the arm to get his attention.

"Come Ash, I will introduce you to TC, and then we can mingle." As they meet TC halfway across the yard, the two men extend their hands in a friendly shake. But a strange thing happened.

Sam noticed what seemed like a scowl on both their faces, as they were shaking hands and saying nice to meet you. Yes, it was a definite scowl! That was truly odd she thought. But with no time to ponder it any further, she turned her attention to TC's question on where Dakota was.

"Oh, she should be here in about an hour; she had to work a few hours over today, one of the shift nurses had car trouble, and she didn't want to leave the hospital shorthanded."

Sam was just a little nervous. "You know, duty calls." She lifted her drink as though in salute to TC.

TC smiled at her, lifting his own beer in the same gesture. "Great! I am looking forward to meeting her." TC notices Ash's beer is empty. "Hey Ash, looks like that one has gone dry, let me get you a beer."

Ash looks at his empty beer bottle and replies. "Thanks, but I will get it. I think I see an acquaintance of mine. I should probably say hello to them. Excuse me."

TC nods an affirmative to Ash and looks at Samantha. He loves her bedroom eyes, they drive him insane with desire on most days. So much so, that he finds it hard to look directly into them.

"You look...." He stops short as he feels a hand on his arm, TC instinctively knows it is Jan's. He turned to see Jan was looking at Samantha.

"Jan honey, this is Samantha. Sam, this is my wife Jan." The two women smile at each other.

"So nice to finally meet you Samantha. TC speaks very highly of you."

"Thank you Jan, as he does you."

Jan smiles. "I hear you have been a great asset over at River House. Congratulations on the partnership." She looked up at TC, slips her arm into his, as though to show ownership and smiling back sweetly at Samantha.

"Thank you Jan. Yes, it has been a whirlwind summer for sure." Sam notices how pretty Jan is. And how very tall! She suddenly felt very short in her flat heeled sandals. I knew I should have worn the ones with a little heel. Secretly cursing herself, feeling a bit nervous in Jan's presences. She also felt a little vulnerable in her peach sundress that doubled as a swimsuit cover. TC noticed Ash had stopped to chat with some others, another beer in his hand. "Well, looks like Ash has made himself right at home."

Sam looks in Ash's direction and then back at TC and Jan. "Yes, it is true, he never met a stranger. Oh, Jan I um should introduce you to my husband..." as she turns again toward Ash.

"No worries Sam, he looks like he is deep in conversation. I'm sure our paths will cross paths before the night is over. As she turns back to look at TC, Gunny walks up and extends his hand to Samantha.

"Why hello! Sam is it? TC speaks very highly of you. I'm the damn old Gunny Sergeant that he probably doesn't speak that highly of!" Giving Sam a little wink.

TC sighs quietly to himself. Good old Gunny, always coming to my rescue. Although from what he wasn't quite sure.

Sam is immediately put at ease as she shakes Gunny's hand, noticing the little twinkle in his eyes, not unlike that of John Rivers.

"Gunny Sergeant, may I call you Gunny?" Without waiting for a reply she continued. "Now I am sure you absolutely know that is far from the truth! TC is your biggest fan!" She gives Gunny her best winning smile.

Gunny grins at Sam, and turns to TC. "I see you've been telling lies on me again TC! Building me up like that to this woman." TC raises his beer to Gunny as if in a toast.

"Well if the shoe fits Gunny." About that time Jan excuses herself from them as she is being beckoned by another guest for her attention. TC too, is pulled away to help Andy and Dalton with the grills, filling ice buckets and general host duties. Leaving Gunny and Sam to get to know each other. It is not long before Gunny is really smitten with Sam.

"Oh excuse me Gunny, my cell, it must be my friend Dakota." As she reaches into the pocket of her dress. "Sure thing, I need a refill anyway and to find that missing wife of mine." He winks at her. "Pleasure missy!" He leaves in the direction of the house. She looks at her phone and sees it is a text from Dakota telling her they are out front in the driveway. Putting her phone back in her pocket, she sat her drink down on a nearby table. As she goes out the side gate and down the path to the driveway, she noticed all the pretty flowers that adorned each side, wondering if that was TC or Jan's handiwork.

Dakota was Sam's best friend of many years. They shared a lot together. She was a very tall drop dead gorgeous blue eyed blonde with a perfect body. Sam had always envied her height and perfect looks. Although Dakota always denied she was far from perfect. Her husband Ron, was also a blue eyed blonde and about the same height as Dakota, with a nice build to boot. They seemed to be quite the perfect couple, not just in looks but personalities as well. A happy second marriage for the both of them.

Entering the back yard, Dakota exclaims "Wow! I thought this was going to be a quaint little BBQ, with just a few friends!"

"I know, I was quite surprised by it as well." Sam replied.

Ron spied Ash talking to a mutual friend and excused himself to go join them.

It wasn't long before the party was kicking in high gear; seemingly most folks had introduced themselves, if not properly introduced by someone else. The sun had long gone down, leaving way for the stars to light the night sky.

Eventually the food was devoured, the fireworks depleted and the pool now empty in the coolness of the night. Candles and lanterns lit the back yard and deck. Sam had taken a seat at a table far from the center of the crowd, sipping a rum and pineapple concoction that Andy had insisted on making for her. It was actually quite good, she thought, as she took another sip.

TC appeared from nowhere. He smiled at her as he pulled out a chair.

"Mind if I join you"?

Sam smiled back at TC.

"This has been a really great party TC, just great. You have a lovely wife and such a nice group of friends."

TC doesn't reply. He is just looking at Sam thinking how

beautiful she looks in the candle light. Her green eyes dancing from the flickering flame. Sam's eyes met his; they are both held spellbound for a moment. TC's eyes seemed to envelop her entire being, touching every aspect of her. It was hard not to look away; equally hard to look as well. Her face blushed and she shivered. TC noticed the shiver.

"Sam are you cold? Should I get you a jacket or sweater? I can grab one of Jan's for you." A slightly concerned look upon his face.

"No! Uh I, I mean no thank you." She managed in a much calmer voice. "I am fine really. Just this cold drink got to me and the air is a little cool."

TC grinned. "I guess, that explains the no swimming?"

"Well, I'm not that much of a water person, especially in a crowd."

"Well, yes, one would gather that from the painting hanging in your office." TC theorized comically.

With a devilish smile she looks at TC. "Well, I may just be full of all kinds of surprises TC!"

"I'm sure you are Samantha." He conferred with a wink. "I am sure you are."

She takes another sip of her drink and noticed that Dakota was conversing with a couple of people several feet from their table, but her eyes were fixated on TC and Sam. TC and Sam were unaware Gunny was doing pretty much the same from the opposite side of the yard, intensely watching the two of them.

Before any more conversation ensued, John and Estelle approached their table, thanking TC for the enjoyable evening, food and friendship. They were the first to call it a night. Others soon followed suit, including Samantha, Ash, Dakota and Ron until everyone had pretty much departed. Dalton, Tabitha, Marlena, and Andy all stayed to help TC and Jan with the cleanup.

An hour or so later, TC and Jan were climbing into the respective sides of their bed. Laying there silently for a moment, Jan turns to TC who was on his back starring up at the ceiling.

"Well, we had a good turn out tonight TC."

"Yes we sure did." TC replied without turning to look at her.

Jan was watching TC's naked chest move ever so slightly with each breath while he lay there in what seemed like deep thought. She wondered what was on his mind.

"It was good to finally get to meet Samantha. She and her friend Dakota seemed to be very pleasant." She waits for TC to respond, but he does not. "You never mentioned how pretty and petite Sam was, and how stacked! I wonder if those boobs are real. And Dakota, now there is a gorgeous lady." TC had grown annoyed with what seemed like Jan's rambling on and on when he was trying to clear his mind to go to sleep, that and the fact that he had a few too many beers.

"Yes, Samantha is beautiful. Dakota is pretty enough, if you happen like your women extremely tall..." before he had finished he was fast asleep with only a gentle snore left for Jan's ears. The results of too many beers, a big meal, not to mention a very busy day.

Annoyed as well, she turns to her other side away from TC mumbling to herself.

"Well, I guess he forgot that I happen to be tall!"

Although angry, she soon succumbs to sleep as well.

Chapter 8

Months had flown by since the cookout and business had recovered to some normalcy. Normal enough to give both Sam and TC a little breather, which also meant more time for socializing during their visits. Any time he had a free moment, he would find himself drawn to her office. During their visits they would be engaged in a normal conversation and without fail flirting would ensue. It was as if they had no control over it, no matter how hard each of them tried to resist. Intense flirting would take off at the most innocent comment, almost as if it was its own wild seductive being, with a mind of its own. No matter how dangerous they knew it was, they both enjoyed it immensely. Their emotions were like a rollercoaster up and down, winding around one curve to another, wildly exciting, and frightening at the same time. Each visit they tried to ignore the attraction, but it was bigger than the both of them. No matter what tactic they tried, how much they both brought up stories of their respective spouses, and TC his kids, nothing worked. Even recent sermons from a Sunday church service wandered into their conversations, trying desperately to be good God fearing Christians, all to avoid their attraction to one another. Each secretly wanting so desperately to take it a step further, neither of them daring to make the first move. Oh sure, there were the friendly hello and good bye hugs, but those were not like real embraces. Those were only courtesy types of hugs, resembling the kind you give your brother or sister, just a quick touch then release, appropriate for business acquaintances and the like. However, it wasn't long, before one particular visit changed it all for the both of them.

It was late one afternoon, TC had not been by Rivers Title in a couple of weeks. He had been out of town on another seminar and with catching up on everything, he had just not found the time. As he entered the front reception area, he passed Deidra, with her purse in hand on her way out. "Hello TC, Sam is in her office. Everyone else has gone home for the day, me included." As she kept walking toward the door. "Tell Sam I will lock you two in, not to worry about the door."

"Thanks Deidra, you have a good evening and be safe getting home."

She nods her head in acknowledgement. TC paused for a moment before heading to Samantha's office. As he stood watching Deidra, now on the outside, insert her key in the door, he heard the click of the lock. Deidra gave him a last smile and waved goodbye before she turned to go to her car.

For some reason TC was especially anxious to see Sam today. "Hope you're not on your way out too, Sam?" he said as he stuck his head around the corner of her office door.

"No, TC, you know I would always make time for you anyway." Smiling sweetly back at him. "Come in please. Would you care for some bottled water? I know it has been a very warm day." Smiling,

TC replied, "Yes, I believe I would, thank you."

Sam smiled and walked past him, out her office door and down the hall to the kitchen, not realizing TC had followed close behind her. As she turned from the refrigerator, with the ice cold bottle of water, TC was practically on top of her. She suddenly reached out and gave him a full frontal hug, bodies touching. TC reciprocated the embrace. Sam whispered softly in his ear, "I've missed you." And just as quickly she released him and stepped back. It happened so quickly, and just as quickly it was over.

Sam immediately heads back to her office somewhat embarrassed by what she had just done. As for TC he was pleasantly surprise by her actions, and totally shocked by his own feelings while he was holding Sam in his arms. Hearing her actually say she had missed him. Her soft body pressed gently against his own. Yes, he had feelings alright, feelings that would never be the same again.

It was a late September morning, TC was still in bed, not really sleeping but just resting and preparing for what was going to be a hell of a day.

"Terrance Chadworth Martin!" Are you walking your daughter down the aisle today or not? For heavens sakes! I do not have time for this today!"

Throwing back the covers from his naked body TC gets up and puts on some shorts. He could tell Jan was thoroughly pissed, that was quite clear from not only what she said but her tone of voice as well. Not to mention the stomping of her feet as she made her way down the hall to their bedroom.

"Damn, it's only seven a.m.! The wedding isn't until four in the afternoon!!" He yells back at Jan. In a less audible tone, as though to himself. "It's going to be a day! That is for sure. Heaven help us all!" Then in a louder tone for Jan's benefit. "I'm up damn it! I'm up! You want to come back to bed baby and see how 'UP' I am?" Half-heartedly joking and the other half being very serious, after all it had been awhile, Jan just never seemed to be in the mood anymore. Suddenly Jan appears at their bedroom door, cooking utensils in her hand.

"Is THAT all you ever have on your mind TC? Sex! Really? You would think you are reverting back to your twenties instead of a middle aged man! What with everything that has to be done before this afternoon! I mean really? You would think you would have the decency to cut me some slack and give me some support. Today of all days! Joseph just got home on leave and there is just no time! No time for anything!" Jan was nearly in tears by the end of this tirade. TC reaches out and gives her a hug, making sure the utensil is tucked away at her side, least she decide to make a weapon of it.

"Jan, honey it is all going to be ok. Everything has been prepared for this day, almost from the day Annalisa was, what five old! Now come on baby, chill out a little." Then he teasingly grins at her. "May be a roll in the hay is just what you need, to relax you." Jan pulls away. "TC, you are incorrigible to say the least! Go take a cold shower." She turns and goes back to the kitchen to check on their breakfast. Satisfied that the egg casserole needed a few more minutes of cooking time she shuts the oven door and resets the timer for twenty minutes. As she was sitting the table with her best china her mind rambled with thoughts. Why doesn't TC understand, I wanted to make the entire day extra special for Annalisa. A day to remember more than just the wedding its self. I will certainly miss that spunky little girl being around, that's for sure. A tear streamed down her cheek as she placed the napkins neatly beside each plate. She didn't know why she was so emotional of late. Everything seemed to be going awry. Work, TC and the kids with this issue or that. Someone or something constantly pulling at her. Never enough time for herself. Never enough time to be Jan. Not someone's mother not TC's wife not the executive, just plain Jan.

After a very quick shower and shave TC heads down the hallway to Annalisa's room. Just as he is about to knock on the door he pauses for a moment. Memories come rushing back on all the times had entered this very room to check on his little girl. Whether it was to read her a nighttime story, look for monsters under the bed, a tooth ache, a stomach ache, or to fetch a glass of water as that last excuse to not fall asleep. To console her after a fight with her best girlfriend or not making the cheerleading team her first tryout. To congratulate her on her straight A report card and the list went on and on. Taking a deep breath TC knocked on the door. "Annie are you there?"

"Come on in Daddy the door is unlocked." TC enters the room; Annie is lying across her bed on her stomach looking at family photos on her lap top. She looks at TC and pats the side of the bed.

"Sit Daddy, Look! Remember teaching me to ride my bike?' She flips to the next photo and it is of Jan doctoring up her skinned knee and elbow, with the disheveled bike in the background. They both laughed. "What a day that was. Your momma was so mad at me."

"I know Daddy; I remember it like it was yesterday." Her eyes became misty at the thought. "I remember all the wonderful things you did for me over the years. And for Davis too. You were...are. The best Dad to me and for Davis, He thinks of you like a second dad, you know that right, Daddy?" TC reaches over and gives her a big hug tears filling his own eyes.

"Of course I do sweetheart, of course I do. You and Davis will have a wonderful life together, I'm sure of that. And someday you will get to share all these wonderful memories with your own children. And on the slight chance that he doesn't make you happy, well I will wring Davis' scrawny neck!" He makes a twisting motion with his fist and contorts his face horribly.

"Oh Daddy!' Annalisa falls off the bed with laughter. Just the thought of her Dad saying that to Davis would probably cause him to freaking pass out! The mental vision was too much for her on this day of already heightened emotions. TC was laughing too, knowing exactly what she was thinking he reaches down giving her a hand back up to the bed, and another hug.

"You better get you act in gear, girl. Your Momma will be up here screaming in a minute. She's already yelled breakfast is ready twice! And we both know when we get down there she will say well 'almost ready'." He chuckled and added. "I already got my yelling for the day." Anna laughed. "I know Daddy, I know I heard. Tell her I am on my way, please." As he got up from the bed he reached over and tasseled the top of her head, just like he used to do when she was little, knowing she still hated it. "Will do." Laughing at her as she frowned and slapped back at his hand. He headed downstairs to face Jan.

TC walks into the kitchen to find Jan has a huge omelet on the stove and a huge pile of toast sitting beside it. A large bowl of fresh strawberries and melons dressing the center of the table. Joseph and Joshua have both already helped themselves to a big portion. Nodding at both the boys he looks at Jan. She looks really stressed and tired. He thought, as she hands him a plate from the table directing him toward the stove. He takes the plate and her other hand with his, directing her to her own chair.

"Jan, honey you need to sit and eat too. I know how you are. You won't eat all day trying to take care of everyone else." He pours her a glass of juice, insisting she take it in her hand. "You will do Annie no good if you pass out at the wedding."

He proceeds to fill her plate with food sitting it in front of her. Joey and Josh both nodding in agreement at their mother. She smiles and makes a feeble attempt at consuming some of the egg. TC sits down beside her with his own plate. Anna enters the kitchen. "Good morning everyone!" a big smile adorning her face. Giving both her brothers a pat on the shoulder she then fills her own plate and takes a seat by her mom. Jan smiles at her and reaches over giving her hand a squeeze.

"I am so happy to have all my children home at one time." Smiling at each of them.

"Well, where is Audra?" Joseph asks.

Looking at the clock Jan replies "She should be here in about an hour."

"She... um... spent the night with a friend." Annalisa chimed in.

"She better be! She is my maid of honor and she has duties!"

TC is shaking his head no as if to get Anna to hush least she give her mother something else to worry about. Both boys just grin as they load their empty plates into the dishwasher. "Thanks for a great breakfast Mom, Josh and I got a few errands to run we will be back by one." Giving Jan a kiss on the check they are both out the door. Anna finishes her nibbling leaving most of her food on her plate grabbing a slice of melon as she takes off upstairs.

"Got stuff to do thanks Mom!" she yells over her shoulder. Jan starts to reply to her and TC gently puts his fingers to her lips. She takes his hand and attempts a smile back at him.

"Don't worry honey it is all going to be fine. You and Anna have planned this down to the tee! It will go off without a hitch!' Jan looks at TC and for a moment he thought she was about to burst into tears, instead she broke out in laughter at the pun of without a hitch. Relieved TC began to laugh with her giving her a hug and kiss on the forehead.

As planned the wedding was perfect. It was as though the cosmic gods knew they had best not test the wrath of Jan! TC laughed quietly at the thought as he looked at Jan sleeping beside him. She was exhausted, he was sure, as she had fallen asleep as soon as her head hit the pillow. His own sleep was not forthcoming; in lieu of waking her he decided he'd go downstairs for a while.

Slipping from the covers he looks back at Jan, her steady breathing told him she was sound asleep. Grabbing some lounge pants from the dresser he closes the bedroom door behind him, he goes downstairs to the kitchen retrieving a beer from the fridge. He stands looking out the door to the back deck taking a sip of his beer. Quietly opening the door he steps onto the deck taking a seat in the chaise lounge, his favorite spot for star gazing. The night air was perfect, a little breeze blowing just enough to make it pleasant. As he sat there drinking his beer his thoughts turned back to the wedding.

Yes, it had indeed been a good wedding and Annalisa was a

beautiful bride, just as Jan had been so many years ago. Where had all those years gone? Time is sure slipping by me. Sighing he looks up again at the night sky. It looked like the stars were now covered up by a few clouds. He could smell rain in the air even though it had not yet arrived. This was all it took for his RTP to kick in and fill his mind with thoughts of Samantha. Smiling to himself as he saw her beautiful bright green eyes and pretty smile. Sighing a much heavier sigh he whispered. "Sam, Sam, Sam what am I going to do about you? What am I going to do?" Sighing again. What is the pull I feel every time I am in near you Hell who am I fooling what is the damn pull I feel even when I am not with you. TC was frustrated that he hadn't been able to figure out this relationship. What is it pulling him to her? What about Jan and his family? These thoughts have haunted him for some time now. How could it ever be anything but a strong bond of friendship? But he knew in his heart that was not the case and he knew ever since that hug in the kitchen. That innocent hug was pretty much what did it for him.

Deep down he knew it had all changed at that point and was much deeper than just friendship. One day neither of them would be able to deny it or run away from it.

"Hell fire! Samantha Montgomery! I've been trying to get you out of my head for years now. That night on the beach, well, it didn't happen for nothing!" He growled angrily. Angry at his thoughts he takes the last few sips of his beer, trying to direct his thoughts away from Sam.

"Got to chill out here, time to hit the sack myself. It's been a hell of a day." Placing his empty bottle in the trash TC goes back inside and heads upstairs. He quietly slips between the covers with Jan. His back to hers, he soon drifts off to sleep.

Chapter 9

"Hey Samantha.' Sam hears Dakota's voice on the other end of her phone just as she was about to head out for lunch. "Hey Dakota, what's up?"

"Sam, you want to meet me for lunch I was just about to head over to Angelo's, want to join me?'

"Well, Dakota you know I can't turn down an offer of pizza! Sure! I can be there in ten."   Angelo's being centrally located made it a favorite haunt for many in downtown Nashville. The atmosphere was great. A locally owned quaint little pizza and sub restaurant complete with checkered table cloths and fat little ceramic chefs adorned the walls on each side of the eating area. You always got a pleasant happy feeling when you walked in.   In less than ten Sam arrives and sees Dakota in their usual booth, she takes a seat across from her.

"I am so glad you called, I needed a break today Dakota." Dakota smiled back at Sam and hesitated for a moment before speaking.

"I have to say Sam I've been a little worried about you lately. You seem, very, um very distracted the last few months. Are you ok?

Are you and Ash having problems again?"

Sam nervously looks at Dakota as she plays with the straw in the drink the waiter had just sat in front of her. Sam takes a sip of her drink. Before she has a chance to answer she sees TC walk through the door with Andy, Gunny and Dalton. They take a table in the middle of the restaurant. TC is facing Sam. As Sam is looking at him he is looking at her and Dakota is looking at the both of them. TC nods a hello at them and they both give him a little wave.

"Do you think we should go over and say hello, Sam?' Sam quickly looks at Dakota. "No! No I don't think so. We acknowledged their presence. I think that is good enough."

"Ok, Sam." Dakota shrugged her shoulders. She thought it was somewhat odd that Samantha didn't want to, however she didn't press her on it.

During their meal Sam and TC could not help but to exchange several looks at each other, although they tried not to. Dakota picked up on the looks.

"Sam, Ok like I said before TC and the guys came in. You seem a little distracted of late, is everything ok with you and Ash?" Sighing Sam pushes her plate to the side as she tries to ignore that fact that TC is only a few feet away. She could feel his eyes studying her. Trying to act nonchalant she looks at Dakota.

"Well, you know Dakota, Ash and I never really get along. We have our good days but mostly we have our bad days. We haven't even been intimate in months. Ash doesn't seem to care, either. I tried talking to him about it but he showed no interest. All he does anymore is work and come home and bury his nose in a book or his lap top grading papers for work."

Again Dakota notices Sam's eyes cut over to TC. "Hum."

94

Dakota murmured. Looking back at TC then at Sam.

"Wonder could that handsome hunk over there that you keep looking at might have anything to do with the situation?"

Samantha is aghast that Dakota would even say such a thing. "Dakota! Really?"

"Sam! Really yourself! Ever since the BBQ last year you two have been, well been, different. See, he is looking over here now. With the same longing look on his face as yours!"

Sam leans across the table to whisper to Dakota while giving her a stern look. "Well Dakota! Probably because he sees you keep looking over there! Please stop it."

"Oh no Sam, trust me it has nothing to do with me. I actually noticed it at the BBQ last summer. Something going on between you two? Sam? Come on you know for God's sake that you can trust me!" Sam couldn't lie to Dakota; she was after all her best friend in the world. And knowing it wouldn't do any good anyway, Dakota would see right through her lie.

"Well, no nothing is going on, per say. Just, well, I don't know just a strong attraction I guess. We have become quite close over that last year or so and well." She stops.

"Come on Sam, finish." Dakota prompts her to continue.

"Well, I don't know there is." Sam pauses. "A well a, um a strong kind of weird pull to him and I think he feels it too. I never told you this but remember my Florida vacation before taking the job at River House?"

Dakota wrinkled her brow in deep thought for a moment. "Yes, I remember." She looks at Sam, who is not saying a word just giving her that "you know" look. Dakota's eyes grew wide with excitement.

"Oh my, gosh! You aren't saying he was the guy on the beach

that night? The one you thought was struck by lightning and when you came back with help he was walking back to his cabin? That guy! Sam! That guy?"

Sam could only manage a nod in agreement at the moment. But, Dakota didn't skip a beat.

"Sam, that guy that you swore was your soulmate, something about his eyes that night? Really? That guy? I can't believe you have never mentioned this to me!" She leaned back in the booth a look of discernment upon her face.

Sam was finally able to answer. "Yes Dakota! That guy! I know it sounds crazy but the moment I saw him in my office and Uncle John introduced us, I knew it was him. Strangely I am not sure he even remembers it. He has never hinted at a memory of it, even when we talk about my ocean painting in my office. I was afraid to bring it up. He probably thinks I just ran away and left him to die."

Dakota with a genuinely worried look on her face reaches over to squeeze Sam's hand for a moment. "Oh honey. That is good, I mean that is terrible. I mean good and terrible. Are you sure? Has he made a move?"

"No, no move. We have been doing a lot of innocent flirting with each other almost every time we are together. And I don't know, it is just, well you know it is just, just weird I can't seem to help myself! There is this magical pull to him."

Shifting in the booth Sam obviously is a little distressed. She raises her hand up in the air as if in dismissal.

"Really Dakota! I'm crazy! Don't pay any attention to me. It is nothing just a strange attraction. We are just friends that is all. TC and I, we are just friends! My goodness he has a beautiful wife and a passel of kids, yes they are all grown. Well, all but one, but still. We just have a close working relationship with a little friendship and a little attraction that causes us to innocently flirt; nothing will ever come of it." Dakota just looks at Sam for a moment, one eyebrow raised as in a questioning look. "Hum, yes I see." About that time the waitress came by to check on their drinks. "Could I have a tea to go and the check please?" Sam says as she looks up at the waitress.

"Yes ma'am I will get your tea, but the gentlemen over there." Pointing to TC's table "They took care of your bill." And off she went before Sam could reply.

Dakota looks at Sam with that knowing look of hers. "Yes, I see. Looks like we have to stop by on the way out at least to thank them."

"Yes, yes of course we do." Sam says as the waitress returned with her tea. "Well, let's do it. I have a two o'clock closing and I need to get back."

Dakota and Sam go over to the table to thank the guys for buying their lunch. It was a quick exchange of pleasantries and both women were out the door, each back to their respective jobs.

Samantha and Dakota having left the restaurant TC returns his attention back to his pizza.

"Some damn good looking women there, eh TC?" Andy says with a mouthful of his own pizza. Dalton nods in agreement.

"Can't argue that." TC replies as he tries to appear indifferent. Taking a sip of his tea noticing Gunny is looking at him kind of strangely; therefore he avoids eye contact with Gunny.

"So, which house is the poker game Friday night?" TC asks in hopes of changing the subject knowing very well it is at his own.

Andy replies. "Oh don't even start that TC you know it as your house and you promised to provide the beer. So don't even try to weasel out with a lack of memory excuse! Right Dalton?"

"Yeah, TC you dog, don't even try it."

"Just seeing if you guys are paying attention or still thinking about women!" TC laughs.

Gunny is still just listening, and silently watching as he is finishing his last piece of pizza. After paying for their share of the meal Dalton and Andy say their goodbyes leaving TC and Gunny lingering over their iced teas.

"So, TC, how are things at home these days? You and Jan pretty much have an empty nest except for Jacob. You guys been handling that ok?"

TC is a little taken back by the surprise question. "Yeah, yeah sure Gunny, it's ok. Kind of settled down a little since the wedding."

Gunny is watching TC intently, a slight scowl to his face. "Hum, yeah well you know, marriages can be tough sometimes what with all the distractions in life. You got any distractions, to mention of TC?"

"Nothing but the normal ones Gunny, just the normal ones." Taking his last gulp of tea TC sits the glass down on the table as he looks at Gunny.

"You ready to blow this place? I got a few errands to do this afternoon." TC is still seated and reaching his hand is his back pocket for his wallet, while holding the check in his other hand.

"Sure thing, TC." Gunny stands and gives TC's shoulder a gentle but firm squeeze.

"I will see you come Friday, be sure to bring lots of money, you'll need it." He chuckles as snatches the bill out of TC's hand and makes his way to the register.

Chapter 10

The winter months had long passed and it was again early spring, TC and Sam have had many visits in her office during those long cold winter days. Many days of flirting and teasing one another, days of growing closer and closer in friendship. Today was no different. TC was at her office doorway and she motioned him to come in and pointed at the chair across from her desk. She was on the phone obviously helping a client. So he slipped into the chair across from her desk, intently watching her. She glances up giving him a smile, and then her attention was back to the call.

As he sat there, his mind absorbed every inch of her. She looked beautiful. She had her hair pulled up on her head in was of those twisting styles, except she always seemed to have that rouge strand or two of hair that refused to hang with the rest and thereby trickled down the edge of her shoulder. Her neck was soft and supple looking. He wanted to touch it. She was wearing a slightly low cut purple top. It showed just a hint more of cleavage when she reached across the desk to retrieve her pen, smiling at him as she did so. TC's heart began to pound a little faster in his chest; he could feel his temperature rise. His RTP thoughts had taken him off into a fantasy of the things he would like to do right now. Things he would like to do to her. He fancied walking up behind her chair and taking her long dark hair and moving it away from her neck, imaging the feel of his lips upon her.........

"Hello, TC so sorry you had to wait and hear all that."

Startled TC is brought back to the here and now. Shifting in his chair a bit.

"What? Oh, the phone call. Oh no. That no, I wasn't even paying any attention. My mind was on something, err I mean somewhere else." Avoiding eye contact with Sam as he spoke, hoping she didn't notice the reddish tint to his face as he could obviously fee the heat himself. He then cleared his throat.

"Where is everyone? Deidra wasn't at her desk that was why I came on back."

"Well you know that is fine TC after all this time you hardly need to be announced." Sweetly smiling at him again. "Deidra was the last to leave this evening I was about to go lock the door then the phone rang." She adds seductively. "Luckily for you." Fluttering her eyelashes at him.

"Indeed!" He replied with a grin, raising one of his eyebrows in the same flirty manner.

"So what brings you to see me today TC?"

"Oh, nothing really Samantha. Honestly I, just thought I would stop in and say hello, see how you were doing."

"I am glad you did. I always enjoy seeing you and the time we spend together. Unfortunately, I do need to leave though; we are meeting Dakota and Ron for dinner and a movie. I'm sorry, can I have a raincheck?" Smiling sweetly at him. TC stands and watches as Samantha is getting her purse.

"Oh, yeah sure." Hoping the disappointment did not show on his face. "Shall I see you safely to your car?"

"Of course TC! That is very sweet of you."

After securing the office for the night Sam and TC are at her car, he opens the door for her; she gets in placing her keys in the ignition. Before starting the car she looks up at TC. Those sexy bedroom eyes get the best of him. He thinks he recalls her saying thanks and him saying goodbye. But all he really had on his mind at that moment was that he wanted to lean down and kiss her lips. But he knew it was too soon. He was afraid of her reaction. Unsure of the consequences. A part of him also held back knowing what a mess it could all end up being. He respected her and didn't want to hurt her in anyway. And he certainly wasn't ready to risk losing their friendship. The thought of that was totally unacceptable.

The next morning Ash left extra early. Telling Sam that he had to grade papers that he had put off in order to have time for their dinner last night. She thought it was a pretty lame excuse, but no matter to her, she was long past the stage of caring about what Ash did or didn't do. Dakota swore he was probably having an affair, acting the way he was. Sam didn't know and oddly she really didn't care if he was. She had grown weary of begging him to be with her, not only physically but mentally as well. The distance between them had definitely grown larger. It seemed nothing she did or said affected him one way or the other, he was in his own little world. Seemingly content with their relationship just as it was. She honestly didn't care if he did have a lover. She wasn't really sure why that thought didn't affect her adversely.

Sam finished her coffee, rinsing the cup and placing it in the dishwasher. Taking one more look in the mirror at her outfit of choice, deciding it was sufficient. She left for work. It's going to be a beautiful day. Sam thought as she pulled out of her drive heading for town.

"Good morning Deidra, do I have anything special going on today?' Sam inquired as she entered the office.

"Nope Ms. Sam, just a normal day, kind of quite actually. Oh, and Mr. Rivers called and said he was taking the day off." Shuffling the mail Sam stops to look at Deidra.

"Oh? Is he ok?" "Why yes! He said he had promised Ms. Estelle they would go to Gatlinburg for a weekend shopping trip and she wanted to get an early start."

"Oh yes, I do remember him telling me she would probably insist he take off Friday as well. That is good he deserves to enjoy himself, he has spent many years working very hard."

"Yes, Ms. Sam. He surely has and with you being here, he's certainly been less stressed, for sure. You are a big help to him. He has become very dependent on you."

"Yes, I know Deidra. I know. And I am very glad that I was able to step in and give him that help. He is a wonderful man."

Smiling at Deidra as she then proceeds on to her office, and begins to tackle whatever tasks were at hand. Sooner than she expected it was lunch time. She lets Deidra know she will be gone for a couple of hours. She needed a bit of a break herself and she had nothing pressing at the office. Time for a few new outfits she thought as she drove past the mall. Whipping in she was lucky to find a really close parking spot. Wow, must be my lucky day. She made her way into the mall. Surprisingly it wasn't crowed for a

Friday. After picking out a pretty coral button up blouse and a skirt to match. She managed to find a sleeveless straight lined dress in a slightly huggable material, in a pretty shade of deep blue. Hum, I like this color, it reminds me of TC's eyes. Delighted with her find, she takes it to the dressing room to give it a try. Yes! It is perfect. She smiled at her own image in the mirror as she turned this way and that as she ran her hand down her side feeling the softness of the material. The fit of the dress nicely accentuated her shapely curves perfectly. Yes this will work just fine, and a perfect length for me too.

With a matching pair of blue and coral heels happily purchased she looked at her watch. No time to stop for a bite to eat, better get back to the office. Samantha was mindful to never abuse her position in any way, she respected her Uncle John way too much to ever do that, she knew he was appreciative of her diligence. Once back at the office she settles in to complete a few mundane tasks while time is affordable.

It was late afternoon, Deidra looks up as TC enters the front door. "Well hello TC! Here again? You need Ms. Sam?" Smiling as though knowing something he didn't and it sounding more like a matter of fact statement instead of a question. It slightly perturbed TC, but he didn't let her see it. "Yes is she available?"

"Yes, sir she is. You can head on back and I will let her know. She will be delighted to see you."

TC nods and makes his way down the hall, hearing Deidra announce to Sam that he is on his way. That woman scares me sometimes. Thinking of Deidra and her sixth sense or whatever it was she seemed to possess. Anticipating seeing Sam's smiling face he quickened his steps down the hall. Sure enough that beautiful smile was waiting for him. Seeing her always made his day a better one. The smile on her face told him she was just as happy to see him. She looked pretty as a picture in her bright yellow dress and turquoise jewelry. Always so feminine, he thought as she greeted him at doorway offering him a little hug.

"Hello, how are you? Come have a seat, tell me what has been happening since I saw you last. Are these files you are carrying for me?"

"Yes, yes they are just a couple more closing for you to squeeze in if you would."

"Of course! Thank you." She smiles sweetly as she takes them from his hand.

"They are both Justin's so you know everything is in order." He takes his usual seat.

"I most certainly do." She says as she reaches for the lid of her candy dish siting by her phone. "How long has it been since you had a kiss TC?"

He has a slightly shocked look on his face at first and then he sees she is offering the chocolate candy kiss to him from her open palm.

He smiles as he takes the candy. Purposefully and slowly slipping his hand across hers as he takes the candy, eyes locked on her face the entire time. Then with a little smirk.

"Well, it has been a while." He opens the candy and plops it into his mouth.

"Oh really? And whose fault is that TC?'

"Why yours Sam!" His blue eyes sparkling with naughtiness. "You haven't asked me for one!"

He cracks up at the shocked look on Sam's face. Realizing of course that he is joking Sam laughs too. She nervously focuses her attention back to her computer as TC asks her a question about an upcoming closing. She feels his eyes studying her while trying to remain focused on the business at hand. After, another twenty minutes or so of taking care of business TC rises.

"Well, I best be on my way." Knowing full well that his resistance to her was very weak this visit he figured he best end it.

"I'll walk you out TC. I need to stretch my legs a bit."

TC laughs. "Well they are a bit short, a stretching my do them some good." He winks at her. "Although I kinda like them just the way they are."

Sam smiles at him with a slight blush.

Having arrived at his truck TC gives Sam a friendly goody bye hug catching himself just before he almost kissed her right there on the parking lot in open site for any and everybody to see! Thank goodness, she turned her head in just the nick of time or it would have surely happened.

With Sam's office being his last stop of the day TC heads home. Andy and Marci, Andy's new love interest, along with Gunny and Martha are expected at their house for a cookout that evening and he knew Jan would be impatiently waiting on him with a list of chores. Even though, aside from Marci, they had all been at their house millions of times, Jan still thought everything should be perfect.

On his drive home he kept thinking of Sam and their little game with the chocolate candy. Her smile, her face, her body. The thoughts were causing some issues in his current seating position, shifting himself in his seat with a seat belt, while driving wasn't easy.

Damn I need to chill. Hell fire! Chill? Don't know how I am

supposed to do that when that woman heats me up like a flame. Sam, Sam, Sam! What is going on? I only wish I knew what it is between us. You have an unperceivable power over me, my sweet little Samantha. That is for certain. Sighing as he pulls in his driveway a little agitated with his thoughts.

TC enters the kitchen as Jan is sitting the table for dinner. She looks up at him in her own aggravated stare, stopping for a moment with a fork in midair.

"Andy and Marci will be here any minute, do you think you could possibly go light the grill instead of always leaving it for Andy to do?"

"Yes, I suppose so. Don't know why you get in such a rush. Besides Andy likes taking charge of the grill, he does that for a living you know. He's a chef!"

"TC don't be an ass. I know that! Perhaps you need a shower before they arrive, maybe to wash off some of that grumpiness." Frowning she continues to stir the dish she is preparing.

"Yeah a cold one." He mutters under his breath as he heads up the stairs. "I've got plenty of time to take a shower and change clothes first. Be back down in a minute." He hears Jan hotly slam a piece of silverware onto the wood table.

While in the shower he thinks of Sam again. Frustrated, he forces himself to think of the yard work he has planned for the weekend in order to get her out of his mind. Or else he really would have needed a cold shower. Once finished with his shower, and dressed he went back downstairs only to be greeted again, with the wrath of Jan.

"Well don't rush now TC! Andy is here and has started the grill already. Gunny and Martha just stepped outside too." A seething look on her face.

"Excellent." He smirks as he grabs a cold beer from the fridge. "Do you need me for anything in here?"

"No, I have everything handled." She grumble back at him.

He could tell she was really pissed, but he didn't have time to ponder on it now. It was all he could do to keep Sam out of his thoughts.

Somehow, TC managed to make it through the evening, but not without some tense looks from Jan. Tense enough to let Andy and Gunny know that all was not well in the Martin household. She had finally cooled down toward the end of the evening and everyone seemed to have had a pleasant enough of a time.

As they are saying the last goodbyes TC shuts the front door turning to Jan.

"I'm going to bed. I want to get an early start on the yard work tomorrow."

"Fine, I'm going to read for a while, I'll be up later."

He nodded at her in acceptance. Fine. Definitely means things are not fine! TC thought as he climbed the stairs and headed to their bedroom. He was too tired to worry about now; he just wanted a restful night of sleep. Sleep, however was not restful. He dreamt of Sam.

She was standing on the beach facing him, with her arms outstretched as though beckoning him. The wind was blowing fiercely; her clothing was being wildly whipped around her. The waves were splashing up behind her like some fierce monster about to attack. He tried stepping toward her but the wind was making it too difficult. Suddenly he heard someone screaming his name, but it wasn't Sam, her mouth wasn't moving. He saw a giant teardrop fall from her big beautiful eyes, as though in slow motion, he watched it fall straight down to the sand and splatter in a million little pieces as though it were a piece of crystal glass. The fractured pieces bounced back up into the air and were snatched by the ocean's waves as though they were hungry little hands. He then realized Samantha was looking at something behind him. He turned around to see Jan. Her arms were outstretched to him as well and she was yelling his name. Her face was so distraught. Undecided as to what to do, he turned back to look at Sam, but she was gone! No sign of her just the abominable waves pounding the shore where only moments ago she had been standing. An immense fear comes over him as he screamed out her name! Samantha!!!!

TC suddenly shot up in bed his heart was pound in his chest he couldn't breathe. His body was wet from sweat. Daunted, he gets out of bed and goes to the window on his side of the bed, opening it to allow some fresh air in the room, taking a couple of deep breaths to calm himself. He could usually feel a PTSD episode when it was starting, it didn't feel quite the same. He wasn't sure what this feeling was all about.

As he turned back toward the bed he realized Jan was not there. He checked the clock, to his surprise it was three a.m.

"What the hell?" he grumbled putting on his robe he decided to go downstairs to see where she was. As he walked into the den all was quiet and seemingly empty. The only light was from a small lamp on the corner coffee table adjacent to the sofa. As he walked around to the front of the sofa he saw Jan laying there. She was curled up in her favorite positon with her book still in her hand and flopped over her chest. She appeared to be in a deep sleep. Reaching over her for the throw that was draped on the back of the sofa he gently covered her. He stood there for a moment, just starring at her. Finally turning off the lamp, he went back upstairs.

Chapter 11

It was Monday morning Sam was on her way to work when her cell rings. She sees it is Dakota.

"Well hello there Dakota! How are you on this lovely morning?"

"It is only lovely because I am off at four today and Ron is hanging with some guys tonight so I thought my best pal Sam might want to have a girl's night? Dinner? My treat!"

"Well how could I pass up on an offer like that? Sure! Where and what time?" "Well, you know it is early, and I may change my mind ten times before supper time so why don't I just swing by your office after my shift, then we can decide."

"Okay sure, I can't wait. Oh! And have your big pocket book ready cause I think I shall be really hungry since you are paying!'

Dakota laughs "Sam, really? No more than you ever eat that is the least of my worries! Okay I will see you then."

As the morning turns into afternoon Sam looks at her watch it was mid-afternoon. Wow, I didn't realize it was that late, I never even broke for lunch. Hum, surprisingly Deidra didn't remind me fifteen times to do so. I guess she realized it would be of no use anyway.

About that time the intercom sounds with Deidra's voice. Startling Sam so that she actually jumped and spilled the water she was about to drink.

Damn, how does that woman seem to know when she is on my mind? Ge'ez. Finally she answers. "Yes, Deidra, what do you need?"

"TC is on his way back to you, and I need to make a quick bank run that leaves just you and TC here you ok with that till I get back?"

"Oh, ok Deidra; just lock the door please, since we don't have any appointments this afternoon."

"Will do Ms. Sam, I will only be about twenty minutes."

By this time TC is at her doorway and has heard the conversation. As he takes the seat across from her he grins. "So, we are all alone eh? Interesting! What shall we do with ourselves?"

Leaning back in her chair Sam replies. "Well, TC whatever did you have in mind?" She gently takes her hair and clears it from her neck to behind her shoulder, as she reaches her other hand into her desk drawer for a piece of chocolate candy. All the while giving TC a teasing smile as she opens it and places it upon her bare shoulder, gently caressing her neck with her fingers. Before she knew what had happened TC was no longer across the desk from her but at her side. To her surprise he leaned down and let his lips ever so gently retrieve the chocolate candy from her body and then on to gentle kisses upon her neck. She sat there not moving, shocked at first, then enjoying every moment of it. He then lowered down to her shoulder. Warm tender kisses hardly touching her bare skin. She could feel his breath upon her and her own breath quickened. Then another soft brush of lips just at the edge of her breasts.

Sam responded by taking her left hand and gently fondling TC's neck in soft tender touches, as he continued to nibble at her skin with his lips. Her hands moved to the top of his head running her fingers through his curly dark hair. It was almost taking her breath away.

Oh my God! She thought. Her body was hot with desire, as was his. His lips found hers for the first time and they kissed for a very long moment.

Then just as suddenly as it had happened TC stood up and backed up with almost a look of shock on his face. "Bet you never expected that!" TC exclaimed with heightened excitement in his voice as he stepped back another step from her.

He was almost like an excited youngster who had just managed to do something unbelievable for the first time. TC was obviously shocked by his own actions. Sam was at a loss for words, all she could manage was a faint. "No. No I never expected that."

TC quickly returns to his chair. They both sit there motionless and lustful, eyes locked on each other. Perhaps both, somewhat in shock.

Finally TC smiles at Sam and she smiles back at him. They hear the bell of the front door realizing that Deidra must be back.

Before either of them could speak Deidra was at Sam's door with the bank receipts. She gives them both a strange look. Maybe she sensed the electricity in the air. Before Sam could address Deidra, TC excuses himself to them both and he is out the door and gone.

Once to his truck he starts the engine. With trembling hands he reaches over to turn the AC to full blast. He sits there for a minute, letting the cool air hit his face, his eyes closed and head leaned back upon the headrest. Suddenly his eyes fly open. He looks down at his hands as though in disbelief. "Holy shit! Did I just …did I just do what I think I did? What the hell was I thinking?" He questioned.

Numerous thoughts ran wildly through his mind, jumping from one thought then quickly to another. Damn her skin is soft as silk, just like I imagined it would be. The smell of her clean skin was like an aphrodisiac to him. No perfume, he mentally noted. What a nice change from Jan's sometimes overwhelming scent of choice. So soft, her skin was so soft. His mind was racing as fast as his heart. His head was full of questions.

"Where is this leading? What is wrong with me? What the hell am I doing? Holy shit!" He exclaimed excitedly.

Samantha wasn't in much better shape herself. After Deidra left her office she had sat back in her chair turning it around to face her ocean painting. Usually if she spent any length of time focusing on it she would have a sense of calming, but not this time. If anything, it seemed to quicken her pulse, as though the waves were taking her breath away. But she knew it was not the imaginary waves that left her breathless, it was TC!

How on earth did that just happen? What just happened? Perhaps a better question might be how could she have let that happen? The effect on her was intense.

Not that she was a prude or anything like that, but she had never condoned cheating. That was after all what had ended her first marriage, an unfaithful husband. The other shocker was that she enjoyed it immensely; it aroused something in her she had never felt before in her life!

Finally able to calm herself she turned back to her desk. Spending an hour or so trying to complete a few things she had been working on but her mind would not allow it.

She finally gave up and reached for her purse. Guess I will freshen up a bit before Dakota gets here. Taking her compact and lip gloss from her purse she walks over to the large ornate mirror that hung behind the seating area. She sees her own reflection in the mirror and seemingly freezes, just starring at her own reflection. Big wide eyes staring back at her with a blank stare. "What have you gotten yourself into, Samantha Montgomery?" she quietly whispered. She had no answer forthcoming.

Freshening up her makeup she turns to go back to her desk, putting the items back into her purse. Leaning on the edge of her desk as she looks at her painting again thinking about what had just transpired between her and TC. Closing her eyes and about to relive the moment she instead hears the irritating buzz of the intercom.

"One of these days!" she says through gritted teeth. Taking a deep breath she answers.

"Yes, Deidra what is it now?" "Ms. Dakota is here."

"Yes, well you are fully aware there is no one with me so why does she need an intro? Send her back. And bring me the checks you needed me to sign."

"Yes ma'am." Sam hears Deidra's slightly timid reply.

Deidra was just a bit confused by Sam's tone of voice. She looked up at Dakota, realizing she had heard it too. Taking the checks she walked with Dakota to Sam's office.

Sam was in no mood for Deidra's silliness and nosey games, but she also realized she might have been a little too harsh with her.

Deidra and Dakota entered Sam's office. Deidra handed Sam

the checks she turned without a word. Dakota and Sam made eye contact with each other without saying a word. Dakota gave her that wide eyed what the hell was that all about look. Yes, the one Sam knew all too well. With the tiniest curse under her breath, Sam calls out to Deidra. "Deidra, wait please. Give me just a minute and you can take these checks back as you go."

"Yes ma'am." Deidra replied as she stood there starch and stiff, her hands folder together in front of her. Her lips set firm. Sam signs the checks hands them back to Deidra and in doing so she gives Deidra smile.

"Deidra I am sorry. I didn't mean to snap at you." She hesitated for a moment. "Please accept my apology. I have a lot on my mind and I am sorry I took my frustrations out on you. Please forgive me; I truly appreciate your tenacity." Sam managed another half of a smile at Deidra.

Satisfied with Sam's apology, Deidra smiles back. "No problem Ms. Sam, we all have our days. Can I get you and Dakota something to drink?" Sam looks questionably at Dakota.

"Uh oh no, thanks Deidra but I am fine, we are about to go eat so I am fine." Deidra smiles at Dakota and looks at Sam.

"No, thank you I am fine as well, Deidra. Please close the door on your way out. I am gone for the day if anyone should call. Thank you again, Deidra."

Deidra obliges but not without giving Sam that frowny look of "how do you expect me to eavesdrop if the door is shut?' Of course she purposefully, doesn't quite close it all the way. Dakota quickly goes and shuts the door behind her then opens it slightly to be sure Deidra is not listening at the door. Peering around the edge of the door she sees no sign of Deidra. She shuts the door and rushes to

Sam's desk pulling up a chair in closer proximity to Sam.

"Ok, okay Sam! Give it up. What is going on with you?" A worried scowl upon her face. Sam takes a deep breath leaning back in her chair. Dakota anxiously awaits Sam to speak. "Well! What is Samantha? The way you just talked to Deidra along with the look on your face I see something major is going on! Don't even try to deny it."

"TC kissed me." Sam blurted out before she realized it. Dakota jumps to the edge of her chair in excitement and practically yells at Samantha. "What! He kissed you?" A true look of shock on her face.

"Dakota! Shhhh! We have ears remember? Lower your voice, please!' Sam nervously looks at the closed door and back at Dakota.

"Oh my! Oh shit!" Dakota pulls her chair closer to Sam leaning in toward her. "So tell me! What? How? When?"

Sam was really in no shape to recant the entire episode to Dakota, she was really just as upset with herself for blurting it out to Dakota anyway. Even though Dakota was her best friend and she knew without a doubt that she could be trusted. She really wished she had not let it slip out. "Dakota, I err, I well, I well I really don't know."

Wide eyed Dakota exclaims. "What!" What do you mean you don't know? Of course you do! Tell me Sam!"

"Well, um... one minute we were talking then playing my little chocolate candy game and well, um well the next minute TC's lips were all over me! And well things just kind of got out of hand."

At this point Dakota could not contain her excitement and jumps to her feet. "Oh my God! You made it in the office?" The look on Dakota's face was quite hysterical and Sam couldn't help but fall back in her chair with laughter. Mainly because of the need for humor when she is on the spot. After she managed to quit laughing she leaned in to Dakota as though about to tell her something really big.

"Dakota! Really? In my office, a nooner? With guard Deidra on duty! Are you kidding me? Dakota, really?"

Dakota was a little put out at Sam's laughter but she blows it off knowing Sam wasn't laughing at her, it was just Sam's need for humor when on the spot.

With an elated look on her face she leaned in to Sam. "Tell me more! What did he do? What did he say afterward? What did you say? Did you kiss him back? Was it great? What..."

"Dakota! Really! Stop! I haven't even had time to process it myself! It literally just happened this afternoon. I haven't even caught my breath as yet." Dakota leans back in her chair crossing her long lean legs, clasping her hands over her knees. With a confused look on her face, she calmly responds.

"Ok, okay Sam. I get it. I understand. I just got excited for you."

The more she thinks about it the more Dakota gets excited and she starts to ramble again.

"Well, I guess I should be excited or should I be worried? I knew there was chemistry between the two of you! I knew it! Well, he is very married! And oh my goodness, all those kids! And wow what a history that is! And Ash! What about Ash and...." "Dakota, please! Stop! I will share my thoughts with you, but not right now. I don't even know what they are yet."

They both hear a slight knock at the door and Deidra pokes her head in before Sam can respond.

"Sorry to interrupt, but I thought you two might have changed your mind, maybe Ms. Dakota would like a diet coke, or something."

Sam looks at Dakota motioning for her to take Deidra up on the offer; otherwise she will be back every ten minutes. Dakota quickly picks up on Sam's cue.

"Yes, Deidra I would love a diet coke and please bring Samantha her usual, she looks thirsty." Smiling at Samantha.

"Yes ma'am Ms. Dakota I shall return momentarily with refreshments".

Turning to look back at them as she walks toward the door. "It's a shame TC had to leave so quickly you all could have had a little party." Chuckling to herself she exits the room. Sam waits until she is sure she is out of earshot before speaking. "Really Dakota? You had to add that last bit! Om my God do you think she heard us?'

"Calm down Sam, I am pretty sure I heard her shoes clicking down the hall just before she opened the door, so no, I don't believe she heard a thing."

Dakota sees the look of relief on Sam's face. She was secretly hoping for Sam's sake that what she had just said was true. No need in worrying her. That is what friends do after all, protect each other. In her mind she was protecting Sam from more worry.

"I hope you are right." Sam decided they best change the subject as Deidra would definitely be back in a moment with drinks.

"So Dakota, how is Ron? Where did you say he was tonight?" "A friend of his from college is in town so they all went out for beer, food and a pool game or two."

Deidra had returned with their drinks, as she takes her diet coke from her she nods a thanks. Returning her attention back to Samantha, she adds wryly. "Not necessarily in that order." Raising her coke in a cheering gesture to Sam before she takes a sip.

"Thanks Deidra, you can go ahead and shut it down for the day.

Dakota and I will be leaving soon so just lock the door behind you."

"Yes ma'am thanks!" Deidra leaves the room again not bothering to shut the door. Sam rolls her eyes and Dakota starts to get up to shut the door but Sam motions her back down in her chair. It wasn't long before they heard Deidra yelling goodbye and the exit tone on the front door.

Settling back in her chair Dakota asks. "Now, where were we?' Sam reaches for her purse before responding.

"We were about to finish up these drinks and get out of here ourselves."

Their dinner is uneventful, as Dakota knew not to push Sam on what had happened with TC she would just have to be patient, which was not an easy task for her. She knew Samantha would fill her in soon enough.

Chapter 12

A few days had gone by and Sam has not heard a word from TC other than a couple of texts with neither of them mentioning what had happened between them. She went over and over in her head what might happen on their next visit, wondering if she should apologize or just leave it alone. If he would apologize and if so, how she should react. She was beside herself with worry but at the same time relished every memory and sense of what had happened that day.

Abruptly without warning TC sends a text asking if she is busy, she replies no and he responds that he will be there shortly. Sam is nervous to say the least. TC is nervous as well, he was unsure of what her reaction would be like, seeing her in person again. He takes a couple of deep breaths before entering her office. Sam as always, greets him with a winning smile. She was indeed happy to see his smiling face looking right back at her. From that instant they both relinquished their worries as though nothing had ever happened. All it took to put them both at ease was the happy look on the other's face.

"How are you TC?" "Great! Thanks, and you?" before she could answer he added "Oh and Deidra said to tell you to lock up when we leave."

"Oh goodness, I almost forgot I have to run some papers over to the Westside office, care to take a quick ride with me, TC?"

"I'd be happy to Sam."

Once in the car and on their way the usual small talk ensues of families and recent activities. After delivering the papers they are on their way back and Sam pulls through a local drive-through for an iced tea for herself and TC. She reaches toward the console for her wallet and accidently brushes TC's hand. He quickly moves it back, as though to avoid touching her.

This is not a good sign. She thinks to herself as she maneuvered her way back through the traffic and back to the office, all the while attempting to make more small talk.

Finally back in their comfort zone of the office, her desk separating the two of them as though it were some sort of safety net. TC picks up his cup taking a long slow sip of his tea, Samantha does the same. He sits his cup down leans forward and intensely looks at Sam. She is peering at him over her cup, her eyes wide and questioning. Oh God! She thought. Here we go again! THAT look! Sam couldn't take it, no not now, not after what had transpired in their last visit.

"TC! Stop looking at me like that!" TC acts as though he is taken aback for a moment. "Sorry Samantha, I didn't realize I was looking at you in any special way." A devilish smile comes across his face. She nervously shuffles papers and pens on her desk. Barely able to look at him she replies.

"Well you were! You were looking at me with that piercing all the way to the soul look and I just can't take it anymore."

TC smiles. "Sorry, I will try to compose myself" He rolls his eyes and sticks his tongue out of the side of his mouth while trying to coherently say "How's this look?' Laughing Sam replies. "TC you are a true mess! I love how you always make me laugh!" Their conversation goes back to normal and TC is telling Sam all about his golf game last Saturday with Andy and Dalton. Telling her how Dalton spilled his beer all over the crotch of Andy's white pants and what a funny mess that was. She is listening but then her mind wanders. She envisions her and TC lying in a bed with a crisp white sheet draped half hardly upon TC's buttocks, he was laying on top of her own naked body. Her arms wrapped tightly around him. ..... "SAM!' She hears TC almost shout at her. Blinking innocently she looks at him and barely manages an audible "Yes?' TC chuckles, obviously he had lost her somewhere in her own case of RTP.

"Where were you just then Samantha?' Sam decides to give him a taste of his own medicine so she looks at him, fluttering her eyelashes as she replies.

"Why, TC I am right here with you." Smiling as sweetly as the tea they are both drinking.

"Well, Darling if you were just right here with me, looking like you were looking, we wouldn't just be talking and drinking tea." "Well, TC." Sitting her cup of tea on the desk and leaning back in her chair giving him the full benefit of being able to see her nicely tanned and bare legs as she uncrossed them. She gives him a demure look of innocence.

"Whatever do you have in mind?" TC smiles and without hesitation he moves over to Sam's side of the desk. Leaning over her his lips gently touch her shoulder, then her neck and ever so lightly upon the edge of her breasts. This time instead of an abrupt halt and TC backing away he pulls her up to him and their lips meet, again and again and again. Her lips were like none he had ever felt, so soft and sweet. The passion was growing in him not only emotionally but physically as well. It was taking every ounce of restraint he had to be gentle with her even though he hungered to take her to the floor and rip every piece of clothing form her body. He ached to feel her naked body against his. But he was scared. Scared if he showed Sam his true passion for her it might just scare her, hell it scared him! So he kept his kisses sweet and gentle. Holding her firmly he pulled her body against his. He felt her body respond to his own and he could stand it no more, he pushed his tongue inside her mouth only to feel her own accepting to his. Long lustful kisses followed. At one point Sam released from him, she needed to come up for air. His hands reached for hers, gently caressing them as though he had never felt hands before. One finger at a time they both gently absorbed the feel of the others skin. To Sam's surprises TC asked.

"Did you ever think after all this time it would lead to this Samantha?"

"Not even in my wildest dreams TC."

Her lips meet his again, her body presses tightly to his. She hears TC let out an audible moan of sheer pleasure as her lips move gently to his neck, then to his face taking in all she can of the feel of him, and the intoxicating smell of him. She teasingly goes around his lips, not quite letting her lips fully touch his. Picking up on her tease, TC grabs her petite body all with one swoop of his masculine arm and pulls her tightly against him again. Causing her to gasp with excitement. TC could feel every curve of her body as he pulled her in, it was intoxicating to him and he craved for more. His lips overpowered hers for more long and sensual kisses. Sam slides her hands up along TC arms. She reached under each sleeve of his knit shirt finding a set of very muscular biceps. She couldn't help but wonder why she had never noticed the size of those arms before. How amazing! She thought, as her hands continued to explore. His skin was very warm to the touch and as she reached his shoulders toward his back she felt him breakout out in tiny little chill bumps. Both their bodies were on fire with passion. Sam felt her knees grow weaker and as their lips were still locked in passion she sat down in her chair. TC still smothering her in kisses. After a few minutes he released his hold on her taking each of his hands and gently slid them down the length of her bare arms. He leaned in for another kiss but Sam playfully avoids his lips again, she only manages to get away with that for a moment before TC takes his hold on her with another breathlessly long kiss.

"We better stop before we both get into trouble." TC mumbles as he is kissing her cheekbones. Although the look in his eyes gives way to Samantha that this is not want he really wants. Sam nods her head in agreement "It could get really bad." as she is still kissing his face and then brushing her lips against his neck.

"TC you bring out the bad girl in me."

"Well, you do the same to me Sam. So I guess we are both bad."

She whispered. "I've never done anything like this before."

"Me neither." He stated, as he pulled her back in for yet another kiss. They both stopped suddenly.

"Was that the front door?" TC asked as he releases her and quickly moved toward his chair. With a look of fright on both their faces they wait for a moment in silence, listening. After a few minutes they realized it was nothing. Just as Sam was about to say something TC's cell phone rings causing them both to jump. Frowning he reaches down and removes it form its holder.

"Who is looking for me now? Ah, it is my wife." He puts the phone to his ear to answer Jan's call. Only to hear her babbling on about the menu for Saturday's cook out.

"I don't know can we discuss this when I get home? Ok, see you soon." He replaces the phone to his holding place on his belt. He looked at Samantha. "Well, I guess that was my cue to leave." Sam smiled back at him and got up to walk him to the front door. Just as they arrived there they see Deidra pulling in. Sam looked at TC and smiles. "Have a good afternoon, TC talk to you soon."

"See you soon Sam." TC passes Deidra in the parking lot. She acknowledges him with a nod of her head and a smile on her face.

Chapter 13

"TC are you and the guys leaving in the morning or the afternoon?" Jan is folding the laundry, in the laundry room, while TC is checking on the roast in the crock pot.

"Jan, honey, again. In the morning. We all took off work and I have already loaded the truck and I pick Gunny up at six a.m. I have told you this multiple times."

"Well, damn TC. I guess I have forgotten it multiple times." As she walked past him with folded towels in hand, on her way to the main bathroom.

TC just looked at her and shook his head. Yelling after her "Where is Jacob? Is he going to be home for supper tonight?'

Jan re-entered the kitchen looked at TC. "No, TC. I've told you multiple times this was the weekend he was going out of town with his friend Gary and his family. Remember? To Gatlinburg? You had him clean out the garage to earn extra spending money just last week! Have you forgotten already TC?"

TC looked at Jan, the smirk on her face made him realize she was not really angry just poking fun at him. He gives her a look, she starts screaming and runs around the kitchen island with TC right behind her, but to no avail he catchers her and tickled her relentlessly. When she could take no more and was begging for mercy he released her. He started to kiss her at that moment but something halted him, he paused and kissed her on the top of the forehead instead. He playfully slapped her ass with the kitchen towel as he turned to go back over to the stove to check on the veggies. Jan didn't seem to notice the hesitation. They enjoyed a pleasant enough of a dinner and evening before turning in for the night.

The next morning TC was up at the crack of dawn ready to be on the road. He loved his guy trip getaways and everybody was going this year, even Dalton, which was amazing in itself. He arrived at Gunny's about a quarter till six and of course Gunny was waiting for him on his front porch, duffel bag by his side. As usual Gunny was in rare form.

"It's about damn time you got here." As he tossed his duffel bag in the back. "Dalton called said he would meet us at Andy's, so one less stop for you TC."

"Sounds good to me Gunny, one more stop and we are on our way!"

Just under a five hour drive with only one pit stop and no traffic delays they arrived in Gulf Shores with plenty of time to confirm their deep sea fishing trip scheduled for in the morning. After which, they grabbed some lunch and checked into the hotel.

"Let's go check out the beach we have a couple of hours to kill. Might be some available chicks around."   Dalton looked at Andy shaking his head.

"And you wonder why Tabitha doesn't like me to come to the beach?"

Tossing a cold beer in Andy's waiting hand. Grinning Andy just motions for TC to join them, he agrees and turns to Gunny. "You coming Gunny?"

"Nah you guys go ahead, think I will take me a little siesta before supper." He yawns and heads down the hall to the room he is sharing with TC.

Once on the beach the guys go for a long walk up one end and down to the next. TC sees a shell floating at the water's edge he stops and picks it up. It is a pretty enough shell, an Irish Flat Scallop by name; however it was broken on one side. As TC tossed it out to sea he couldn't help but to think of Sam. She knew he was going, he had called and told her. He didn't however manage the time to see her before he left. He realized he missed her. Catching up with Andy and Dalton he takes his cell phone out of his pocket handing it to Dalton.

"Here, snap a couple of photos of me and try to get my face this time and the water in the background. Then we need a couple of group selfies for the photo album."

Dalton obliges snapping a few photos of TC then they do a couple of series and goofy ones of all of them. Once back at the room while waiting on his turn in the shower TC is out on the balcony overlooking the water. He retrieves his phone and texts the picture of himself to Samantha. It is only a few minutes and she replies back telling him he looks very handsome. How the water looks so inviting and that she wanted to hear all about it upon his return. He replies back that he is looking forward to the return himself and would see her soon. With a satisfied grin on his face he tucks the phone back into his pocket.

The next day went way too fast to suit all the men, aside from Andy; he spent half the day puking over the side of the boat. He finally took some meds and a short nap and was fairly human again by the afternoon. He then manage to catch the biggest fish just before quitting time.

Unbelievable was the only word Gunny could manage as they exited the boat. A few dozen beers between them all and some fresh fish for supper and their sunburned and spent bodies were out like a light by nine o'clock.

Sunday morning they managed to get up and out just before the eleven o'clock deadline. Filling up on coffee and gas they were homeward bound before noon. TC enjoyed the trip that was for sure, as he bid the water's edge farewell for yet another year. He spent the drive home thinking of Sam.

Sam turned to Ash. "Ash, would you zip me please?" Holding up her tasseled curls so as not to get them in the zipper. Ash noticed the smoothness of her back and the pretty red bra and matching panties she was wearing as he zipped her dress. But, he only lightly squeezed her shoulder before walking over to the dresser to retrieve his wallet and his keys. Coming back to give her a goodbye peck on the cheek before leaving.

"Have a nice day Ash." Sam called after him, sadness in her voice as she looked over her shoulder at him while slipping on her heels. He shouted back the same sentiment to her.

She remembered all the times in the long ago past that when she had asked Ash to zip her up and instead he undressed her followed by a quick romp in the bed, causing both of them to nearly be late for work. Those days were long gone. She didn't understand. Their sex life had always been fantastic. Ash was a good lover and he had told her many times that he enjoyed making love to her. It just suddenly stopped, without warning. Just a cold stop by Ash. As though a light had been turned off, just that simple. Sam had long sense quit trying to make him interested in her again. She assumed it was his age, or so she guessed. She was really at the point of giving up on him and their marriage altogether. She had talked to him many times and fought with him too. Not just about the sex but their marriage in general. She told him it was dying and she felt like his sister instead of his wife. Not only did they not have sex anymore but they didn't have fun either. He would scoff it off each time and each time he would swear that he loved her and that he did not want a divorce. And each time Ash would be a little nicer for a few days and then slip back into his old routine of distance or grumpiness. Sam was never sure which one to expect. She had grown weary of it as well.

TC knew he would not have time to get by to see Samantha on a Monday, so upon arriving at his office he sent her a text.

"Good morning! How was your weekend?"

As usual Sam responded quickly. "It was good TC Welcome home! Welcome back to the real world, I was just thinking of you!"

"Yeah, I know that is right. I have a lot going on today and tomorrow but Wednesday, if you could swing it, how about I take you out for a little Mexican dinner? I know this quaint little place kind of off the beaten path. Jan will be at a seminar that night."

Oh, okay yes I am sure I can manage that, just send me info on where and time."

"Will do Sam, have a great day!"

Sam was excited at the thought of seeing TC a little nervous about it, but she didn't really think anyone would think much of it if they saw them out in public after all they were work colleagues.

To Sam's surprise the time seemed to fly by and Wednesday had arrived before she knew it. She had been extremely busy at work mainly due to the fact that John had only been in a few hours each day. She was glad. Glad she could afford her uncle some extra time off, he had always been good to her as had her Aunt Estelle. She was thankful he had offered her the position in order to move back home. She was truly blessed to have both of them in her life. Ash was getting ready for his usual departure for work, he looked at Sam as she stood there in her black lace panties and matching bra, starring at her closet, her hands on her hips.

"Sam, what is this mess with all your cloths strung everywhere?'

"Well Ash, Just my once a week fight with the closet, when I can't decide what to wear!"

"It looks like the closet is winning Sam!" He laughed as he looked at the disheveled mess, picking up a navy blue dress as he pointed it toward her. "I always thought you looked very professional in this one."

Sam takes it from him.

"Thanks, but no it will be too hot for this one."

She hangs it back in the closet, thinking a definite, no!

"Got to go I will leave you to the mercy of the closet. Oh, and don't expect me for supper, I'll grab something before my late class."

"Oh, yes I forgot about that class, ok see you late then." Smiling Sam picked a pretty bright blue button front blouse and a matching short knit skirt. Ah! Finally, the cosmic Gods are with me today! I didn't have to make up an excuse to Ash for tonight and this outfit will be perfect!

Sam arrived at the restaurant first. She had been there before with Ash. It was an average sized restaurant and the food had always been delishous. It was tastefully decorated with live plants in giant colorful containers. Pictures of Cacti adorned the walls, which were painted in bright oranges, yellows and greens. The front of the restaurant had a large glassed area facing the sidewalk she asked for a booth in the corner of the room that faced that window. Having settled in for only a moment she saw TC as he walked down the sidewalk to the doorway. What a handsome man! She thought. A very special man for sure. Her admiration for him had no words. She just knew in her heart he was a good man. And if it was one thing she did well it was listening to others when the talk. Some people took that to mean shyness; but they couldn't have been more wrong. She figured out a long time ago that you learn a lot more when you listen that when you speak. In all those visits to her office, he had shared some wonderful stories of his life, family and friends.

A few seconds later TC was slid in the booth facing her. Although he had much rather sat next to her, it was too risky. He knew they were taking a slight gamble as it were. Sam smiled at him. He noticed how pretty she looked in the blue top and how it really made her eyes look blue instead of their usual green. He loved her smile it was so warming and so genuine, never a doubt that she was indeed always happy to see him.

The waiter took their orders and left plenty of chips and salsa for them to munch on, along with a cold beer for TC and a raspberry daiquiri for Sam. TC told her of his fishing weekend in between bites and caught her up with the kids and even mentioned Jan here and there. Sam listened intently. Watching TC as he took a drink of his beer, she was absorbed in his every action and word, content to be spending time with him. Just as TC was about to speak again the waiter arrived with their meal. TC picked up his fork, then glanced at his plate, he paused and looked up at Sam.

"Ok, so we both know we want each other. Neither of us wants to face it though. What is this thing between us Samantha?"

Sam wasn't able to reply she was caught by surprise. It didn't seem to matter though, he didn't really wait for a response from her before he spoke again.

"I have no idea Sam." As he shakes his head in denial. "But it is sure there, and on my mind all the time, it really messes me up."

For lack of knowing what to say she lightly mumbles. "I know what you mean TC, it is on my mind a lot too."

TC placed his fork on his plate and picked up his mug and took a drink. As he sat it back on the table he looked at Sam. Not ready to continue the conversation in the direction it was going as now his RTP had taken off again. Thoughts caused him to question the serendipity of their relationship. Thoughts of, Damn why does she have to stir me up so? What is it about those gorgeous bedroom eyes of hers? So mesmerizing, so damn pretty! What is the magical power she seems to have over me? Questions with no answers, at least not now.

The sound of Sam's glass clinking as she almost sat it down in her plate, brought him back to the conversation.

"I don't know Sam but there is definitely something going on here. I don't understand it myself. I have a good marriage. There isn't anything wrong with my marriage. There is just something special about you Sam. You have some kind of pull on me. I have no idea what it is. Just something about you."

He retrieved his fork and started to eat, as though he again wasn't expecting an answer. Just getting something off his chest, sort of just putting it out there, she assumed. It was a good thing because Sam was so shocked that she really didn't quite know how to handle his comments. Certainly a surprise that he would just bring it up like that. After a few moments of silence while she was eating, along with some heavy thinking on her part, Sam looks at TC; she chooses her words very carefully before she spoke.

"I understand my side of it TC. I mean my marriage with Ash isn't really a good one. It isn't really that bad, I suppose, in the all and all. I do love Ash, as a person and another human being, I just am not in love with him"

TC is intently listening to her, seemingly focusing on every word to its fullest meaning. She takes a deep breath before continuing. "But, what I don't understand is why I do not feel guilty about the feelings I have for you? I mean, well I do feel badly TC, I feel badly about putting you in this position. I feel badly that I am not strong enough to back away from you. I don't want to cause you pain or hurt you or your family in any way. Most importantly, I don't want to lose your friendship."

She reaches over the top of the table to let her fingers gently touch the top of his hand, TC reached for her fingers, giving them a slight squeeze before they each released hold.

"Well, that is good to know Sam. I've been wondering how you have felt, well after our little encounters. She knew he was referring to her emotions on the few times they had sort of made out. It was as though she could read his mind.

"I'm ok with it TC. I know it can't be anything more and that it is not going anywhere permanent. I also, know for some strange reason I don't want it to stop."

Sam could sense that TC was genuinely worried about her, that he didn't want to break her heart. The distraught look on his face confirmed that. TC nods his head in agreement. They are interrupted by the waiter asking if everything is ok. TC lets him know they are fine as he finished the last of his bear. Sam takes a nervous sip of water. They sit in silence for a few minutes looking into each other's eyes. It was as though they were two lost souls searching for the answer to some unknown question. As abruptly as their conversation had become serious it again took off on a lighter note, joking and laughing again. TC goes into an in depth description on how or why someone is left handed or right handed. Laughingly he stops. "How did I get onto that one!" shrugging his shoulders.

"See, Sam my RTP takes me places sometimes." Smiling he reaches for her hand giving it another little squeeze. "I don't know Sam, it just happened all of a sudden. All the playful flirting and joking back and forth after all this time and then." His face slightly flushes red.

"Well then that day in the kitchen, when you hugged me. Well I just felt something, it happened for me right then and there Samantha. It all changed. After that it escalated so quickly before I knew what was happening it had a hold on me. Whatever, **it** is!"

"I know TC! I know! I was in total shock that day you actually took me up on my playful dare with the chocolate candy on my neck. How many times had we played that game all in fun? I had never expected you to do that at all, not at all." Smiling sweetly at him she added. "Although, I must say I enjoyed it immensely, even in my state of shock."

TC grinned back at her. "Yeah, that kind of took me by surprise too."

TC motioned for the waiter to bring their bill. Once that was taken care of they left the restaurant to the dimly lit parking lot. TC had parked beside her but when they got to his truck he opens the back door. "Would you like to sit a while?" Smiling at Sam he holds the door open. Again Sam was surprised by TC's actions.

"Yes, yes TC I would." So she climbs into the back seat with him getting in behind her and closing the door. In only a moment he has her totally wrapped up in his arms kissing her passionately. His lips move gently down her neck, his moustache slightly tickling her with each movement. He moves the collar of her blouse off her shoulder to smother it in kisses, as his hands move to the buttons on her blouse. Sam's hands were gently gliding through his hair; she loved the feel of it between her fingers. She was in awe of how much it excited her. Maybe it was just the simple fact that she was touching him, whatever the reason, it was exhilarating. Having totally unbuttoned her he stops to look at her breasts. Just enough light from the street coming through to see they are indeed as beautiful as he had anticipated. The sexy black lace bra exposed them beautifully; his lips wasted no time giving each breast its turn of sweet kisses. He was thankful his windows are darkly tinted so there wasn't much fear of them being seen. As he kissed Sam's lips again his hand works its way to the back of her bra. Sam lets out a little laugh and quietly says to TC.

"It is a front closure." He kind of snickers himself and

immediately both hands are grasping the front of the bra to release her breast. As he does so his lips covering each of them in kisses and then gently and teasingly tickling each nipple with the tip of his tongue, one on one, as he lovingly caressed them in his hands. Sam was melting with pleasure, her body moving with his every touch. Occasionally they were interrupted by car lights coming and going; they would stop and duck down to be sure they are not seen through the clear front glass. However, it was only a momentary break and they were right back where they left off. Sam's hands fumbled with TC's belt she was not able to unfasten it, all the while they were entwined in hungry kisses. TC finally assisted with the belt and Sam then managed the zipper. He raised himself enough to slip his jeans down to release his rock hard erection. The touch of Sam's hand upon him gave him chills. Holding and kissing her he whispered.

"We better quit Sam, before we go too far."

Sam pulls away from him.

"Yes, TC we had better stop." She is fidgeting with her bra and top while he is fastening his pants.

She hears TC sigh, she looked up at him. "I want to be in you Sam, I really do. I am just not ready yet." She is again shocked at his honesty. Knowing he was thinking of Jan and his marriage. She reached up with her hand and gently stroked the side of his face, his soft beard tickled each finger. In a low soft voice she replied.

"I understand TC it is ok. Please do not worry." TC sighed again as he reached for her leg and gently stroked it from her toes all the way up to her thigh. Gentle caressing strokes. A look of regret upon his face.

He wanted her so badly, it was true. But the ties to Jan and his family, well, what about those? At this moment he wasn't sure about anything. He gives her a last kiss and they both exit his vehicle. He walked her to her car opening the door for her. He stood there and watched as she took her seat. He wished things were easier.

No goodbye kiss was exchanged; they both knew it would only lead to another and another. Sam stared the car engine. TC followed the hint.

"I will talk to you soon Sam. Have a safe ride home." A slight look of sadness on his face.

"You too, TC."

He carefully shut the car door. He watched as she left the parking lot, then returned to his own truck.

On his drive home TC could think of nothing but what had just happened. He couldn't seem to get her out of his head. He became angry, frustrated and elated all at once! His mind was racing from one emotion to the other. It was on overload. What is wrong with me? What am I doing? Am I willing to throw over twenty five years of marriage to Jan, down the tubes like it was nothing? I had said a long time ago I would never let anything like this happen. I'd made up my mind to stick with this marriage no matter what! Why does Samantha have this hold over me? Why are we being pulled together? Damn I wanted to make love to her so badly! Finally getting so worked up he yells out to his own reflection in his rearview mirror. "Shit! I'm and idiot!"

Knowing he is getting too upset and that he needed to calm down. Sometimes extreme anger does trigger a flashback and he hadn't had one in a while, for which he was very thankful. He reached over to turn on the radio to calm him and get his mind off Sam, as though some sort of cosmic joke he hears Cher bellowing out "If I could turn back time". He looked at the radio. He was really pissed now, he angrily turns it off. Just as he glanced back up something large and dark jumped out in front of his truck. "Shit!" He hit the brakes and swerved just in the nick of time and managed to not lose control as he veered over into the other lane.

"Damn deer! Thank God another car wasn't coming! I know better than to swerve like that! Shit! TC gets your act together!' He cursed at himself.

His thoughts then went right back to Sam. She haunted him. What is it about her that makes me want to tell her everything? Hell, I don't think I have ever been this candid with Jan. He slammed on his breaks as he realized he had passed his street. Damn it! Better get my act together! He backed up and turned down his street and into his driveway.

It appeared Jan was home. He wasn't ready to go in just yet. He wasn't sure how he would handle it. He had never cheated on Jan, not that he and Sam had actually had sex, yet. But it was still wrong and he knew that. His emotions were running wild. He killed the engine and leaned his head back on the headrest for a moment looking out the window at the stars. So, so mysterious, just like Sam he thought. TC closed his eyes trying to clear her out of his mind so he could relax and go in and face Jan. But his thoughts would not cooperate. Every second they had just shared was on rewind in his mind. He broke out into a sweat.

Unbeknownst to him Jan had seen his lights in the driveway. It had been a while and he never came in, concerned she turned on the porch light and went out to see what was wrong. When she got to his truck she could see from the light that his head was leaned back and his eyes closed, she could see the sweat trickling down his temple. Fearing he had either passed out or having a flashback she franticly reached for the door handle it was locked so she tapped on the door. TC didn't respond. She continued to yell at him but TC was so absorbed in his thoughts of Sam that he didn't hear her. She finally tapped on the glass. Startled he jumped with fist in hand at the glass, only to see Jan standing there with a frantic look on her face. He opened the door of the truck as Jan stepped back and then rushed to him.

"TC! Are you ok? Are you having a flashback?"

TC looked at her for a moment as though he doesn't know what to say. He then replied.

"No babe, not a flashback. I think I just had one too many beers." He reached for her and she wrapped her arms around his waist as though to assist him in walking to the door.

"Sorry I worried you babe."

"Well you should be." She said in a relieved tone.

Once inside TC went straight to bed. He laid there feeling guilty. He wrestled with the lie he had just told Jan, knowing all the while the beer had nothing to do with it. He had just had too much of the exhilarating Samantha. He had let Jan think it was the beer. It was a quick and easy out for him. One that he was thankful he had.

Upon arriving to her own home Sam pulled in the driveway noticing Ash's car was not there.

Hum, no Ash yet. That is odd I would think he would be home by now. Oh well, probably a good thing. Instead of going inside, she decided to take a walk down the curved sidewalk that led to the back of the house. The area was well lit from the path lights she had installed last year. They led her to her favorite swing on the back deck, which faced her rose garden, one of her favorite spots. A spot she had spent many hours sitting watching the birds or reading. It was a comfortable oversized swing with a big thick floral cushion. The wooden arbor that it sat under kept it dry and free of debris. The area surrounding the deck was adorned with a bird bath, feeders and various yard art. Her little angles she called them. The overseers of the garden, she liked to tell Ash, who would rarely sit there with her.

Oh, Ash why can't you be TC? The night's events rushed through her thoughts over and over, until she could take no more.

Guess I better get inside before Ash does get home. Going inside she turned on the lights as she made her way to the bathroom.

As she placed a warm wash cloth upon her face she could still smell TC's cologne. She relished the smell for a moment before she continued. Finally her face washed and teeth brushed she looked at her reflection in the mirror. It was a blank stare. She turned out the light and opened the bedroom window for some fresh air. She took a last look at the night sky, the stars were still twinkling beautifully. A cool refreshing breeze is gently filled the room. Smiling she turned toward the bed. Hopefully. I will sleep well tonight. She pulled back the spread to leave only the sheet to cover up with; she snuggled into the bed slipping into the softness of her pillow. Just as she was about to doze off she hears Ash coming up the stairs. She turned over on her side pretending to be asleep as he slipped in the bed beside her. She felt his hand on her side as he gave her a gentle little pat, as though to say goodnight.

Chapter **14**

A few weeks later TC stopped in again to see Sam, there had been many texts back and forth since the restaurant night. It was uncanny how so often one would be thinking of the other and suddenly the other would make contact. They both were keeping up with each other's lives.

It was the middle of the day and the office was full of people coming and going. Sam was happy to see him and she could tell from the look on his face he was elated as well. She greeted him with a big hug, squeezing her tightly for a moment, before he released her and took his usual chair.

"Would you care for some water TC?" She asked before she took her own seat.

"Yes, Samantha that would be great. She went over to the corner of her credenza where she had just placed a fresh pitcher of ice water. She poured TC a large glass of the sparkling water. Even though her back was to him she could feel his eyes upon her.

She turned to him, her lips slightly curved in a smile as she offered him the ice water. "I thought you might be thirsty, TC."

When took the glass from her he made a point of his hand

lingering on top of hers as he gave her that drop dead gorgeous I want you look that caused Sam to melt every time.

She smiles at him in acknowledgement of his little tempting game.

"Well TC tell me what has been going on in your world? What had you so upset the other day when you text me?'

TC kind of sloughs it off. "Oh, Sam, you know the usual day to day life things. Jan had been on my ass majorly, just enough to keep me agitated then the usual crap with the kids, again just enough going on to keep the agitation level up. He looked at her with a slight melancholy look on his face, pausing for a moment.

"Then there is that devil woman thing. Me wanting to see you. Me handling the guilt of wanting you so damn bad like I do! Sometimes, Sam." He paused again. "Sometimes it is all hard to handle, kind of like a devil on one shoulder and an angel on the other, both whispering in my ear at the same time telling me what to do."

Sam was surprised.

"Oh, so I am a devil woman now, hum?" She smiled as devilishly as she could at him trying the humor thing again, in order to make him laugh, for lack of not knowing what else to say.

"If you weren't so damn handsome, maybe I wouldn't be a devil woman TC!"

TC laughed at her reasoning. Seeing her had definitely made him feel better. He started telling her about how he cleaned out Gunny, Andy and Dalton in a poker game. She wasn't really listening, not that it was a boring story. It was just that he was so close yet so far away and she really wanted to touch him. She wanted to feel him in her arms again. But, with an office full of people she knew this was not going to happen. She imagined the soft touch of his lips gliding upon her skin, tickling her earlobe.

Suddenly she realized she has slipped into a fantasy and that TC had quit talking and was just sitting there looking at her with his sultry eyes, melting her to the core.

Both of them yearning for the touch of each other. TC smiled at that moment and simply said. "Me too Samantha, me too." He discretely slid his hand across her desk, touching the edge of her finger tips. About that time John Rivers entered her office. They quickly moved their hands away from each other, in hopes that nothing had been seen.

"Sam I need your assistance." John then turned his attention to TC. "Hello TC, sorry for the interruption. Sam, I am with the Alexanders, and they seem to be having difficulty understanding the closing procedure. Could you come assist me please?" A look of despair on his face.

"Of course John, I will be right there." Sam felt the blood rush to her cheeks; she hoped they were only a slight pink and not the beastly red she was feeling!

"Excuse me for just a moment TC?'

"Sure Sam, I need to make a few quick phone calls if you don't mind me using your office? I will wait for you."

"Of course TC, make yourself at home."

In less than five minutes, Sam was back in her office with TC. They chatted for a few moments about the closing and then TC got quiet. She could tell something was on his mind.

"What are you thinking about TC?"

A slight frown was upon his face as he answered her.

"I am thinking about how to be good...but I can't, my mind is racing with a million thoughts right now." He rose from his chair. "I better get out of here. I hope I made your week Sam."

"You certainly did TC, and I look forward to more!" His face changes to a very somber and worried look. "Yes, but we have to be careful, this could really go somewhere."

Sam didn't reply, as usual she was caught off guard. A quick goodbye hug and he was out the door. As Sam watched him leave she was thinking about his statements, they had certainly surprised her. Was he telling her that he really wanted her in hopes of her making the moves first? Or, was he hoping she would take the higher road and be strong enough to resist temptation for the both of them? Or, could it possibly be he just needed to share his feelings with her? She was so confused! Damn it! Why does it have to be so hard?

The days come and go and it is business as usual but not a word from TC. Not being able to stand it any longer she sends him a text: "Hey, how are you?" In was but a few moments and she heads his special tone, the one that always made her smile, and ok admittedly sometimes made her nervous. She quickly looked at her phone.

"All is good. How are you?"

She text back "Great now that I am talking to you, you have been quite lately."

It is a moment before he answered. "Just trying to be good."

Sam doesn't know how to respond, so she doesn't respond at all. After a few minutes her phone rang, it was his ring tone.

"Hello TC." She answered.

"Hello Sam. Yeah, well it has been kind of a crazy few weeks but

I am free tomorrow night if you might happen to be? I could meet you at the office after five?"

It seemed to Sam that he was almost worried he had upset her, without thinking on it further she replied.

"Yes, yes that would be great TC, I look forward to seeing you." Her emotions had gone from devastation to elation in a matter of seconds, she looked up at the heavens, smiled and said thank you. Something in her gut just told her that her mom had her heavenly hand in putting her and TC together. She knew TC wouldn't understand her feelings regarding that and she had never shared it with Dakota either; in her entire being she felt it was the truth.

It is after five in the afternoon and everyone had departed for the day at River House. Sam is anxiously waiting for TC to arrive, she watched for him out the front window. She saw his red truck pull in the parking lot so she opened the door to let him in, locking it behind him. Smiling at each other they go to her office. TC had no sooner taken his seat when he received a text message. He looked at his phone. Still reading the message he tells Sam. "It is Jan; she is waiting to pick up Jacob from ball practice. She must be bored she keeps texting me."

"Oh, thought he wasn't into sports, he is growing up I guess?" Sam inquires.

"It appears so." He replied as he is finished his own reply text to Jan. Once completed he lays his phone on Sam's desk. He smiled at Sam and abruptly picked up his chair bringing it around to Sam's side of the desk, turning her chair around to face him; they are touching knee to knee. He reached down and picked up Sam's feet and removed shoes, all the while a playful smile on his face. Astonished Sam asked. "Oh! TC what are you doing?"

"Giving you a foot massage." He stated simply, then smiled a little more mischievously as he started to massage each foot. Slowly and tenderly at first, knowing just when to apply the right amount of pressure to really make it feel good to her.

"Oh! TC that feel so wonderful, you really do have magical hands."

He smiled as he worked his hands on up to the calf of her legs massaging them tenderly, then to her knee and finally to her outer thigh before going back down to her toes again. With each movement of his hands Sam was truly melting. It had been so long since someone had touched her, touched her, in that way with loving caresses and actually caring about how she was feeling and not just themselves. She was reeling in the pleasure of his touch. She saw him sneak little peaks under her skirt when she moved each leg according to his touch and the smile that came over his face when he realized her pleasure. Sam pulls herself closer in to TC, the rollers on her chair afforded her to do so with ease. He assisted by pulling her in closer to him.

"Are you okay Sam? That position isn't hurting you is it?" She could hear the concern in his voice.

"No, no TC it is fine."

She looked at him alluringly as she reached for the top button on her blouse. She unfastened a couple just enough to tease with a little cleavage.

"Oh dear! I came undone." Giving him her most demure and innocent look.

TC smiled and both hands reach for the other buttons on her

blouse as he slowly undoes them all, until her breasts are fully exposed. He leaned in to her gently kissing them, his lips soft and warm. Sam rises up to meet his lips with hers. Their passion is burning inside them. TC undoes the front clasp on her bra and released each breast into his hands, it gave him great pleasure. He could feel his own desires heighten. He let out a slight moan as his lips brush across her satiny bare skin. Sam's body responded accordingly, and moved under his every touch. He pulled her legs around his body as his hands slid down her stomach. He paused for a moment at the feel of her plush soft panties before moving on to her inner thigh.

"Are you comfortable Sam?" He is continually moving his hand along her inner thigh.

"Oh, yes, I am fine I just am having a little difficulty with this chair and don't want to slip out of it." She was also a bit nervous, to say the least.

With the chair being on rollers it was a little difficult to remain in it, not to mention what TC was doing to her.

In a deeply masculine voice he replied. "Not to worry Sam, I will not let you fall."

His hands moved from her inner thigh reaching her panty area. His fingers found their way beneath her panties, stroking her gently as he watched the lustful look on her face, knowing he was giving her pleasure. Sam's body was overflowing with rapture; she let out a faint moan of bliss.

TC suddenly pulls her into him she can feel his hardness even through his clothing, they got so caught up in the heat of the moment that Sam's contorted body started to slip from the chair. TC stopped her from totally slipping out of the chair in the nick of time; they both let out a little laugh. He moved his chair back and began to clear off a corner of Sam's desk then gently guided her to the top of it. He is standing against her, fondling her breasts. Sam's body bows upward at TC inviting him for more.

He reached under her skirt and began the downward decent of her panties.

"Let's get these off." He smiled lustfully at her. Sam lets out a gasp as TC's lips touch her. She feels the tickle of his tongue then his lips again. TC is steadily unfastening his pants and has quickly dropped them to the floor, never stopping the pleasure he is giving her. He is all over her with unsurmountable passion. Just as Sam feels him about to enter her he stops short groping himself with his hand.

"Oh shit, I can't it is too late! Damn it! I feel like a teenager experiencing his first time! Shit!"

Sam lets out a little laugh. "It is okay TC, here let me get you something to clean up with."

"I'm sorry Sam, really." TC didn't seem to be the slight bit embarrassed. Which to Sam just solidified just how comfortable they were with each other.

"It is fine TC, no worries; really you did give me pleasure. It is ok honestly."

Afterward, he reaches for Sam's panties and gently slid them back on her. She fastened her bra sitting there on the edge of her desk her blouse still gaping open, they are both still fondling each other's body, arms hands anything within reach, with tender loving caresses.

"I don't know what happens Samantha. I have the intent of

seeing you just as a friend, but once I am within touching range of you, I just can't hold back. Once I see you I want to touch you."

He paused for a moment, a confused look upon his face.

"I don't understand it. I have a good marriage with Jan. A good family life, a happy one. I don't know what draws me to you Sam. I try so hard to resist you, but I can't!"

Sam reached up and gently took TC's face in both her hands. She looks him directly in the eyes.

"TC, there must be something wrong, somewhere or you would not be here with me."

She released him from her hold; he nodded his head in agreement. Sam trying to understand it herself continues.

"Is there something missing with Jan? Maybe the excitement?"

TC looked down. "No everything is good. All is really good as a matter of a fact." He emits a little half smile at her.

"That is why I don't understand the draw to you."

Sam knew that was his way of telling her their sex life was not suffering as hers an Ash's.

"Then what is it TC? Just the lust for my body?"

TC became serious again and a disheartened sigh was released before he answered her.

"Sam, if I knew the answer to that, I'd have all the answers, to all the world's questions. I just do not know. I just know that I like giving you pleasure. I like knowing I please you. Something pulls me to you. I don't know what it is I feel. I know it is not love, we can't fall in love! It's complicated."

The early morning sunlight came filtering through Sam's

bedroom window it provided a warm feeling upon her face, a gentle awakening that she always enjoyed. She was definitely a sun person; she could never get enough of it. She lay there for a moment basking in the sun's warmth. Slowly drifting into her consciousness was the dream she had last night. She knew immediately it was of TC. She remembered the feel of TC's muscular arm across her waist as they lay there asleep on the bed together. The thought made her smile, but then, she started to recall the rest of the dream...

"Instead of being in a big soft comfy bed she and TC were laying on what seemed to be a hard stainless steel type of surface with a white sheet covering their naked bodies. They were both peacefully sleeping each laying on their side, with TC snuggled up to her back, his arm possessively over her waist. Suddenly Jan enters the room and they both awaken and quickly rise form the bed. Jan is aghast at the sight! She had missed TC not being in bed with her, and had come to look for him. TC immediately heads out the front door telling Jan he must go to his meeting. Jan tells him that is fine babe I will see you later. Sam is left to contend with Jan on her own. Jan glares at Sam as TC shuts the door behind him. Sam begins to explain to Jan that nothing has happened between them, that she thinks Jan is crazy for not trusting TC; that he loves her and that she is all he talks about. It is me! My entire fault! Do not blame TC! Sam tries to take all the blame. Jan just stands there with her hands on her hips without saying a word, just looking at Sam.

Sam was sure other words were exchanged in the dream between herself and Jan but her mind would not retrieve them. Instead, she focused on the odd parts of the dream, not that the entire dream had not been odd. Frowning, she just realized that they had been in her parent's old house in the dream. The last house they had owned when they both passed away, many years prior. I know Mom would have loved TC she thought, her own RTP taking over again. She frowned at she got out of bed heading toward the bathroom, as she thought how strange this dream had been. Maybe later she would see if she could analyze it. Something she loved to do, as she dreamt quite often and not unlike this dream she knew there was always a hidden meaning, secret messages from the subconscious. Although, there wasn't much needed to analyze this one. It is obvious to her that it was on guilt overload.

Going back to the bedroom in dawned on her that Ash was not there. She assumed he had left early for his golf game, again.

For a Sunday afternoon things appeared to be normal at the Martin house. Jan was gone shopping and Jacob was at some friends for the weekend. TC was in his garage not doing anything really just puttering around trying to keep his mind clear of Sam. It doesn't seem to be working so he went inside and changed into his swim trunks.

Maybe a few laps in the pool will expend some of this energy and my crazy thoughts.

Afterward he was sitting in the lawn chair enjoying a cold beer he looked at his phone laying on the table beside him. He wanted to call Sam, but he resisted, instead he called Gunny.

"Hey you old fool, if you're not doing anything come on over for a swim, Jan is gone and I need some company."

In an apologetic tone he hears. "Sorry TC, can't make it today. Martha has me out with her shopping for furniture."

TC was disappointed to say the least and Gunny could hear it in his voice. "Oh, okay well, you have fun and don't pick out anything too weird, you old fool."

"I'm sorry TC. Um you okay? I could probably get away, if you really need me?"

"No, no Gunny it is fine I was just a little bored, nothing serious. I'll talk to you next week."

He hung up with Gunny and called Andy, no answer, he then dialed Dalton's number, same no answer.

"Well shit! Appears everybody is doing something except me!"

After a thirty minutes or so, with his beer bottle empty he got up to go inside. Hell, guess I will go start some supper. At least that should make Jan happy. Although these days I'm not really sure what makes her happy. Within an hour or so TC has supper ready but there is no Jan. He sends her a text.

"Supper is ready. Are you on your way home?"

A few moments go by and Jan replied. *"Oh sorry TC thought I told you to fin for yourself. I won't be back for a bit, sorry."*

TC, angry now doesn't even bother to respond, instead he fixed his plate grabs two beers and goes out on the back deck. It is a perfect evening for eating outside he thought as he tried to get himself into a better mood. He certainly didn't need or want another fight with Jan.

Sam slipped back into his thoughts, as she always did. Before he knew it, like a thief in the night the devilish angel woman was there in his thoughts, in his soul.

I wish I could be enjoying this meal with her right now. I wonder how she prefers her steak? Wonder if I could entice her to go for a skinny dip afterward! He smiled at that last thought as he finished up his meal. After a bit he went back inside to clean up and get another beer. Hell might as well grab a bucket of ice and slip a few more beers in there and chill outside a little longer.

Several beers later Jan arrived home to find him sound asleep still in the chaise lounge.

"TC, honey wake up. Come on inside and go to bed." He felt her tug on his arm. Only semi awake he muttered "Sa...."

He looked up realizing it is Jan, and changed that almost Sam to a 'Sure, oh, ok Jan I'm coming."

Things are buzzing at River House; they usually do on a Monday morning. Sam's cell chimes with TC's text tone and she immediately looks at the message:

"Good morning! How is your morning going?'

Happy she text back. "Morning! Just a normal busy Monday morning, trying to detour thoughts of a handsome man I know."

TC smiled when he reads it. "Well I just drove past your office. That must be why all of a sudden the temperature feels hotter, closer to the source!"

She replied back: "Well if you had stopped in I would have offered you some cold water, or something."

Hoping he would be able to catch that little flirt through a text.

"No time this morning Sam. Close your eyes lean your head back and let your imagination flow for a minute or two, and I believe you will have a wonderful thought and a good day."

Sam replied. "Whoa, my imagination is on overload! What a wonderful thought TC, will you do the same?"

"Already been there Samantha, just wondering if you would enjoy it."

No further exchanges were made, she knew that meant he was busy and that was enough to make her day brighter, just knowing he was thinking about her always made her very happy.

Several days go by before Sam hears from T.C .again, then without warning the special tone is on her phone and TC is asking if she is available after five, she tells him she is.

TC arrived just a little after five. Feeling safe they are secure and alone TC was sitting across the desk from Sam making small talk. There is only a small lamp on in her office to afford them a little light. They are catching up and making small talk as Sam wonders if he is going to make the move or not. Finally, she goes over to join him as she reaches the front of her desk she innocently asked. "May I sit over here a little closer?" He replied of course and keeps on talking about the past few work day events. Sam could sense that perhaps he is trying to 'be good' as he puts it, trying to resist the temptation of her. He barely even makes eye contact with her, another sure sign he is in resist mode. She sat there for a moment contently listening to him. After a bit she got up and went back to her chair on the other side of the desk. She pretended to look at something on her computer all the while she was making small talk with him and very much engaged in the conversation. She was hearing his body language loud and clear of being good and she started to oblige. But knowing their time was precious, she didn't want to waste a minute of it, so she went back over to TC's side and sat on the desk in front of him, her skirt tantalizingly raised just enough to be sexy. TC could not resist, it was just seconds and his hands were stroking her bare legs, enjoying the feel of her supple skin. After a few affectionate strokes he moved his way up to the buttons on her blouse. As he unfastened the first four buttons and was working on the rest Sam commented.

"TC we don't have to do anything if you don't want. I enjoy being with you no matter what we do." He doesn't reply. Instead he was gently gliding his fingertips across the exposed tops of her breast, just along the edge of the lace scallops of her bra. His mind salaciously focused upon Sam's breasts.

"What a beautiful sight, they are Sam. Perfect, the way they are spilling over the confinement of your bra, begging to be released."

TC could feel his temperature rise, among other things, as he fumbled with the bra's front closure. Once he released them, he gently fondled each breast, he looked Sam in the eyes as he did so. Her eyes met his with the same sultry passion.

"You have some kind of crazy hold on me Samantha." He said, as he gently kissed her breasts. She didn't comment she was too absorbed in his touch.

"Do I make you feel good Samantha?' He whispered softly to her as he is moving on to her neck.

Knowing her neck that was a major weak spot for her, one of the many, places his lips drove her crazy with desire.

"Yes! Yes, you do TC! You know you do." She stammered barely above a whisper.

TC Looked up at her, and gently started to remove her blouse. Sam was just as busy with his clothing until they were both naked from the waist up. TC placed his body against hers, pulling her in as tightly as he could. He wrapped his arms around her waist as he gently but firmly pulled her to him. This movement excited Sam so, that it almost took her breath away, causing her to gasp, which excited TC all the more. He loved pleasing her; it was almost like an addiction, knowing he was giving her pleasure.

"Someday, I'm going to go all the way Sam." As his hand gently approached her stomach, pausing for a moment, as he enjoyed the feel of her.

"Why are you holding back TC?" His hands had now reached her inner thigh. "Just wondering if the risk would be worth it Samantha."

Sam takes her legs and wraps them around TC's back pulling him in closer to her.

"What risk would that be TC?" Gazing up at him with a seemingly innocent look.

"The risk of getting caught." He mumbles as he gently kisses her neck again.

Sam knew this was not the only risk TC was worried about. She knew the risk he was really afraid of was his heart. His heart getting so attached to hers that he wouldn't be able to let go. She also knew that maybe he didn't realize it yet, on a truly conscious level, but it was there all the same, eating at him. Instead of saying what she was thinking she simply asked.

"Then why are you here with me TC?"

"I still don't know the answer to that one. Something keeps drawing me to you." He sighed.

"It's complicated Sam."

He pulls her in against him, her warm breast gently pressed against his own bare chest. He relished the feel of her naked breasts against his.

"It's not love. We can't fall in love Samantha."

TC was intent on giving Sam's body all the pleasure he could with his hands until she is exhausted in a blissful euphoria. That was his intent, to give her pleasure. They shared a few more kisses then

TC reached for his shirt, handing Sam her blouse. Sam gets dressed except for the buttons on her blouse.

TC reached for the disheveled items on her desk.

"I must put things back in their respective places."

Sam looked at him then down at her blouse. "Well, I guess you need to put me back together as well."

TC obliged with a smile, trying to button her blouse as she is gently stroking his shoulders and his neck with her hands. After he had buttoned a couple at the top, he was working on the lower ones and she reached up and unbuttoned the top ones again.

"Oh! Look TC! They came undone again!" She gave him a pouty little look.

"Yes, with the help of someone, I see." He smiled as he continued to struggle with the tiny buttons. Finally through joyfully fighting with Sam he manages to clasp the final button. They are sitting in the chairs beside each other and Sam noticed he was avoiding looking at her; it frustrated her, she didn't understand.

"TC you are doing it again!"

"What?" He looked at her unknowingly.

"Not looking at me when we talk! Why do you do that?"

"You know why Sam, because I can't resist you when I look at you."

On that note his cell phone rang. TC sees it is Jan, he tells Sam who it is before he answers it. Sam sits quietly and patiently beside him as he talks to Jan. He makes up some excuse for his whereabouts, telling her he is on his way home and hangs up. Shaking his head in disgust he looked at Sam.

"I had to lie again." He puts his phone back into the holder on his belt.

"I'm sorry TC, I really am." She turns her eyes away from him and they both head toward the door, TC just a step in front of her.

"You need to quit thinking about me so much Sam."

She stopped and reached out to touch his arm, he turned to look back at her.

"Is that what you want TC? For me to stop thinking about you?" "Well it would probably be safer that way Sam. But I can't tell you to quit though."

"Well you just did TC. Are you going to quit thinking about me?" "Probably not" Giving her a half sheepish grin he continues. "But it would be safer if I did."

Chapter 15

In the interim, there have been multiple other visits with TC, nothing leading to a true consummation of their affair. There have been plenty of flirty texts, sexy photo sharing and the song of the day game. On a lot of mornings he would text and ask what color clothing she was wearing that day or to tell her it was cold or hot and that she should dress accordingly. It always warmed Sam's heart when he would advise her to dress one way or another due to the weather, as though he were taking care of her. They would flirt relentlessly and the next minute they would be making each other laugh foolishly, just enjoying their friendship. She was always ecstatic to receive his texts and always worried when days would go by without one. Sometimes she would think she should break ties with him, but that thought never lasted for very long, just like TC; he always tried to be good, it just never seemed to work out for very long. He too would worry on those days that would go by with no word from Samantha. He would always call in lieu of a text if he thought for one minute that he had upset her.

Sam had agreed to meet Dakota for lunch. As she took her seat across from Dakota she was barely seated before Dakota had leaned over toward her.

"Well?! Tell me? What has been happening with TC? Well? Tell me about it! What?"

"Well geez Dakota give me a chance!"

"Oh pooh Sam! You know you are dying to tell me!" She leaned in even closer to the table. "Give it up girl!"

Sam tucked her purse away on the seat beside her about the time the waiter walked up. Dakota placed her order as Sam muddled over the menu, she peeped over the top of the menu and sheepishly smiled at Dakota. Dakota realizing she is toying with her, looked at the waiter as she snatched the menu from Sam's hands.

"She will have the same thing as me! Thank you." She handed the menus back to the waiter. Then gave Sam an evil eye.

The waiter stood there and waited on approval from Sam. She smiled at him and nodded in agreement. As the waiter leaves Dakota leaned back in her chair, arms crossed, giving Sam her all-knowing look.

"Cute Sammy pooh cute! You have stalled long enough! Now spill!"

A little devilish smile escaped Sam's lips.

"Okay." Taking a deep breath she begins.

"Well, we have had more than just a few visits, it always starts the same. TC tries to resist me, not that I am doing anything to entice him, well, not much." She grinned sheepishly at Dakota.

"I was good this time I really didn't do anything, but thirty minutes into the visit we were in each other's arms kissing and one thing led to another, until, well, you know."

Dakota let out a squeal of delight.

"Dakota! Really? Keep it down!"

Sam looked around the restaurant to see if anyone noticed. Satisfied that no one was paying them any attention, she continued.

"So afterward, well I mean not after sex. We didn't exactly have sex we just, well sort of made out. After we are dressed and cooled off.

"What! You were naked!" Dakota yelled out, not remembering where she was causing several patrons to turn and look at them. Sam kicked her hard underneath the table.

"Ouch!" Dakota exclaimed reaching down to rub her shin.

Samantha was beyond embarrassed and a little perturbed with Dakota to say the least, but she continued on.

"Dakota, I can't remember exactly what was said to start it, but TC again mentioned how he always comes to see me with the intent of resisting me but he just can't and he doesn't know why. I remembered early on he had told me that he erased my personal cell number from his phone in an effort to resist temptation, but that didn't last long.

He goes on to say he worries not only about our respective families, should the truth come out but our careers as well. I asked him if he was breaking up with me and he immediately and very vehemently said NO! I told him good because it would make me cry. He said he didn't want that either. He said he still didn't have a reason for the draw to me. I told him I thought it was a higher up kind of thing, if you will. That we were brought together for a reason. He stated he didn't know about that."

Dakota waited for her to finish, knowing there was more.

"Dakota, I could tell by the look on his face that he meant all that he was saying."

"So, what did you say after that Sam?"

"Well, I don't know exactly at that precise moment. But I told him that he knew it too, that it was in his heart, just not in his head yet."

Turning a little pink Sam added.

"Well I did lean into him about that time nibbling on his ear and kind of whispered something sexy like he'd miss me."

"Samantha! You are too much! Tell me more!"

Dakota was smiling with anticipation. Sam sighed a heavy sigh as she looked at Dakota, thinking that she really didn't feel comfortable telling Dakota a lot of the intimate details, even though she was her best friend. Before she had a chance to speak the waiter arrived with their food. Sam was thankful for the momentary distraction. Just as they finished their lunch Dakota looked at her watch.

"Damn it! How can the lunch hour go by so quickly? I've got to scoot back to the hospital! I can't be late for my shift. I'll talk to you soon and we will finish this lovely conversation!"

She smiled at Sam as she laid her money on the table for her lunch, giving her a quick hug goodbye and was out the door.

TC and Sam are at her office, after five, everyone else is gone. With the excuses for being late to their respective spouses taken care of prior to their meeting, everything seemed to be in place. Sam turned on her CD player and offered her hand to TC.

"Dance with me TC?" As she looked at him with a sultry smile.

TC accepted her offer, taking her hand as he stood up.

"I'm afraid I am not a very good dancer Sam." As he took her in his arms.

"I will teach you." She looked up at him, her eyes bright in anticipation.

He pulled her in closer, it is only a matter of seconds before he was kissing her forehead, her cheek, nibbling on her earlobe. Finally, he made his way to her lips, but she playfully avoided him. He half grinned and sort of shrugged his shoulder, as if to say, no matter to him, and started to gently kiss her neck. Both of his hands gently strummed up and down her back, she could feel the warmth of them. She takes her own hands and guides them up and down his muscular arms. The sexy saxophone music filled the room, they were lost in their desire for each other. TC's lips gently brushed her cheek again and then her neck. Meanwhile, his hands have traveled from her back down to her buttocks he squeezed her tightly. Excitedly, their lips met in a much anticipated kiss. The cd had stopped but neither of them cared. It is just their own bodies they were interested in at the moment, until, they hear someone bang on the front door! They immediately stop and back away from each other like two teenagers caught in the act. They looked at each other, both wide eyed with fright.

"Was that someone knocking on the door?" Sam asked as she looked at TC.

"I think so. Holy shit!" He stepped into the darkened hall trying to get a glimpse of the door to see who it might be, but the door was not visible from Sam's office. His cell phone rang. He looked at it in horror, it was Jan! At this point he was not really sure what to do, fearing if he answered it she would say she was out front and demanded to be let in. Not to mention wanting to know what the hell is going on. He had a sick feeling in the pit of his stomach.

None the less, he decided he'd better answer. When he does he hears her say.

"Hey honey I was just checking to see what time you would be home, dinner will be ready in about 20 minutes and I was going to wait on you if you were on your way."

A silent sigh of relief and a quick look at Sam as though to relay the same relief to her, he replied.

"No babe, I will be a bit longer go ahead without me. Just put me a plate in oven."

Sam noticed there were no sentiments expressed at the end of the call, like I love you, just a simple goodbye. Maybe some people just don't do that, like she and Ash do, what does it mean, after all?

TC went to the front door and saw a brown delivery truck had backed up to the front door. The driver was just stepping out of the back of the truck with a package in hand. TC opens the door and the driver hands him the package.

"Hey man, sorry to disturb you. I just happened to see Ms. Sam's car out front. I'm their regular driver and I took a chance that she might still be here. Hope I didn't disrupt anything. Would you sign here please?"

With another sigh of relief TC took the package and his shaky hand signed for the receipt of it, bidding farewell to the driver, he locked the door. TC turned to see Sam standing at the edge of the hallway, as though she were hiding.

"Oh my God TC! That scared the hell out of me!" A slight look of relief on her face.

He placed the package on the front lobby desk.

"You got that right! I just knew it was Jan at the door and about that time she even called me! I just knew I would hear her demanding to be let in. I think that was our warning Samantha. We'd better call it a night."

"Yes, TC I agree, we best call it a night."

With the office secured for the night, TC walked her to her car.

"Have a good evening Sam." He smiled at her.

She reached for his hand and pulled him down to her for a goodbye kiss, albeit a quick one.

"Call me TC."

As TC shut her door he replied. "I will Sam."

Samantha left the parking lot, but not before she took a last glimpse of TC in her rearview mirror. On her way home she was thinking of him. Stressful thoughts were swimming wildly in her mind the entire drive home.

Could it be? Would that little scare be enough to take TC away from me? Will it make him realize the dangerous game we are playing? Oh Shit! What if it reminds him how much he does not want to lose Jan? What will happen then? Will he call it off? Will I lose him forever? It obviously scared the shit out of him. Of course neither of us wants to get caught. This can't cause it to end, my gosh it is too new! Surely it is not over before it has actually begun!

Sam is immensely disturbed by her thoughts. The thought of TC backing away from her was more that she could bare.

"Life is just not fair!" she yelled out angrily as she pulled into her driveway. Ash's car was not there yet again. Good, she thought. I really need some down time.

She stopped by the kitchen to mix herself a very large pineapple and rum concoction; Andy's recipe, that she so loved. After a sip or two she took it with her upstairs to the bedroom, sitting it on the table by the entry to their master bath. She walked over to the dresser beside their bed and removed her jewelry. She placed it neatly in the glass tray, as she looked at the bed; it reminded her of how hard a time she had in convincing Ash to let her decorate it in a beach motif. It was a massive California King with tall wooden posts on each corner. She had decorated it with a pretty teal spread and white bed skirt with matching pillows tossed here and there. She loved this room. It relaxed her, much like her painting at the office. She removed her clothes and dropped them, one by one, on the bench at the foot of the bed. Then, taking her drink with her into the bathroom she ran a nice hot soaking bath. It was the only time she preferred a bath over a shower. Nothing like a hot tub and a cold drink to make one feel better, she thought as she retrieved a hair clip from the vanity. Taking her long curls she piled them on top of her head, in hopes of keeping them dry.

She lit her favorite candle; the aroma soon filled the room as she slipped her naked body into the welcomingly warm water. She leaned back against the tub; the water gently roll over her breasts, they slightly jiggled in the water as the Jacuzzi jets gently massaged her body. Sam closed her eyes relishing in the moment and in hopes of forgetting about TC, but he would not leave her thoughts.

Before long the water had turned cooler than she liked. She reached for her drink taking the last sip. She noticed her fingers were now wrinkled from being in the water much too long. Sam reached over to extinguish the candles, as she lifted the lever to allow the water drain, exiting the tub.

She shivered as she wrapped herself in an oversized towel. It made her wish TC's warm arms were around her. Sighing again as the night replayed in her mind.

Putting all her attention into the task of drying off, and applying lotion to her body, she tried not to think about TC anymore.

Suddenly, it dawned on her that it must be really late. She didn't think Ash had come home while she was bathing. Worried she looked at the clock.

My goodness it is after midnight! I wonder why Ash is so late. She picked up her phone and sent him a text, asking of his whereabouts. He replied he was on his way and would be home shortly. Satisfied, she dropped her silk robe on her side of the bed and slipped under the covers. She was met with a fitful night of sleep, with TC in her every thought.

TC's drive home wasn't much better than Sam's. He couldn't get Sam out of his mind along with Jan, the kids, they all whirled around in his thoughts. As he pulled in his driveway it suddenly hit him.

What if this is to be the last time I ever walk through these doors? Am I ready for that? Do I want that? This is my home, my life. Jan and the kids...they have all been my life for so long. His thoughts were distressed until he thought of her; Samantha, the woman he longed for. His feelings bounced from anxious to serene and back to anxious again.

Damn it! What the hell is wrong with me? Am I having a, so called, mid-life crisis? Or am I just a lust filled fool! His last thought as he exited his vehicle, going inside his home, to Jan.

It is the following Wednesday, an entire week had gone by since Sam had heard from TC she was beyond the point of worry, but she wouldn't allow herself to make the first call. She was scared. Scared of what he might say. She looked at her office door thinking she heard someone; she hoped it was TC, but instead it was John Rivers.

"Sam dear, Estelle is coming to take me to supper would you care to join us? It is almost five thirty, you know.

"Thanks for the offer but I have a ton of work to catch up on before my 9:00 a.m. closing in the morning. I do appreciate it though." She smiled impishly at him and adds. "A rain check please?'

John smiled back at her with his twinkling blue eyes that she dearly loved. They always reminded her of her father's.

"Of course Samantha of course! I am sure Estelle will stop by to say hello before we leave. You and I are the only two left in the office so I will be sure we stop in before leaving you."

"Thank you Uncle John."

John nods and returns to his office. It was just a few moments later when TC arrived at River House on the pretense of checking on the morning closing. He wasn't sure if the office was still open, there was no sign of Deidra's car, but John and Samantha's were still in the parking lot. He entered the building, as he expected there was no sign of Deidra, he was glad. The day had been stressful enough without her watching his every move. Not that he didn't like her; she gave him the creeps sometimes. As though she was always reading his mind or something, creepy definitely creep. Going on down the hall, TC stopped at Sam's door. It was open and he just stood there for a moment looking at her. She was so beautiful! He thought as he stood there with his hands in his pockets like a gaping fool. She had not yet felt his presence, however he knew she would, much like their first encounter on the beach.

Had it really been that many years ago? When did she start here at River House, what was it, two years now? Damn the time is flying.

He frowned, but as he stood there watching her his frown turns to a smile. Yes, indeed she was in her own little world sitting there with her back to the door starring at her water's edge painting. Apparently in deep thought about something, or perhaps daydreaming, he wasn't sure which.

TC heard footsteps coming up behind about the same time John Rivers called his name. "TC! Is that you?" TC turns to see John and Estelle coming toward him but not before he catches a glimpse of Samantha whirling around in her chair to look at him as well.

Reaching his hand out to John they share a friendly handshake. He then reaches over to give Estelle a hug.

"How have you been little missy? You keeping John on his toes these days?"

Estelle hugs him back with a big smile on her face.

"You know it, TC." In her crackly little voice.

"Between myself and Samantha he hasn't got a chance!" she winked at Sam.

John chimed in, "I know that is right!" A broad smile beamed across his face.

"TC I'd invite you to supper with us but something tells me you are here to see Sam, yes? And unfortunately, she has already declined us."

"Yes, John I fear you are correct. You know what a workhorse I am I stopped by to check on our closing in the morning. But, I'd sure like a raincheck on that dinner invite, if I may?"

"TC you sounded just like Sam! Alright then, you two don't work too long. I will lock you in."

Sam and TC in unison reply "Thank you." John laughs. "See what I mean! No wonder you two work together so well."

Sam gives her Aunt Estelle a good bye hug before they are on their way.

After they have heard the door chime TC looks at Sam.

"Where is my hug?" A big grin on his face.

Sam happily obliges and they embrace but only for a moment and Sam pulls away taking her seat at her desk.

She was nervous, not knowing what to expect from TC. He sat in his usual chair and a little sheepishly asked.

"So is everything good for Brinkman's closing in the morning?" Knowing full well that Sam would not fall for this lame excuse for a visit.

"Yes, TC it is all good. As usual Justin has done a superb job. He makes my job so easy."

She leaned back in her chair in a much more relaxed manor, feeling more confident that things are okay between them. She smiled at him with a raised brow as though to dare him to admit that wasn't the real reason for his being there. He knew he had been pegged.

"So how was your weekend Samantha?"

He couldn't help but notice how beautiful she was in the coral colored dress, a very good color for her. And a very flattering style for her voluptuous figure. He was pleased at what he saw. Sam blushed under TC's stares.

Sam smiled, getting up from her chair.

"Hold that thought TC I'm going to the kitchen to get us a drink.

I am suddenly very thirsty."

"I know what you mean Sam, I always get a little dry mouthed around you." He winks at her knowingly.

She returns with two ice cold bottles of water, sitting them beside TC as she takes a seat on the desk in front of him. She lets her heels fall to the floor exposing her coral polished toe nails. TC watched the shoes as they gently fell to the floor one by one. Taking note of her petite little feet. Very sexy. He thought as she placed her feet in the chair beside him. She opened her water to take a long drink of the cool liquid before finally answering TC's question.

"It was a good weekend, nothing exciting to speak of, but a good weekend on the whole."

TC attempted at more small talk, his arms folded across in front of him as though that were the only way for him to keep his hands off Sam. He seemed a bit nervous. She wasn't sure if that was because of what happened between them the last time or because she had pulled away from his embrace earlier. So, to break the ice and put him at ease she asked him if he wanted a kiss. As he smiled he extended his hand to her.

"You know I do Sam." She gives him a devilish look and handed him a chocolate candy.

TC unwrapped the candy looking her in the eye the entire time. He placed one end of the candy in his lips offering her the other tip. She takes the cue. She leaned slowly toward him, her lips gently curled over his, retrieving her share of the sweet chocolate. TC pulled back for a moment. They both take the opportunity to take a drink of their water. TC sat his bottle on the desk then looked at Sam, his eyes intense.

"If we truly consummated the relationship." He stopped short, fear in his eyes.

The source of the fear Sam was unsure. Is he afraid of a possible emotional attachment to me? Or fear I will become more attached than he wishes. Not that there was not already an attachment. Or perhaps the fear was that they would both change. She wasn't sure and he didn't seem able to finish the statement, so she prompted.

"What are you afraid of TC? Are you afraid it would be a onetime thing and then we would not be friends?" She looked at him in bewilderment.

"No, no not that Sam, just, well if we did....."

He could not finish and Sam felt she should not push it, not right now anyway. TC sensed this and pulled her in for a long embrace and then a kiss and then another. Soon they totally wrapped up in passion. Each wanting the other so badly. TC gently guides Sam to lie back upon her desk. He is leaning over her kissing her ever so gently. His hands gently pull her blouse off her shoulders slipping out each arm then tossing it onto the chair beside them. Moving on to her bra, he released her breasts and grasps one in each hand.

"Sam your breasts are so beautiful!"

Sam surprised by his comment sheepishly replied with a simple "Really?"

As she looked at him she couldn't help but think that he seemed to be in a state of erotic madness. It was as though he could not get enough of touching her breasts. Almost like a miser groping his gold in his hands for the first time. Letting each coin side between his fingers to feel the cool slick metal upon his skin only to be retrieved and repeated again and again. It was as though her breasts were taking over his entire mind and body; his every sense seemingly focused upon them. Sam closed her eyes, her body relaxed under his touch. She could feel his strokes suddenly change from urgency to soft loving pleasure. After a few moments she opened her eyes to look at him. He was still entranced by the sight of her well-formed breasts. His voice heavy with emotion. "Samantha, what am I going to do with you?"

Sam doing what she always does when she is blindsided by a comment she is unsure on how to respond, resorts to humor.

"Well I could think of several things at this point."

Teasingly looking up at him. She arches her back to the sensual feel of his hands upon her.

"You are trouble."

TC replied, as he smiled back at her while he was steadily fondling her breasts in every way possible. She responded accordingly, to his touches.

He continued the conversation.

"Well, you kept teasing me, placing that chocolate candy on your body Sam, until I could no longer resist the temptation."

"Oh, so that means you like a challenge, do you TC?"

Again smiling teasingly up at him while trying to keep the conversation on a less serious note.

His lips suddenly devour hers in heated passion. Within moments TC hands released her breasts and made their way down her body to her skirt, raising her skirt up he gently removed her panties. He then unfastened his belt and dropped his pants to the floor. He gently glides his manhood against her, although it is only semi hard. After some coaxing on his part he is finally fully engaged. Stroking her, he moans with delight. Again before he realized it he has reached the point of no return, he has not even been inside her as yet. He just got too excited.

"Damn it again! I am sorry about that Sam. You just got me too worked up."

"That is ok TC I understand no need to apologize." Although secretly she felt a little disappointed to say the least, she so wanted him to make love to her.

"It's hard on a man my age, loving two women."

He reached to help her up and they both return to their proper attire. They sat there for a moment cooling off and replenished their heated bodies with some much needed water.

"At my last checkup I was going to talk to the doctor. You know they have medication for those problems now. But it was the female tech and I didn't really feel comfortable asking her."

Sam is again surprised by his sudden frankness, and pleased at the same time that he could confide in her. Suddenly his cell phone rings. Looking at it he sees it is Jan.

"Um, Jan" he looked at Sam.

Sam moves to the other side of the desk. She straighten items to try to avoid hearing his conversation. It is a short call and he tells her he will be home soon and had made up some excuse to her as to what he was doing. After he disconnects the call. He lowers his head as if in shame.

"Damn, I hate d to have to lie to her, again."

Sam sat down in the chair next to him.

"I am sorry TC."

There is silence for a moment before he speaks again.

"Sam, I don't understand what is going on with us. I mean I try so hard to do the right thing, to be a good person. I talk myself into leaving you alone, into remaining just friends. Telling myself I am not going to call you so often. Then the next thing I know I am calling you or stopping by with some lame excuse to see you. I can't seem to get you out of my mind."

He appeared to Sam to be frustrated and truly tormented. Which made her heart ache for him.

"I don't know, Samantha I really don't know what it is! I have a good marriage."

Sam interrupts him at this point.

"TC, I was going to ask you about that. You had said that the other day and I am just wondering, if you have a good marriage then what is this?" She gestures at the two of them before she continues.

"What is this that is going on between us?"

TC shaking his head in denial.

"I don't know Sam, I really don't know."

As he leaned back in his chair he ran his hands through his hair, as though in exasperation, and looked at Sam.

"It's complicated, Sam. It's complicated."

"Well, TC for some reason we have been thrown together. I'm not sure why either. Maybe we are just meant to have that connection, you know, like that old movie something about in September or whatever it was."

Sam lets out a little laugh as does TC. Him knowing she could never remember movie titles or the like: one of the things about her that he found very endearing.

"I care about Ash and I don't want to intentionally hurt him, but I am definitely no longer in love with him. We hardly even touch each other. I don't think he even finds me attractive any more. TC's RTP takes over and he is wondering how any man in his right mind could possibly not find Sam attractive. That just didn't make sense to him.

"He may even be having an affair for all I know, Dakota thinks he is.

"Well, Sam I must say Jan and I have had our share of problems over the years, what with the kids and life in general. I suppose everyone has, at one point or another. We even separated once for a short time, but managed to work it out. We've made a good life out of it. I decided a long time ago that I was not going to just leave; I wasn't going to just walk away. I was going to do what I could to make the best of it; there isn't anything any better out there."

Samantha just sat there looking at TC somewhat offended in the 'nothing better out there' comment. What did that make her? Maybe he just didn't realize how it sounded or maybe she just took it wrong.

As though they had exhausted all avenues of thought on the situation, the conversation changed to the personal things happening in their lives in the upcoming future. Soon after, they called in a night.

Sam quietly slipped into bed next to Ash; he had gone up way ahead of her. She could tell from his gentle rhythmic breathing, that he was sound asleep. She lay there hoping for a good night's sleep or at least a night filled with happy dreams of TC She soon realized neither of which was going to happen any time soon. She couldn't help but relive the feelings the evening had released in her. How good his lips felt upon her and how his masculine hands made her body quiver in sheer delight. She loved how the muscles of his arms automatically tightened when she touched them, exciting her all the more. Yes, he enjoyed it too, that was obvious. Suddenly feeling a little too warm she pushed the bedcovers from her body, leaving only the sheet draped over her. She hears Ash start to breathe more heavily, which soon turned into an irritating snore. She reached for her cell phone and earphones. She tuned in to her favorite radio station app knowing the music would certainly lull her to sleep and hopefully drown out any more thoughts of TC along with Ash's snores.

But the thoughts of the conversation with TC both before and after their sexual escapade would not leave her. His comment on loving two women perplexed her. Did he mean that in a sexual sense? There were so many correlations in their lives it was uncanny. His and Jan's wedding day was only 10 days after hers and Ash's, and even in the same month. His wedding date was also her life path number. They were crazy about the same music groups, they slept on the same brand of mattress, and Jan's birthday was the same as her mother's birthday. She was terrified by spiders and he didn't care for them either, they both owned Pit Bull Terriers who were sweet as could be and the list went on and on. It was certainly interesting to say the least. Not to mention that they seemed to be cosmically connected, how she would be thinking of him and he would text or call either at that exact moment or not far from. Sam was convinced that it was not all coincidental. That there was a higher power guiding them. TC had said he didn't much agree with that theory, it was probably more of a test, which they both horribly failed. Even so, neither of them wanted to stop it.

It was all too much for her mind to absorb, frustrated she changes positions. Crazy thoughts still filled her head. Why on why couldn't they have met sooner? Why couldn't I have been the one he said yes to all those years ago? Why could it not be me making vacation plans with him instead of Jan? Was it serendipity that the damn radio station will not quit play music by his favorite artist! Really? How is a person supposed to sleep with all this going on? Is it profound providence trying to tell me something? I don't need any help keeping him on my mind, thank you! She looked up at the ceiling as though talking to the heavens.

She quietly whispered. "He is always there, on my mind and always in my heart, always."

Angrily she shoved her arm under her pillow, as she turned over on her side, and tried to find a more comfortable position.

I should break it off with him, this is just too hard and so unfair! Closing her eyes as they filled with tears, she lay there quietly sobbing. Sleep eventually followed.

A few weeks later, it was barely breaking dawn, Sam awoke abruptly, eyes wide from yet another dream of TC. She had not heard from him in days. She was growing weary of his hot and cold treatment. Yes! It was complicated! As he would always say. She just wished he would elaborate on his definition of complicated, she knew her own. She wished he would elaborate on his comments of how he thinks of her with 'random thoughts on a regular basis' and how or what the something is, that keeps drawing him to her. Sure she could fill in the blanks to suit her own needs, but she wanted to hear him say the words. She recalled the dream...

She was in her office, only instead of the usual furnishings there was only a large bed, not unlike that in her own bedroom. She awoke to find TC lying beside her. She immediately looked around the office for fear someone else might be present and their affair would then be discovered. But the office was dark and no one else in sight. She snuggled back under the covers and next to TC. He woke feeling her movements. He wrapped his arms around her pulling her naked body in close to his own. "I'm sorry if I startled you Samantha, I just needed to be with you." Gently kissing her forehead he continues. "I've missed you so much till I ache. I just couldn't go another day without seeing you, being next to you, touching you. I try and try to be a good faithful husband to Jan, but I just can't get you out of my head Sam, those random thoughts on a regular basis, get to me." A mischievous little grin upon his face as though to tease her, then pulling her even closer. She feels the warmth of his body. "So, where are you tonight TC?" "I told Jan I was in Dallas." He was quite for a few moments deep in thought, his face becomes very serious. "Samantha, I love you! I want you to stay in my life. I want us..."

That last statement was what caused Sam to wake up so suddenly. She lay there rethinking the dream. Yes, it is a nice thought and it was certainly what she wanted to hear. She so wanted TC to proclaim his true feelings for her, in terms she could understand. Yes! She wanted him to say those words. To tell her he loves her and needs her. She needed to hear it from him, even though she knew, all the way to her soul, that TC did indeed have feelings for her. Feelings that went much deeper than friendship or lust, she just wanted him to realize it and say it. But he was fighting it and she knew it.

"Damn it! Why does it have to be so complicated?"

She groaned as she angrily kicked the covers to the floor, and climbed out of bed.

She went downstairs to the den, thinking perhaps she may rest on the couch for a while, but after checking the clock she realized it was almost time to get up anyway. So she went to the kitchen and made a pot of coffee. Sitting at the kitchen island and enjoying her first cup when Ash comes down the stairs.

"Good morning Sam. You are up early!"

As he poured himself a large coffee and sat down beside her.

"Not that early Ash. I woke just a few minutes before the alarm and figured I may as well get up. I usually just feel worse if I go back to sleep anyway."

"Not for me Sam I could sleep anytime. So what has been going on at the office?"

Sam a little startled, and somewhat still sleepy, looked at Ash questioningly. She tried not to show panic. She was never very good at having a poker face; she was usually as readable as an open book.

"What do you mean Ash?"

"I mean how is your Uncle John and have you been swamped lately or what? Just the normal stuff.   Just inquiring, we haven't talked much lately." As he placed the morning paper under his arm.

Sam was relieved, to say the least. She was also glad he had not been looking her in the face at that moment. Realizing it is her guilt, rearing its ugly head again,

"Everything appears to be running smoothly, Ash. What about with you?"

"Nothing exciting on my end either Sam."

H gave her a kiss on the forehead before he exited the room, coffee cup in hand.

Chapter 16

It had been a busy morning, Christmas week; so of course everybody was wanting it done yesterday. But in all the chaos, TC managed to find the time to take care of a few errands, he had just left from lunch with Gunny, Andy and Dalton. While wishing them a Merry Christmas and a long weekend. He had thoughts of one very important meeting that had been on his mind for weeks now. Smiling at the thought of seeing her. He slowed his truck down in order to stop at the red light that had just caught him. He was only a few blocks from Sam's office. He glanced at the multitude of files on his seat next to him, files for Sam. His body started to tingle from sheer anticipation of seeing her, being close to her, it had been awhile. He could almost smell the intoxicating clean smell of her long curls and the silkiness of it against his touch.

Suddenly a loud horn blasted in his ears! He looked in his rearview mirror then quickly up at the signal light it was indeed green. As he accelerated he looked back into his rearview mirror, and waved to the seemingly angry lady behind him in acknowledgement.

"Ok okay, damn! A guy can't even wander off into his RTP

without someone interrupting!"

As he pulled into the parking lot at River House, TC couldn't help but recall their last phone conversation regarding his absence from her. He had told Sam he was "trying to be good" translation a faithful husband to Jan. Albeit it was a little late for that. It wasn't so much his love for Jan that caused these torn feelings but more so the love of his family. It is not easy to just wash away an entire lifetime, it was complicated to say the least. He knew delivering the files in person in lieu of using a runner was just an excuse to get to see her and he knew Sam would realize it too. He also knew it would be a safe opportunity to get to see her, after all there would be an office full of people and he'd have no choice but to resist temptation. Maybe even to be able to be in her presences without thoughts of undressing her. He needed to prove this to himself, he had to. He wanted to remain friends no matter what; he had to have her in his life in some form or fashion. He couldn't bear the thought of never seeing her. The thought of not looking into those gorgeous eyes, not feeling her silky soft skin beneath his touch....

"Damn it! There I go again!"

He slams his hand against the steering wheel in frustration.

"Shit! Why am I even trying to do this? I already know I will fail! I should just walk in her office throw her on the damn desk and make mad passionate love to her, right there for all to see!"

Thinking about the look that would most likely befall Deidra's face, he chuckled.

He smiled at the mental picture he had just conjured up in his head and suddenly he felt much better, he went into the office.

Deidra is just exiting Sam's office when she sees TC.

"Well, hello there TC, how are you?"

"I am well Deidra, and yourself?"

"Oh you know me TC I'm always happy! Are all those files for Sam?"

"Yes Deidra, they are. I plan to keep that woman very busy." He glanced at the stack of files in his arms.

"Well from the looks of all that, you will! Here sit them on my desk and I will do the preliminary work up on them."

"Happy to oblige, Deidra, is she in?'

Oh, yes, she is in her office go on back I will lock you two in. Everyone else has gone for the day."

A little perplexed, TC takes a step toward the hall and Deidra called back to him.

"Oh and TC Merry Christmas!"

He turned and smiled at her, as he replied.

"Merry Christmas to you too Deidra."

Sam had overheard the conversation and she met TC at the office lobby just as Deidra was exiting the front door. She was very nervous, but manages to hide it well.

"Hi, I am glad you stopped by." She said to him with welcoming smile on her face.

"Me too!" His steel blue eyes looked straight into hers as he smiled back.

They go back to her office and TC is all business talk.

"Wow, everyone left early today? For the day?" looking a little perplexed at Sam.

"Yes, TC we have all been busting butt to get things in order before Christmas. It is only two days away you know, so we thought a long weekend was in order. You know for family time."

TC turned a little pink. He was not even sure of where his thoughts had been, of course it was Christmas!

"Oh, well yeah of course. Don't know what I was thinking."

Sam became slightly worried. TC was acting rather strange, almost like they are just business associates. She tried not to let it show. She looked at the papers on her desk she then looked at TC through lowered lashes only to see him sitting there giving her that look again. That deep to her soul I want you look!

"What is on your mind TC?"

TC smiled that sexy little smile of his as he pushed his chair back and made the gesture for Sam to come join him.

"Why don't you just come over here and show me what has been on your mind Samantha?"

Sam walked around her desk and faced TC in his chair. He motions for her to sit on his lap. Although her dress is a tight form fitting one that nicely showed off her curves, luckily it had little stretch to it, allowing her to raise it up to her mid thighs as she straddled TC's lap. His hands reached for the curve of her waist, and he pulled her into him. She looked at him with a naughty little smile as she slipped her hands up the sleeve of his shirt.

'Why, I have been thinking of your wonderful muscles TC. Where ever did you get them?"

"Just from being a hardworking man, I guess." He smiled as he enjoying her touch. Pulling her in, his lips met hers in a fever of passion. Lips that were sweet and supple just as he remembered. One kiss followed another and another, and then TC breaks the silence.

"I've been thinking about you Sam."

Still kissing her gently between words.

"I've been thinking about you too TC, probably more than I should."

TC acknowledged that as a fact for him as well, with a nod of his head.

"You probably shouldn't risk falling in love with me Sam." A concerned look on his face.

Sam was gently covering his neck with kisses as he was speaking. At that comment she stopped and looked into TC's eyes, her own eyes wide with expression and exclaims.

"Why, TC! What if you fall in love with me?"

Before he had a chance to reply Sam smothered his lips with hers giving it her all. She was afraid of what his reply might be. TC moaned with great pleasure. Their bodies entwined as best they can, giving their sitting positions. TC's hands moved down Sam's side to the edge of her dress. He wondered should he go further, but only for a split second. His hand under her dress, pressed against the restraints of the material until he felt the soft lace of her panties.

"What color are you wearing today Sam?"

"Hum, I'm not really sure TC. I guess you shall have to find out for yourself." As she is nibbling on his earlobe.

TC's mind was racing, his heart pounding and he became a little over zealous with his movements, unknowingly about to push her completely off his lap. Sam broke from him with a slight chuckle. "TC! You're about to make me fall!" He grasped her tighter, and pulled her back into him. She was totally aware of how aroused he is. The very large bulge in his pants gives way to that. He immediately lifted her up onto the desk, eagerly pulling her dress over the top on her head and without skipping a beat freeing her from her bra. She is doing the same releasing him from his jeans, both in a heated frenzy, as though their hands could not move fast enough. He removed panties, slipping them from her. He felt the warmth and moistness of her passion as he made her moan with ecstasy. Followed with more fervent kisses.

He whispers softly to her.

"Where do you want me Sam?"

"Inside me TC! Inside me!"

As he enters her she moaned with pure pleasure. His passion is hard and strong. Her legs are wrapped around him, pulling him in tighter and tighter, he was grasping them with one hand in order to help her to hold on against the wrath of his frenzied pushes. His thoughts were raging, realizing she was so moist with desire for him and so damn tight too! So damn tight, he thought he wasn't going to fit for a moment! It drove him wild with passion. His body pounded against hers until they both shrieked with euphoria. Each of their bodies breaking out in chills of ecstasy. Sam, as she gasped for air managed a raspy, "Oh my!"

TC smiled back at her. "Yeah!" was his only reply.

Sam had never had a man react so vehemently or with such a display of passion, both verbally and physically. She was truly in awe that she could give such unsurmountable pleasure to TC.

With him still inside her, reeling in the pleasure his body was absorbing, his cell phone rang. It was laying on the desk right beside them, he looked down at the phone, and it was Jan. He doesn't answer. Sam knew by the look on his face it had to be Jan.

"Dare I ask who that was?"

"No, you don't want to know."

He released himself from Sam and leaned in for a kiss. Still a little breathless he said to her.

"We have to be careful Samantha."

"I know TC, I know."

Later, as they sat together in silence allowing their bodies recoup and replenish with some cool drinks. Sam could sense TC was feeling a little guilty from the phone call. They sat in silence for a while longer, until Sam spoke.

"TC, I know you are more religious than I, not that I don't believe. I just believe a little differently or maybe more opened mindedly than you do. I'm not really sure how to explain it. But, I do know that there is a Proverb that I think fits our situation perfectly."

TC looks at her inquiringly and somewhat surprised.

"What might that be Samantha?"

She looked at him, his eyes fixed on hers. It takes her a long moment before speaking.

"A man's heart plans his way. But the Lord directs his steps." (Proverb16.9)

"TC you stepped straight to me!" She spoke with great convection.

"Don't you get it? We have both tired so hard to fight it, but to no avail. We have no reasonable explanation of the draw to each other, well; I think this explains it perfectly! Please, please don't say anything right now. I know you need time to absorb that notion. Just think about it with your heart and soul, not your head TC. Just your heart and soul. It is just meant to be! I believe it."

Sam's eyes become teary and she blinks the tears back as best she can. At that point TC swooped her up in his arms holding her tightly, kissing her sweet soft lips.

TC walked Sam to her car. As Sam opened her car door she

turned to look at TC. He was stood there as though mesmerized, he starred into her eyes, with such a look of longing in his. Or a look of love perhaps? She really wasn't positive, as TC surprised her so often with his unexpected comments and deep to the soul looks. She wasn't sure what he was thinking at that moment, especially after she pretty much bared her soul to him. What she did know was that look he just gave her would stay in her memory for a very, very long time.

She finally broke the silence, again.

"Merry Christmas TC."

"Merry Christmas Samantha." He replied as he turned to go to his truck.

It was a very long holiday weekend for Sam. John and Estelle had gone to New York for Christmas to see her sister which left Sam and Ash to fin for themselves for the holiday. She had busied herself most of the day cleaning house and baking, while Ash was gone to finish up some last minute Christmas shopping. They would open their respective gifts in the morning. Ash was always good to her in the gift department, and she to him.

She longed to hear from TC but knew he wouldn't chance a phone call or text, even though she checked her phone frequently.

Who am I kidding anyway; of course he won't text he is after all with his family. All the kids were home for the weekend too. She lay the phone back on the counter and opened the oven door to check on her baking. She longed to talk to Dakota too, but knew that was a bad idea as well. Dakota being the good friend she was would, of course, take the time to talk to her, but Sam knew she had a house full of relatives, and that wouldn't be fair to her or them.

Her thoughts wondered back to TC. I wonder what a typical Christmas is like in The Martin household. I bet he smokes a ham or turkey, while Jan makes all the sides and deserts. The house is probably filled with laughter and the normal hustle and bustle of a big family, something I have so longed for. Strange I have never asked him about their traditions, probably because I don't really want to picture it. I do know he enjoys the season. Oh how nice it would be to have a husband that would Christmas shop with me and go to plays, unlike Ash. Someone who would enjoy looking at all the lights and wonder that is the magic of the season. To wake up next to TC on Christmas morning! How wonderful that must feel. Jan is indeed a lucky lady. Sighing at the thoughts.

"Oh well, I suppose I should start supper, Ash will be home soon." She mumbled to herself as she lit some candles and put on some music. It wasn't long and Ash was home and poking his head in the kitchen.

"Don't be peaking now!" Grinning at her like a fool.

"You know I will Ash!" He is certainly in a jovial mood she thought, as she watched him clamber through the back door packages in tow.

As he headed upstairs, he looked back enticing her to follow. It was a game they played every year. She ran up behind him and banged on the locked bedroom door.

"What are you hiding in there Ash? Let me in! I must get something from the dresser."

Of course he does not fall for that. He yelled back.

"You will just have to wait! It is not Christmas yet!"

She leaned her head against the door and could her the tearing and rattling of paper. She smiled and decided she may else well play along a little longer. Banging on the door again she yelled.

"Ash! Come quick I have set the kitchen on fire! I'm not joking! Ash! " She screamed hysterically.

He fell for it, he ran to the door and flew it open, just as he did Samantha shot past him and landed in the middle of their large bed; laughing hysterically.

"Got cha!" She exclaimed through the laughter.

The look on his face was priceless! It was a rare occasion that she was able to trick him.

He returned the favor by piling the bed pillows on top of her and all the scrap wrapping paper and whatever else that was loose that he could find. Before she knew it she hand to climb from under an array of items.

Having had their fun they returned to the kitchen where Ash made them some drinks and she made some cheese dip. A little snack to carry them over until supper was ready.

After their supper they retired to the den to watch a movie, Ash gave in and let her put in 'Miracle on 34th Street', the original one. She loved that movie. She always wished for the same happy ending in her own life. Ash mostly read, while she watched it until he fell asleep on the couch. He could be a wonderful man when he wanted to; it just seemed he didn't want to very often.

TC's home was filled with family and noise, not a quiet moment to himself. Every time he picked up his phone, to chance a text to Sam, someone was demanding his attention until he finally gave up.

He enjoyed his family, it was a good Christmas with them all home, but he longed for Samantha.

Chapter 17

It was an extra cold winter day, Sam sat at her desk looking out of her window longing for spring to hurry up and arrive, she hated the cold dreary days of winter. Her thoughts were interrupted by TC's text tone. Happily, she looked at her phone.

"Hey, I have some free time, free for a catch up visit after five?'

Sam was excited at the prospect of seeing him, she happily replied. "I would love it!"

Fifteen after five TC arrived, they are alone as usual. Sam greeted him with a smile and welcoming embrace. He held her tightly for a long moment, then gave her a short little hello kiss. She could tell he had missed her.

Once back to her office, Sam decides it was time for a different game of chocolate. She retrieves a chocolate square that is filled with caramel. She walked around the desk and sat atop in her usual fashion, facing TC. He reached for her legs placing one booted leg on each side of him. Which he could tell gave her a bit of an uncomfortable feeling given the short length of her skirt.

"Not a very lady like position, but one I sure do like." He smiled up at her.

He had the most gorgeous smile. One she could never resist. Sam smiled back, TC had put her at ease. With a mischievous look on her face she starts to slowly open the candy, not letting him see it.

"Do you like caramel, TC?"

"Yes! I like caramel."

He says is an almost childlike anticipated manor. As he watched her unwrap the candy he wondered what game she had concocted up this time. Sam broke off a little piece putting it between TC's lips and he teasingly sucked on the tip of her finger, his eyes twinkling in excitement. She took a small bite of the remaining candy and leaned her head back, she moaned in delight at the flavor while looking teasingly at TC He is intently watching, a little smirk of a smile on his face. She drizzled some of the caramel on the exposed cleavage above her blouse and with a despairingly pouty look at TC she said.

"Oh look! TC I have dropped some!"

He immediately moved toward her to lick the sticky sweetness from her skin, while she ran her fingers through his curly hair. She smiled as his beard tickled her skin.

It wasn't long before they are naked and enjoying the feel of each other's body. TC had Sam to sit on the front of her desk again. He directs her back to a laying position. He kissed and caressed her as he made love to her to the point of a breathtaking orgasm for them both. Again his body pulsated erotically, and again Sam is amazed she was able to give him such pleasure.

Afterward, they are dressed and sitting beside each other talking about nothing special just their respective events of the day and the last few weeks. TC retrieved his cell phone off the desk and started to scroll through his photos. Sam is shocked to see he has saved the one she sent to him months ago of her in a black satin robe. It was his favorite picture of her, he had said. He continued to scroll, showing her various pictures of Gunny, and the guys, his kids, and even some of Jan.

A sad look came over his face as he said.

"It doesn't make any sense does it?"

"No TC it doesn't. You seem to have a happy family; I don't know why you are here with me."

She secretly wished she knew the answer to that question, it tortured them both.

"I don't know Sam." As he still scrolled through his phone. She could tell from the look on his face he was telling the truth.

"We can't fall in love Sam, I've told you that." Still looking at his pictures.

"Yes TC, You also said that I should not fall in with you. But you never took into account the possibility of what would happen if you fall in love with me"

TC stopped scrolling through his phone and looked up at Sam, a very serious look upon his face.

"It would be complicated, Sam. Very complicated."

He goes back to looking at the photos in his phone.

"I know. It is complicated! To say the least TC, but something is wrong with your marriage or you would not be here with me after all this time."

He frowned, but did not reply, he also did not look at her. Sam feared she had struck a nerve with TC. In a more cheery voice she quickly changed the subject in hopes that his RTP would kick in.

"So, any plans for the weekend TC? I heard there is an antique car show in town."

TC started to speak then hesitated for a moment. He stopped what he was doing and looked at Sam for a long, long moment. He then stood up and pulled her up to him for an embrace and a very passionate kiss. Afterward, he gently pinched her chin and smiled. "I am not that easily distracted, Samantha!"

Sam shrugged her shoulders, turning a little red, knowing TC caught on to her ploy.

"Well you can't blame a girl for trying, TC." She smiled sweetly at him.

"Yeah, I will give you that."

She leaned in for another kiss, she relished in the softness of his lips pressed against hers with his arms wrapped tightly around her. After the kiss he sat back down in his chair and she walked up to him for another hug. She is just the right height in her bare feet for his head to rest upon her chest. Sam looked down at him as he lay there against the softness of her breasts. His eyes were closed. He had such a serene look of contentment upon his face. It pleased her immensely to see that look, especially knowing it was because he was he was in her arms. She closed her own eyes to savor the moment. She then bends her head down to kiss the top of his. He looked up at her with his soul piercing blue eyes and Sam melted all over again.

That night Sam was restless, it was well after one a.m. before she even went to bed let alone to sleep. Too many thoughts of TC in were in her mind and the fact that she hated sleeping alone. Ash was gone, again on an overnight seminar, she wished he were at home. She knew tomorrow she would feel like hell from not having enough sleep, she dreaded it as she had a busy day planned. After a bit of tossing and turning she finally drifted off to sleep.

The next morning she woke with an immediate smile upon her face, realizing she had dreamt of TC and what a vivid dream it had been! Sitting on the edge of her bed she got pen and paper from the nightstand and began to recall the dream. As she wrote, her smile faded to confusion......

I was at a door. A door to a building of some sort, not an office, not a home, just two rooms. The door opened and I was greeted by Jacob, TC's youngest son. He greeted me warmly and motioned for me to enter the room. I knew it was Jacob although I never actually saw him in the room. TC was lying on a bed and he motioned for me to join him, which I did. We laid lay there together discussing business as though we were sitting at a desk, like it was perfectly normal. I could hear the buzzing of Jan's sewing machine in the back room. Jan knew I was there and I knew Jan was there, and that seemed to be perfectly ok too. I was snuggled up to TC's broad shoulders and before we knew it we were both fast asleep. I remembered smiling at TC just as I succumbed to slumber. I then woke just as TC reaches to smooth my hair from her eyes. We smile at each other. Jan appeared and is about to turn on a lamp for us, but she does not. Then she just disappears. TC and I, realizing we had fallen asleep, abruptly jump up as though we had done something wrong. We head for the front door and pause. I peer around TC and follows the sound of the humming sewing machine. I see only Jan's legs sitting at the sewing machine table. I do not see her face or the actual machine, I am just focused on Jan's legs and the sound coming from the machine. I look at TC and say. "I never know whether to say anything to Jan or not." TC shakes his head no and ushers me out the door. He is walking me to my car, but I can't seem to remember where I parked it. He was holding my hand and leading me through some very tall grass. "TC, where are you taking me?" I remembered feeling worried. We stop in front of a metal parking canopy and TC leaned in for a kiss. I say to him. "TC! Really? Are you crazy? Jan can see us from here! Her window is right there!" We both look at the building which at this point looks like a big apartment complex, the brick pattern seemed to be of some importance in my dream. TC continued to lead me around the parking area to the side of the building. The sun is gleaming brightly on that side of the building, another seemingly important factor to the dream. Samantha stopped writing and thinks about that for a minute, she then continues to write down her dream. TC stops on the concrete steps and pulled me in for a sultry kiss. A very long kiss. Afterward, TC is just standing there grinning at me from ear to ear. He said to me. "Sam my God your kisses excite me so!" About that time TC is about to kiss me again and a stranger appears behind him. It is a man. His hair is long in

Dreadlocks down to his shoulders and he is wearing a black and white vertical stripped shirt. Although his hair texture was that of maybe a Jamaican, his skin was of a much lighter tone. With his back to the stranger TC was kind of crouched down facing me as I sat on the steps, his hands were on my shoulders. Just as he was about to kiss me the man reached for TC's wallet in his back pocket, it was poking out a little bit. TC puts his hand there to stop him, and then turns to look at him. TC ever so politely informs the man that he needs to leave town and not come back. Again Sam stops to think about this part. There was something about the way TC had told the man this, that Sam did not like, but she could not recall what it was. The man smiled and said in his Jamaican accent. "Ah! Man! Be careful, you were just about to lose it!" He smiles and laughs lightly as he turned and disappeared as quickly as he came.   .....

It was at this point that Sam had awakened.   Her first recollection of the dream was that of falling asleep in TC's arms and it brought such a feeling of serenity.   But as she recalled the rest of the dream her mood certainly went to that of sad confusion.   She was sure the fact that she could not see Jan's face was her own guilt of never wanting to face her in real life.   However that thought soon dissipated too, realizing she really didn't feel guilty.   She didn't mean to seem vain, but was it her fault after all that TC wanted her?   That he couldn't get her out of his mind?   That obviously there was something missing in his marriage that moved him to seek her out time after time?

"No! It is not my fault!"

She slings the notepad across the bed in a moment of anger. "There is no blame to be had! It has just happened, for a reason!' She sat there in silent thought for a few moments and the thoughts crept back in... okay, so maybe she should have been strong enough to say no to TC and strong enough not to entice him to come to her. She would admit guilt for that at least. Sam grew angry at where her thoughts had taken her. She knew in her heart that TC was brought to her for a good reason, albeit some pain may come from it. She also knew it felt too right to be wrong. She tried to focus on the dream again.

"Ok let's see, I can do this, I have animalized many of my own dreams in the past."

As she pulled out her dream dictionary from her nightstand she focused on the seemingly significant portions of the dream. Some were obvious, guilt, passion, acceptance, euphoria, fear, they all came into play. There were some though that stuck in her head. She was sure falling asleep meant that they were both comfortable and content with each other. She knew the sunshine in a dream was a symbol of peace of mind and tranquility. It also represented radiant energy and divine power, yes divine power she certainly agreed with that, a good omen indeed.

Excitedly she remembered. Oh yes, and the stranger! That was certainly a weird part to my dream, let me check that out.

Flipping through the page she found it: "to see a stranger in your dream signifies a part of you that is repressed or hidden. Alternatively, it symbolizes the archetypal dream helper, who is offering you insight and advice." She suddenly became very excited talking to herself as though someone else was in the room to listen.

"Oh my goodness! That is it! That is exactly what the strange Jamaican man did, gave TC advice! He told TC, that he had better be careful or he would lose it! Hum, I am sure it wasn't a reference to money. Ah! Wallet": "to dream your wallet has been stolen indicates that perhaps someone has stolen your heart." Leaning back on the headboard of the bed she clutched the book to her chest as she thought about that one, for a moment. Well, it makes perfect sense to me. It wasn't my wallet it was TC's, just proof to me that TC needs to realize that I have stolen his heart! Ok, what are the other crucial segments? Hum, black and white stripes: "close-mindedness and limited way of thinking." Hum confusing that one. What could that mean? Dreams! So confusing. Ok what about the brick building, the brick was very essential. "Brick: to see a brick in your dream represents your individual ideas and thoughts.

Experience and/or heartbreak may have hardened you." Oh, shit! What does it mean to see an entire building of brick! Hardened by heartbreak eh? Well that part is mostly true, from my first marriage, he broke my heart for sure. But that is all over with now. All in the past, that I am sure of! Maybe the building is important.

She looked that up, it was a long analogy that didn't really fit at all. Next she checked out the sound only of a sewing machine that was very prominent indeed, and appeared more than once in her dream. She was unable to find anything on just the sound of it. Sewing, sewing machine was listed, but not just the sound of it. She could interpret it, but it would have to be dissected into multiple parts, sewing, sound, and machine. Oh well, it will take some time on that one! Time I don't have to spare, I'm going to be late for work I don't get my butt out of bed.

She placed the book and notepad back in the drawer. She took a quick shower. In a rush she twisted her wet hair on top of her head and secured it with a clip, to let it dry naturally. She applied a tad bit of eye makeup, she was never one for foundations and all that other mess so a quick five minutes and she was ready. Sam fetched a fresh cup of coffee and she is about to exit out onto the back veranda when she hears TC's special text tone. Smiling she runs for her phone almost spilling her coffee. The text read: "want a hug? I'm in your driveway, is it safe?" What? Oh, my gosh! Surely not! She thought as she sat her cup down and ran to the front door. Sure enough, as she peered out the front window she could see an inkling of a red vehicle in her circle driveway, barely visible from the large Junipers that encased the area.

"Yes!" she quickly text back.

Removing the clip from her hair and shaking the curls loosely before she went out the door. She quickly descends the five or so steps on the porch to the sidewalk. In her bare feet and adorned in only the new purple silk robe she had just purchase when she and Dakota had gone shopping.

By the time she was halfway down the very long sidewalk TC was meeting her, a giant smile on his face. Sam was ecstatic! She ran into his arms, standing on her tippy toes as he wrapped her up in his arms for a very long moment. Finally she pulled back to look at him.

"TC! You are living dangerously!"

"I know. I just thought I would start your morning off right, with a hug." He smiled oh so precariously back at her. His deep blue eyes sparkled with joyfulness in the morning sun. She took his hand and les him into the house. Once inside they go into the den and she motions him toward the large overstuffed sofa. She immediately straddled his lap facing him and gave him another enormous embrace, she could hardly contain her excitement! TC's strong arms held her tightly. She pulled away and looked at him.

"What if Ash had been home, you crazy man!"

He simply but firmly pulled her back in for a fiercely passionate kiss. Afterward, she looked at him.

"I am glad you were missing me TC."

Again he doesn't say anything.

"Even if you won't say it out loud, although you have before."

Her fingertips gently stroked the length of his short beard and around his lips, purposefully tickling his moustache, as she smiled at him.

"If you say so." TC smiled back, hugging her ever so tightly.

"You always make me laugh TC and I love that about you." She mumbled as her lips are covered by his in yet another kiss.

One kiss leads to another until his hand that had been stroking her gently along her back and buttocks, moved to the front of her robe. He reached for the tie, he pulled and it gently and it slid apart leaving her breast exposed for him to admire. He gives each one a kiss.

I better let you finish getting ready for work, don't want you to be late. Mr. Rivers might not like me any longer."

"Okay, but will you come see me soon TC?" All the while placing gentle sweet kisses upon his neck.

"I will do my best Sam. I will do my best." The look on his face assures her that he will. She removed herself from his lap as she put her robe back in order, she took his hand and walked him to the front door. A quick goodbye hug and kiss and he was gone. Sam stands there for a moment, she looked out at the driveway, thankful that she did not have any close neighbors that could have seen his truck or them embracing on the sidewalk. She was also thankful that she knew Ash had a seven a.m. meeting with a student that morning, so no chance of him coming back home unexpectedly. She was still caught up in the exuberance of TC having surprised her in such an unexpected manor.

Wow, he must have really needed a hug from me to take a giant chance like that. And no sex either! Just solidifies that he has feelings for me that go way beyond a casual tryst.

She finished getting ready for work and left with a very happy smile upon her face. Her heart tingling with excitement.

Chapter 18

Several had gone by since TC had visited Sam. He is at his desk looking at a couple of offers that one of his Realtors has presented for approval when he hears Gunny cutting up with Susie.

TC just smiled and shook his head.

"That old flirt!"

Chuckling under his breath just as Gunny appeared at his door. "What the hell are you sitting in here all by yourself laughing about? Reading something amusing TC?"

A knowing smirk on his face as he takes a seat in front of TC

"Yeah, Gunny I was just reading about how old flirts never die!"

Gunny grins from ear to ear.

"Well you know TC, if you got it boy, you got it! He slaps his hand against his own chest.

"How about some pizza and a pool game with me and the guys tonight? You have been absent from us quite a bit lately."

Gunny furrowed his brow and leaned in placing his elbow on the desk to look closer at TC.

"Everything going ok at home? Work?"

TC sat back in his oversized leather chair.

"Yes, Gunny everything is good. Just been a busy time of year."

"Well now, guess I can't complain about that! You need to make all the money you can to support me in my old age."

"Hate to break this to you Gunny, but you are already there!" TC's steel blue eyes twinkled as he looked back at Gunny, with a smirk on his face.

"Yeah, well you only hope you will have the stamina, same as me, when you get my age! BOY!" Gunny laughed.

"Well how about it? Pizza?" TC nods an affirmative.

"I will call Jan and let her know. See you guys at Grandy's about seven?" Gunny stood to leave.

"Perfect TC, I will let the boys know."

He is out the door in a flash. TC's phone rings Sam's text tone. He picks it up to read it.

"Hi handsome! Would love to see you tonight." Sighing he types in a reply.

"Sorry darling, but I just made plans."

"Plans?"

"Yeah, with Gunny and the guys for pizza & pool game. They've been bugging me about it for a while."

"Ok TC hope you have fun! Kick their butts! ☺"

"Thanks'. Was his only reply.

He then called Jan.

"Hey babe, Gunny just stopped by begging me to go have a pizza & pool night with him and the guys, do you mind?"

"Okay TC, thanks for letting me know ahead of time. Tell the guys I said hello, and have a good time. See you when you get home."

He could hear the agitation in her voice, but her reply was amicable.

TC hung up the phone feeling only a slight pang of guilt, not unlike that which he has when he makes up excuses to her when he is with Sam.

After Sam finished reading TC's text about the guy's night she was in a slightly grumpy state, frustrated was more like it. She never knew what to expect from him. One minute running hot, one minute running cold. Distance, then surprise visits! It was hard to keep up with and hard to come up with sudden excuses for being late, although Ash didn't seem to miss her. Having made herself angry she tossed the papers to the side of her desk, grabbed her purse and went down the hall. At the front desk she paused only long enough to tell Deidra that she will be out for a while and will return in a few hours. She could tell Deidra picked up on her agitated state, but she didn't care, she was out the door before Deidra could even reply.

Shutting her car door, she leaned her head back against the seat, the warm sunshine streamed through the window was a welcoming pleasure and helped her mood instantly. After a few moments of thought, she smiled. She wasn't really angry at TC, just highly disappointed.

Time for a little drive in the country! Maybe I will stop by Dakota's house, I think she is off today.

Happy with her decision she started her car and headed out of town. Twenty or so minutes later she is on a little two lane road, the same road TC had taken her down last fall to look at the beautiful colors of the trees getting ready for their winter sleep. It was a gorgeous drive. Green pastures filled with cattle, giant oak trees and flowers adorning the road on either side. She passed the little mom and pop grocery store where she and TC had stopped last year. They had gone in and ordered sandwiches, the old fashioned kind, with the meat they cut off the big slab and make the sandwich while you watched. It was a far cry from a fast food sandwich, but probably how that idea arose. They had gone down a little gravel road after that and TC pulled up to a pasture and a pond and stopped the truck. Getting out he grabbed a blanket from the back, an ice chest and their sandwiches, smiling as he opened the door for her.

As she is stepping out of the truck, taking his offered hand, she asked.

"TC is it okay for us to be here? Who owns this land? Do you know them?"

He smiled and kissed her on the nose.

"Sometimes you worry too much! My little Samantha."

A little gleam in his eye.

Sam smiled and took the blanket from him spreading it out on a nice fluffy area of grass. She no sooner had it spread out to perfection until TC had tumbled her down onto it as he tickled her. Until the fun turned to kisses. She remembered the look in his eyes that day when he abruptly stopped and leaned in for a kiss.

Suddenly there is a loud blare in Sam's ears! She blinked and realized she had crossed the center line of the road and was dangerously facing an oncoming truck! She swerved just in time and his horn screamed as he passed her on his edge of the shoulder.

Oh! My, gosh! I certainly got lost in that train of thought! A little shook up by the ordeal she turned on the next road heading toward Dakota's house.

She called first and Dakota confirmed that yes she was home and it was okay to stop in. Before hanging up she added.

"Tony is here and he would love to see you, Sam."

She pulled in Dakota's circle drive. It was somewhat like Sam's but much closer to the house than Sam's drive. The house sat on two acres; it was beautifully landscaped with magnificent shrubs, flowers and trees everywhere your eyes took you. The home itself was closer to the road giving way to a much larger area in the back, which housed a large in ground pool and pool house. That is where Dakota had told Sam she would be, to come on around through the back gate.

Sam goes through the gate and saw Dakota was sitting in a chaise lounge slathered in suntan oil. Two glasses of lemonade sat beside her on the table.

"Don't you know that sun bathing is bad for you skin Nurse Dakota?"

Dakota raised up lowering her sunglasses to look at Sam.

"Well you are sure one to be advising me! Ms. Sunshine herself."

Samantha laughed and took a seat beside her.

"Are one of these glasses mine?" As she picks up the lemonade filled glass.

"Yep, knock yourself out. Tony has gone back in to get another glass."

She suddenly rose up to look at Sam as though she just realized Sam should be at work.

"Why aren't you at work? Everything ok? You and Ash fussing again?"

Sam took a drink of the cool and slightly tart liquid and sat the glass back on the table before answering.

"No, Ash and I are fine, well as fine as we will ever be I suppose."

208

Dakota still taking a scrutinizing look at Sam before she leaned back in her seat.

"Oh, well then it must be TC, what is up with him? Have you not heard from him again?"

Sitting upright in her chair to look straight at Sam.

"Sam I am worried about him breaking your heart and I swear if he hurts you he will have me to answer to!"

"Dakota!" Sam is laughing at her by this point.

"Dakota, you are so crazy! He has not broken my heart, although I do fear that sometimes myself." Her face becoming more serious.

"Well, what is it then? Tell me."

Sam paused for a moment as if putting her thoughts together.

"Well, I did try to entice him into a visit tonight but he already had plans with the guys. Which nothing wrong with that, at all! Don't get me wrong. It is just difficult to know where I stand with him when he runs so on and off again. It drives me crazy sometimes."

"Well, I can understand that Sam, being a woman and all, I agree with you. Men however, well you know how they look at everything differently than we do. Some little something that is a big deal to us doesn't mean squat to them."

"I know Dakota. Just sometimes it is hard."

"I understand Sam."

About that time Tony arrived back with another glass of lemonade. He looked great in his navy blue swim trunks, and no shirt, nice six pack Sam thought. And a very nice tan going on!

"Hello Tony, love the tan!' Sam smiled at him.

Tony gleamed back at her.

"Thanks! Did you come to join us and work on your own tan? I'd be happy to apply the oil Samantha. So that you won't burn, of course." Continually raising his eyebrows at her.

"Now Tony you know I don't burn! And no I really stopped by on the spur of the moment so no swimsuit. Sorry."

She looked at Dakota who has removed her sunglasses to roll her eyes at Sam. She then looked over at Tony.

"Sorry to disappoint you bro no Sam in a bikini today!" Embarrassed, Sam and Tony both turn a little pink.

"I think my sister has had a few too many lemonades spiked with rum!"

"What! Spiked!" Dakota exclaimed.

Looking at the almost empty glass she is holding.

"I've got to drive back!" Sam looks at Dakota in exasperation.

"Oh please! Sam! It is only slightly spiked and you haven't even had a full glass! Quit being a worry wart and come inside with me while I make us all some lunch and we will trash talk all men!"

As she lovingly rolled her eyes in sisterly love to Tony. Sam mimicked Dakota to Tony followed her inside.

Dakota goes to the fridge and removed various bowls of food sitting them on the large granite island in the middle of her expansive kitchen. Sam loved her kitchen, it is so roomy and has a very comforting feel about it. It was the heart of their home that was obvious.

Dakota started dumping the contents together in one large bowl. A rogue piece of boiled egg failed to make it into Dakota's mixing bowl so Sam reached over to retrieve it tossing the cold egg into her mouth.

"I wish I knew."

She had become lost in her thoughts of TC while she watched Dakota make their lunch and hadn't meant to say that out loud. Dakota unaware and engrossed in her chore of mixing simply replied.

"Wish you knew what? How to make chicken salad?"

Sam sighed.

"No Dakota." Slightly rolling her eyes at her.

"I wish I knew what the future holds for me and TC, are we destined to be lovers forever, or only for a short time. Will we always be in each other's lives or will it end as suddenly as it started?"

Dakota stopped mixing the salad and slapped Sam's hand as she reached in the bowl for a piece of celery.

"Really Sam? After, all this time...you are referring to it as a short time? This..this..this affair has been going on for years now! So I don't think that constitutes a short time."

She winked at Sam and turned her attention back to the chicken salad.

"Dakota, you know what I mean!"

"Yes, Sam I do and you know I was only teasing you. That is the question we all have, is it not? What does the future hold for each of us? And if we could, would we really want to know? I mean doesn't that take all the fun out of it? Knowing ahead of time I mean. Spontaneity is the spice of life, take it as it comes and enjoy it while you can! Don't question, just do! That is my motto, for most everything. Lord knows I see my share of death and sudden endings working at the hospital." She winked at Sam again she motions her head toward the outside patio.

"Now grab the chips and bread, I've got the salad and more lemonade'.

Sam obliged, quickly crossing the wood floor to open the sliding doors for Dakota. As Dakota exits the door she looked back at Sam.

"After we eat, let's go back to that new lingerie store in the mall, you remember the one where you bought your black robe!"

Sam smiled in agreement.

"Oh yeah, that robe!"

Dakota gave her an inquiring look.

"Do you have to be back at work?"

"No, I will text Deidra and Uncle John and let them know I am taking the afternoon off.

The next two weeks flew by for Sam, she had a few text message conversations with TC, some flirty ones and some sharing of sexy photos, each of them doing their share of enticing. She had let him know last week that she really wanted to see him before she and Dakota took off on a girl's only trip to the beach. She pouted, telling him it was because she would be gone so long. Really it was only for three days, a long weekend. When she made the request he had promised that he would try to make it by. She was confident that he would make it, he after all had never let her down in the past. Confident, at the time of asking anyway. Not so confident on the last day he has to keep that promise!

He had been trying to be good, of late as it, would seem anyway. It is Thursday, so if he is going to make it, it has to be today. She thought, as she browsed through her closet deciding on what to wear. Finally, she chose her favorite coral dress, the one that buttoned up the front, for easy access. She smiled at the thought. Maybe I should text him a reminder, like Dakota keeps insisting I do. She frowned as she buttoned each button. Hum, no I think if I am important to him he will remember, I told Dakota I refused to do so. I am sticking to my guns this time. Besides, he has always remembered in the past. Slipping on her matching coral heels and jewelry pieces she is on her way to the office. As she was walking to her car her cell phone chimed. Just like many times in the past she would be thinking of him and he would text or call, it was very uncanny.

The text read: "I will see you this afternoon at the office, close to five as I can. Crazy schedule lately."

She replied by with: "Great! Can't wait to see you but how about I buy you pizza and a beer first do you have time for that?"

He responded: "Sounds great at Angelo's? "Yes I have time Jan is out of town on business, won't be back until tomorrow."

Sam replied: "Yes perfect see you then."

The day seemed to drag to Sam, she was so ready to see TC. When five o'clock finally arrived she left Deidra to lock up. She arrived at the restaurant by a quarter after five, and TC was just pulling in as well. Damn! He looks so sexy in that red truck of his! Smiling at him as they both get out of their vehicles. Once inside and seated TC ordered pizza, salad and beers. Confirming with Sam that they share the salad with Ranch dressing. She agrees. Several beers and food consumed they leave, TC insists on picking up the tab though.

"Well, what now TC?" Looking up at him as they walk toward their vehicles.

"Well, you could take me for a little drive, since I have had a few beers."

"Sure!"

Sam is game she had something special in mind for the evening anyway since both their spouses were out of town for the night. TC directs her to drive down to a local park, there is a walking trail, a bike trail and a large fishing pond. It is pretty well lit, but it made Sam a bit uncomfortable. After all there were people coming and going and they couldn't very well make out in her front seat with the big console in the way.

After a few shared kisses she suggests to TC that they go get a hotel room and be able to make love in the comfort of a real bed. He is all for it and directs her to one in the downtown area. He started to get out to go procure the room, but Sam stopped him.

"Let me do this TC I'm less likely to be recognized than you, what with your real estate signs everywhere."

"Are you sure Sam?'

"Yes, TC. He tried to hand her the money but she shakes her head no. You bought dinner, I can do this." He knew she had her mind set and there would be no point in arguing so he conceded. After taking care of the room she sees a vending machine, she has the forethought to purchase some bottled water for him and a cola for herself.

That done, they find the room and park nearby. Walking to the room together, since it is late and no one is in sight. Once inside, Sam sat the drinks on the dresser and suggested they turn on the television for some music. Least they might make a little too much noise. But TC has other thoughts on his mind he pushes her gently against the room door. Startled for a moment she looks up at him, neither speaks. His eyes are such a deep blue, reminding her of the ocean, time and time again. His look was so very serious. He gently but firmly pins her against the door, blocking each side of her with his arms, hands against the door, leaning in to face her. She couldn't help but notice how sexy his arms looked as his muscles tightened against his weight. Looking back up at him, eyes locked upon eyes, she felt as though she would literally die of elation right there. TC leaned in for a gentle kiss. Releasing her TC smiles picking up the remote he scans through the channels for a music only channel. In the meantime Sam removes her jewelry so as not to get tangled in her hair and plops her shoes on the floor as she drops onto the bed. TC is unable to find music so he turns off the television and removes his shoes and clothes in their entirety. Sam smiles laying there on her back looking up at him as he climbs into the bed.

"I thought it would be more fun if you undressed me." Smiling he climbs over her and is at her feet. Intently working his way from the bottom of her dress toward the top undoing every little button along the way. Once she is down to her panties and bra he sits back just to admire her shapely body. He liked the matching pink panties and bra. Sam knew he would and had paid special attention to pick them when she dressed that morning in anticipation of a visit.

"Nice."

Was all he could reply as his hands gently unfastened her bra, then gently slid her panties from her body. Feeling his own masculinity grow to full capacity.

It was their first time in a real bed. Sam's expectations were heighted at the thought of finally being able to enjoy TC to the fullest. Being able to feel his entire naked body against her own. She had ached for that feeling for so very long.

TC had his own ideas of ecstasy floating around in his head. He wanted to give her more enjoyment than he ever had before. He knew he would certainly not miss having aching calves from standing at her desk, much as he did during their previous sexual encounters. He was excited to show her the full multitude of his lovemaking talents.

Sam enjoying feeling all of TC's naked body against her and his moans of pleasure assured her he felt it as well. Their kisses were many. Their hands explored each other's body to the fullest extent. Igniting them both in a fury of passion. When he could wait no longer, TC takes her legs putting them on his shoulder as he penetrates her. He went deep and hard inside her. Both reveling in desire and passion. Their bodies quavering an explosive climactic ending for them both.

Exhausted they lay side by side. TC is wound up from the excitement of it all, he starts telling her all about his day and other stories abound while gently stroking her back with his hand. She on her side facing him. He was a chatter box for sure. Sam listened intently feeling his need to talk. He talked for a long while about a little bit of everything and nothing that really mattered.

Perhaps he needed to expunge all the extra built up emotions. Or maybe he was just talking because he had someone willing to listen to him giving him all her undivided attention. She wondered if this was part of what might be missing from his marriage. Someone really paying attention to him. Once he seemed to have said his peace she kissed his bare chest.

"Thank you for coming TC. I thought you weren't going to make it."

TC gave her a bewildered look. "Why did you think that?"

Somewhat embarrassed she shrugged her shoulders. "I don't

know, just being silly I guess."

His RTP had taken him to his next thought already.

"Sam, you said once that some people would be shocked to know you are doing this with me."

"Not some people TC! But everyone that knows me would be!"

He continued his hand caressed hers.

"Why did you let me touch you that first time Sam?"

She was caught off guard by his questions. Although she didn't want to tell him the real truth, that she was in love with way before anything transpired between them, she could not lie to him. She looked up at him, her eyes wide in anxiety, at what his response might be.

"Because you are in my heart TC. You really shocked me that day you came around my desk to my chair when I was teasing you with the chocolate candy on my chest. I had flirted and teased with you so many times prior, and you with me. It had always seemed innocently truthful. Based on desires, desires I never thought you would act on, or me either for that matter!"

"I know Sam, I shocked myself that day! I had wanted to touch you way before that. But I was afraid, afraid you wouldn't let me touch you and that I would offend you."

"I could ask you the same question TC, what made you finally touch me that day?"

"I don't know Samantha, I just couldn't resist it any longer. And now, well, I like giving you pleasure. At least I think I give you pleasure, well I know I do by your little moans."

He is gently caressing her breasts now, enjoying the softness of her skin under his touch.

"Do you let your other lovers touch you like this?" Sam is taken by total surprise on this question. She wondered if he was asking because he actually thought there might be others, or because he needed reassurance that she did not have others. She rolls over on her stomach and looks TC direct in the eyes.

"TC, there are no other lovers! There has not been anyone, since, well since you and me. Not even Ash. I am not a slut. At least I don't think I am."

"I know you are not a slut Samantha.' He tenderly kisses her. "I was afraid to tell you TC that you are in my heart. I was afraid it would make you run away."

"I am not going to runaway Samantha. We will always have our friendship. With that Sam exclaims. "See! I knew it! You are going to back away from me now! Afraid I am getting too close. You are afraid I will be too attached!"

TC throws his hands up in exasperation.

"That is not what I said! No wonder men and women have so much trouble communicating!"

Sam has heard enough, she hushes the rest of his words with her kisses.

"I can't stay the night Sam." I have neighbors that might mention to Jan that they didn't see me at home."

A little disappointed she told him she understood. Wrapped in each other's arms for a good while longer, relishing in the precious time they have together. A little later they dressed and left the room key on the dresser.

On her drive home the thoughts of all his unusual and certainly unexpected questions came back to her. It had definitely been a night of surprises. Who would have thought it would all lead to where we are today. What did all those questions mean? Where was his mind leading him? Was he insecure? Did he not trust her after all this time? What did they mean?" If they meant anything at all, she wasn't sure. Why does it all have to be so complicated?

Chapter **19**

Just before dawn Sam's internal clock awakens her, just as it does every morning. She lay there trying to force herself back to sleep, she didn't want to disturb Dakota sleeping in the next room. From the partial open window she could hear the gentle rolling of the waves against the shore, they were beckoning her to the water's edge.

Guess I better go start some coffee, if I want to go scavenge for shells. Putting on her robe she goes to the kitchen, stopping to, peek down the hall to be sure Dakota's door is still shut. After starting the coffee and as quietly as possible she opens the sliding door that lead onto the balcony. Smiling at the beautiful sunrise just starting to peak. Time for one cup of coffee and it should be light enough for me to gather shells. Quickly going back into her bedroom to change clothes. Mornings on the windy beach are a little cool, better grab some long jogging pants and a long sleeved shirt. She tells herself as she rummages through her clothing.

Coffee consumed, cell phone in pocket, net and shell bag slipped over her shoulder, the one Tony had given her the bag a few weeks ago, knowing her love of shelling, he even had her name embroidered on it. He was indeed a very thoughtful man. She remembered he had hinted of sometime all of them going with her and Dakota, meaning, Ron, Ash, and himself of course. Smiling she guessed there were a lot of hints, of how he felt about her, realizing she had overlooked them for years, totally oblivious. She wasn't sure if she actually just chose to ignore them or if it was a subconscious thing. Sure, naturally the thought had crossed her mind on occasion, that there could possibly be something between them if she and Ash were not married. But then TC stepped into the picture. No one had ever excited her like TC did. No one made her feel as complete and content as TC did. Although she did like Tony immensely, he was so kind, a real gentlemen and so tall too! Laughing at that last thought, she shrugs it off, heading out the door in hopes of finding some pretty shells.

After a good hour on the beach gathering what few shells she was able to find she goes back to the room. Dakota is up having had her morning coffee and preparing breakfast for the two of them.

"Good Morning! I thought you might be starving after your adventure on the beach. Let's eat out on the balcony."

Motioning toward the door.

"Dakota, you are too good to me!" Sam states happily.

Once settled and enjoying their breakfast Dakota asks. "Did you find many shells?"

"No, disappointedly, only a slim few."

"Oh well, Sam. You know this is not the best beach for shelling, but it is a good beach for relaxing and sunning!"

Taking her last bite of egg, smiling as she heads inside. Sam follows, with their dishes in hand. They enjoyed a full day on the beach and each only suffered a slight sunburn.

By six p.m. they were both ravenous. Dakota loved seafood, so they decided to eat at her favorite restaurant, Crabs on Us. It was located right on the beach so they could enjoy the view and the outside seating, which they both loved, not to mention they had the best little mixed drinks in town. The fact that is within walking distance of their condo was certainly a plus as well, no worries of drinking and driving.

As the even went by they ate way too much, drank almost too much, and laughed so much their sides hurt. At nine o'clock a live band started up and immediately they had offers from men to dance. Sam was hesitant at first.

"Oh come on Sam! Girls just want to have fun! Ron and Ash won't mind a few dances with nice guys, we don't have to tell them how cute they were! Or should I say Ron and TC?"

Smiling wickedly she convinces Sam to dance with them. By eleven o'clock they were both exhausted. Thanking the guys for a fun evening they returned to their condo. A good night of sleep befell both of them.

The next day was pretty much a repeat of the first day aside from the late night dancing and obtaining a little more of a sunburn. It had indeed been a good girl's weekend.

It had been almost two weeks since their beach trip and no visit from TC. Sam was getting worried that he wanted to end the relationship. She expected it would probably happen sometime, but she had always prayed she was wrong. She was on edge most days, wondering would this be the day. Close to tears one minute, then telling herself the next minute that she was just being paranoid, that he was just busy. She had text him a few times and he replied, but there wasn't much flirting although he had said he would try to get by to see her when he could, but she still worried.

Early one morning, before leaving for work, she got a text from TC telling her he had run out of options to be able to see her this week, as well. To Sam that translated into believable excuses to Jan for his whereabouts. She was disappointed to say the least. She replied back that he was going to disappoint her and included a sad smiley face and of course a sexy picture of herself. TC never responded back.

As the day progressed without another word from him she was a little worried about what he was thinking. Had she gone too far? Had she upset him? Angry thoughts filled her head. So what! It is high time I make some demands on him anyway! I always have to wait! Those thoughts dissipated immediately to thoughts of worry. Worry that he had grown tired of their relationship and would no longer want to be with her. NO! No, that can't be! I know he cares for me. I made a pact with myself to learn patience and trust. She got up to look out of her window. Those are the lessons I need to learn! I must accomplish this before TC and I can be together and be happy. Someday we will. I don't know how on earth it will work out, what with his kids and all, but someday he will come to me. I am sure of it. If I am important to TC and not just a fun time, he will find a way to see me, and soon.

The next morning she was at home sipping her coffee, not yet dressed for work. Thoughts of TC crept into her mind as they did most mornings. Looking at her cell phone at the precise time he would usually text her, their time, at seven a.m. nearly every time. Sure enough his special chime rang through. Scrambling to look at the message.

She reads the text: "Is it safe?"

Excited she knew that meant he was at her house! Even though he had told her he didn't want to come to 'their' house again, hers and Ash's, being the good man that he was it bothered him, knowing it was wrong. So very wrong, but unable to help himself.

"YES!"

Was her text back to him back, elated at the surprise! In only moments he was at her door beaming with a giant smile and she fell into his arms. After their embrace she looks up at him.

"TC you have made my day again! I am so happy to see you!" TC smiles amused that she is so excited and it didn't hurt his male ego any either. It had been many years since Jan greeted him with such enthusiasm and he so enjoyed it.

Sam led TC inside, this time to the guest room. The soft bed was very welcoming. Definitely better that her hard desk at the office, or the hard floor. TC wasted no time disrobing her and her to him. He kissed her passionately again and again. Her hair still slightly damp from her morning shower tickled his nostrils, the aroma of her clean skin pleased him. His lips devoured her neck in kisses before moving on to her shoulders. Nibbling tenderly on each shoulder, as if to tease her, before imposing long wet brushes against her with his tongue all the way down to each breast, and gingerly around each nipple. Her body quivered in pleasurable whispery moans. Stopping for a moment to look at her in her ardent moans of bliss, enjoying the sound. He moves farther down her body to her stomach. He loved the feel of her flesh there, his hands exploring every inch. It was enjoyable to him that she had no hard hip bones protruding, just a soft pleasurable abdomen. He loved the feel of some real flesh beneath his hands, kneading her tummy gently with each hand. Sam had never had anyone quite do that before, but so long as he enjoyed it she did as well. His tongue playfully landing here and there upon it, then infused deliberately into her naval. She quivered in delectation as he reached her inner thigh, then further. His head buried between her thighs, her hands clutched in his hair until neither of them could stand any more. He enters her with great force causing a very loud squeal to escape Sam's lips. Such an unconstrained squeal it gave TC immense pleasure, his body shook, followed by shivers and sounds of culmination from them both, as each reached a frenzied climax.

TC collapsed beside her, his head resting on the pillow next to hers. He lay there looking at her and her at him. Sam knew that look. It was a look of happiness, a look of peace. She knew it meant he was in a happy place with her. Smiling at him with her own look of comfort. She knew he did indeed care a great deal for her, even if he still can't put it into words. After a few more moments of relaxing TC asks.

"Do you ever fear getting caught Samantha?"

"Of course I do TC especially when you surprise me like this."

He smirks a little, somewhat enjoying knowing that he made her nervous.

"Yeah, it is a little nerve racking, isn't it Sam."

"To say the least! TC"

TC always made a point of conversing with Sam after their encounters. Sam appreciated this immensely knowing he was really talking to her and had a real interest in her and what was going on in her life. She appreciated it a lot. What worried her was the no contact for days afterward. She wasn't sure if he was ridden with guilt or just content until the next time. This was a normal train of thought for Sam of late. One minute she would be elated and the next afraid she would be out of his life. It was indeed a difficult situation. She hated feeling insecure, she hated feeling used sometimes, as she did, and she hated that feeling most of all. Knowing all the while it was her insecurities causing her to think in such a way and angry at herself for allowing that kind of thinking at all! She knew in the depths of her being that TC was not the kind of man to just use her for sex. She knew they had a celestial connection that went way beyond that! She hated that they had to live separate lives and the secrecy. She thought a lot about all of the complications they had. She thought about Jan. She used to envy her so very much. Now, most days she felt sorry for her. Not to be confused with pity, not at all. Ironic how things change sometimes. She had actually told TC once that she used to think Jan was the luckiest woman in the world, but not so much anymore. For which he had no reply. She was thankful that he had not become angry at her for saying such a thing. It actually slipped out in one of their strange conversations after having made love in her office. She didn't mean it in a bad way. It was just that she knew the factors in her own marriage that made her want to be in TC's arms. She still, after all this time, had no explanation from TC regarding the matter. Did he still love Jan? Most likely. But maybe he is not in love with her, much the same as her and Ash. Well who knows maybe Jan doesn't even love TC anymore, either. Perhaps she is unhappy. Maybe they have been together so long that they are afraid of change and afraid to face the truth. She did understand how hard it is to walk away after so many years, you settle and it develops into complacency. Yes, you reconcile for fear of change.

Samantha struggled with these thoughts quite often. Some days they were so unbearable that she was in near tears and wanted to break it off with him. The next day or even hours later she would feel quite the opposite, distraught at the thought of losing him, and fighting back the tears over the thought. Wondering what he might be thinking with those random thoughts of her, which he says he has. Would he upset if she broke it off? Would he understand or beg her not to? Or would he be relieved?

"Oh God! How did I get into this mess?" She says out loud to herself. Then looking around slightly embarrassed, to see if anyone noticed she was talking to herself. She had gone to a little outdoor café for lunch and had taken a book with her to read while she had lunch all to herself for a change. Book in hand open to the last chapter, but instead of reading the words on the pages her mind had gone on one of its many tirades concerning her situation with TC. She had become totally consumed by her thoughts even forgetting to eat her salad which was now quite warm and distasteful. Laying her fork back down, she picks up her phone and calls Dakota.

"Dakota, hey what are you doing?"

"Dakota immediately picking up on the tone of Sam's voice asked. "What is wrong?"

Sam knew that she wouldn't be able to sugarcoat her mood from Dakota, she knew her too well.

"Oh, you know Dakota just having one of those days."

"Who has put you in this mood, oh wait why do I even ask? I know it is TC, you don't get this way over Ash anymore. So tell me what is going on?"

"Well, nothing new really. Just the last few times we have made love it has, well it has been different. Not the sex part I mean but the talking afterward. You know he used to avoid looking at me afterward, and strangely that always made me feel cheap and used. Even though I tried not to let it. He would even avoid touching my hand afterward. It was so confusing and I was ashamed to even admit that I thought that way. Now he is touchy, feeling afterward, kissing and generally talking more."

Shaking her head in confusion as though Dakota could see that through the phone.

"It has just been different, in a good way I mean, and it scares me. It scares me that it is all in my head and that he ...well... he."

"Sam! Really! Can't you tell he has falling for you?"

"Oh no Dakota! I don't know. I mean I know he has some sort of emotional attachment to me, but as far as falling in love with me! Um, I don't think I can go there Dakota. Remember he even said in the beginning that we couldn't fall in love. "

"Samantha! Really? Now who is in denial? You can say anything you want to try to justify the both of you. But you have both fallen. It is complicated and the unfortunate part is all the complications that are keeping you both from admitting it! This had been going on way too long now, for there not to be any kind of emotional attachment, for both of you! Three or more years now? I mean really, Sam honey if it were nothing you would have both become tired of it by now. It is not easy after all, to carry on an affair.

And for years to boot! I mean it is a big commitment. The lies, the secrets, the excuses, the guilt! Not to mention the possible loss! That is, if you are in love with your spouse! Don't you realize he is risking it all for you! Even if he doesn't say it, maybe even if he doesn't actually realize it on the surface, but it has to be in the back of his mind somewhere! Didn't he ask you one time if you were afraid of getting caught? Did he say he was? Think about it Sam, if you truly were in love with Ash, could you really be cheating on him with TC? I know you are not the kind of person that takes matters of fidelity lightly. And I am pretty sure TC feels the same exact way. You have shared with me many conversations that prove he is a very decent and caring man. Not a scumbag that would use you for just sex! And certainly not for years! It would have been over in less than six months had that been the case. Don't you know that Sam?"

Dakota hears silence on the other end of the phone, she waits giving Sam a little time to absorb all she has blasted in her ears.

"Samantha, are you going to answer me?"

She hears a sniveling sound in the phone then finally Sam's tearful voice.

"Yes, Dakota I guess you are right, I am such a fool. I know….. I know. Thank you for talking to me. You always make me feel better. You are the best friend I have ever had, female friend anyway."

Dakota could hear the smile in Sam's tone on that friend part and she knew once Sam has added some humor, she is ok.

"Look Sammy Pooh, you know you can always count on me no matter what. Even to tell you the things you don't want to hear. Now call that other best friend of yours and make mad passionate love to him and tell him how you feel. It is time Sam. It is time. Now, I got to go! Ron is waiting for me. Love you!"

"Thanks, Dakota! I love you too. Give Ron a hug for me!" Sam responds.

"Sure thing Samantha, talk to you soon."

Sam thinks long and hard about what Dakota has said. Not sure she is ready to take that step. Not sure TC is ready for her to take that step. She doesn't make the call laying her phone back in her purse she starts to get up and feels a hand upon her shoulder. She turns to see Tony standing there, a somewhat troubled look on his face. In a panic it crosses her mind that he may have overheard too much of her conversation with Dakota. She was petrified at the thought.

"Sam, why is a gorgeous woman such as yourself having lunch all alone? May I join you?" Smiling down at her he pulls out a chair to sit next to her. The smile on his face eased her mind that it was only her imagination and he must have just walked up after she had hung up with Dakota.

"Of course, you can Tony." Reaching her hand to steal one of his fries off his plate.

"What are you up to? Do you come here often?" She asks between bites of the fries he is sharing with her.

"On occasion, when the weather is nice, like today. Was your salad not any good? Doesn't look like you ate a bite of it. Want half my burger?"

Sam looks at her salad and his burger then replies. "Oh no, I just got a little distracted and place her hand on her novel. Thanks for the offer but a fry or two will be sufficient, I had a big breakfast so I wasn't really starving."

Tony proceeds to tell her the events of his day at the shop and a hysterical story about some mice being in a lady's car. They are both laughing and having a really great time. Suddenly Sam stops. She looked past Tony and saw TC walking toward them. TC does not look happy!

He walks up to the table towering over them.

"Well fancy meeting you here Samantha!" TC looks at her with only a half grin.

"Who is your friend?" Sam looks at Tony,

"Oh, this is Dakota's brother, and Ash's best friend and a friend of mine too of course. She stammers it out a little nervously. Tony, he owns Tony's Automotive on Cumberland St. I'm sure you have heard of it, it is one of the best shops in town!"

TC turns to Tony extending his hand to him, by that time Tony has already stood up to greet TC. Standing side by side with TC Sam realizes they are the same height and pretty much the same build too, and both have beards and moustaches! Funny she never connected all that before.

Tony shakes TC's hand and much like when TC met Ash, both men scowled at each other. Sam couldn't believe it. It was so obvious! They were both jealous!

TC introduces himself and explains his affiliation with Sam, being sure to add he is a friend of hers as well as a work associate. A good friend as he put it. They explained pleasantries for a moment before TC excused himself and left. Shortly after Sam did the same leaving Tony to finish his lunch.

Later that evening, she called Dakota.

"Dakota! You won't believe what happened today after I hung up with you!" Dakota could hear the excitement in Sam's voice. "What? You won the lottery!"

"Dakota! No! Although that would be lovely. Tony happened up on me right after I hung up with you and we finished lunch together and guess who else happened up and got very jealous?"

"No! No way! TC? Really? Oh my, gosh what did he say?" "Well nothing really it was more the look on his face and the look on Tony's for that matter. They both had jealousy written all over them, and even scowled like when TC and Ash met for the first time! It was awesome!"

Dakota could hear the smile in Sam's voice.

"Well, maybe now you will believe I am right, on both counts!' Sam laughed.

"Whatever Dakota, whatever. I just wanted to share with you!"

"I know Sam, and I love that you did. I do not love knowing that someday you will be the heartbreaker of my brother's heart, though."

Thinking about that for a moment Sam responded.

"Well, Dakota I have certainly learned to expect the unexpected in all this with TC so who knows what the future will bring us all. Thanks for listening, talk to you soon."

Chapter 20

The very next morning is TC's birthday. Sam assumed he would have a big family celebration and Jan would make it a great day for him. It was her first thought when she woke up that morning.

Then she recalled the dream she had of him last night. She was unable to recall all the dream only the part of her being in the shower. She had one leg on the edge about to shave it when surprisingly the shower door slides open. She turns to look and TC is stepping his naked body into the shower with her.

There was something else in her dream about a window in some older home that was massively leaking water into the house from torrential rain. She could not remember if this was connected to TC in her dream or not, it was all sort of fuzzy and not making much sense.

Oh well, she thought as she lay there a few moments longer in her soft comfy bed. Anxious to get up she turned off the alarm noticing Ash was already gone. Then again remembering it is TC's birthday, she decides she will text him after her shower.

Quickly showered and coffee in hand she takes a seat on her

sofa, stroking the spot where she and TC had sat once before. Smiling at the memory. Although it was a little earlier than their normal time she couldn't wait and decided to text him.

It read: Happy Birthday Handsome!

It wasn't a second and his reply came across her phone to read: "Hug???"

She excitedly replies: "YES!"

It is not even five minutes and he is at her door! She greets him on her tippy toes with an enthusiastic hug and multiple elated kisses all over his face and neck in obvious elation that he has surprised her yet again.

"I wasn't expecting you on your birthday!" she exclaimed happily as she lower herself from her tip toes and taking him by the hand.

He smiled a sheepish grin. "I know, I thought a little spontaneity was in order."

"You do like living dangerously and really enjoy the element of surprise TC."

Still smiling happily at him. "How much time do you have?"

This was her way of determining what kind of visit he had in mind.

"I have plenty of time Samantha."

"Great! Where would you like to go?' Again giving him the opportunity to decide what was going to transpire between them.

"Let's go out on your back deck and sit awhile, it is a nice morning."

She leads him out onto the deck where he takes a seat in the center of the cushion covered swing, motioning for her to sit on his lap. She does so, facing him she straddles his lap in the swing her knees bent. Not an easy task for her short legs. No matter though, as she was certainly enjoying the kisses he was bestowing upon her.

They were kissing and caressing each other in between conversation and at one point TC causes the swing to move. She was a little apprehensive that she was about to fall off the swing backwards and she quickly reached for the back of it to hold on.

"Don't worry, I won't let you fall, I've got you Samantha." A sincere and confident look in his eyes. He pulled her tighter and his lips playfully tickled hers.

"I know it was just an automatic reflex TC. I know you have me." As she placed multiple kisses up and down his neck covering both sides.

It doesn't take long for things to heat up between them. TC has loosened her robe, his hands roaming freely across her back.

Sam's legs could no longer take the seating position. She got up taking his hand as she closed her robe. Pulling TC along with her.

"Oh, are we going to a new location?"

"Yes TC a new location." She leads him into the guest room.

She lies on the bed facing him. Still standing he reaches down and undoes the robe again. Fully exposing her body clad in a new turquoise lacey bra and matching panties. She looks at him and says, "Happy Birthday!"

After their love making, TC is dressing, he stops to look at Sam.

"I sure do like giving you pleasure."

As he reaches for his shoes. "I came with the intent of getting a birthday hug."

Shaking his head in denial.

"But once I am with you for long, I just can't resist." He leans down to give her a kiss.

After he left, Sam's heart was warmed and magically content. It scared her to take such a chance but at the same time pleased her that he wanted to see her badly enough that he would risk the danger. An oddly yet again she was thinking of him and he shows up. They are so connected, so in tune with each other somehow! Laughingly thinking, no wonder he calls me devil woman!

Chapter **21**

TC's nights have been filled with disturbing dreams of Jan and Samantha. Dreaming he lost them both. Dreaming his kids all disowned him when they learned of his affair and the heartbreak he has caused their mother. Dreamed John Rivers no longer wanted to do business with him. That the entire city of Nashville shunned him. His dreams were so disconcerting that he would scream out loud or moan as though in pain, waking Jan in fear many a night. She of course assumed it was his PTSD. She had been begging him to go to the doctor and ask for some medication to ease his nerves, wondering why they were starting up again. It had been quite a while since he had any issues. TC refused telling her it was nothing and that they would go away and not to worry.

He appreciated her worry and realized that she does still care about him even though they have not been happy in quite some time, just existing, which only added to his guilt. His thoughts would then turn to Sam. He didn't want to hurt her either. Although, he often knew what he was doing was indeed hurting her, and would try to stop thinking about her, stop calling her, stop texting her. But it would seem she could almost somehow sense it and she would be texting, flirting and sending sexy photos of herself and he would fall right back under her spell. That devil woman had some kind of hold for sure. There was no plausible answer, hence the nightmares. He also didn't like seeing her having so much fun with this Tony guy, admittedly he was a little jealous.

He thought about the picture frame Sam has sitting on her desk, he had read it many times.

"If you love two people, chose the second. Because if you really loved the first one you would not have fallen for the second one." *(Johnny Depp)*

He knew that rang true and figured she had it there just for him to see, a subtle hint for his heart to realize, but he also knew the assemblage of complications that would arise if he did. Complicated, so complicated and so much easier said than done. Would it be possible to break it off with Sam and remain friends? No, he knew that would be impossible. He wasn't that strong and he knew it. He didn't want to risk losing her, so he bided his time doing what he could when he could, but the stress was becoming too much and his body was paying for it in lack of sleep. What was the answer? He futilely asked himself that question daily. He knew Gunny was worried, Jan, the guys and Sam too, all because of him. For different reasons of course, but they all worried just the same.

He finally told Jan he needed some time alone, to get his mind straight on his shoulders. She although worried, agreed a weekend alone might be in order, so she offered to take Jacob and fly out to visit Davis and Annalisa. She had not seen them in a while. They had just been transferred to Camp Pendleton, Ca. Jacob would enjoy the trip she knew. Although she secretly hoped it would not entice him to join after graduation this summer. When she and TC talked about it they couldn't believe that their youngest child would be graduating and on his own soon. Where had all the years gone? Jan secretly wondered if their marriage would survive the empty nest syndrome, after all they had drifted apart the last few years. She wasn't sure how she felt about that either. She thought the trip might be good for her as well. To give her a different perspective maybe. TC had been so different the last few years, she couldn't really put her finger on what it was, but something felt awry.

So, it was settled Jan and Jacob would fly out Friday morning. TC would drop them off at the airport around six a.m. and pick them back up the following Tuesday at nine a.m. Jacob was out of school for teachers meetings so it would be of no issue with school.

TC was looking forward to the days of solitude, anticipating getting his thoughts in order before Jan and Jacob returned. Friday after work he went straight home, a few beers and a couple of sandwiches and he was out like a light on the sofa the entire night. Waking up with a slight kink in his neck, other than that, his night was restful. Saturday he pilfered around his garage most of the day. He had turned off his cell once he knew Jan and Jacob had made it to the base safely. He had advised Gunny and the guys that he would be unattainable for the weekend. He had however not let Samantha know.

The solitude was comforting and he did a lot of soul searching. Having only had a bowl of cereal that morning, by late afternoon he was starving. Deciding he would grill himself some burgers because he really didn't want to get out. Burgers, beer and the pool. Sounded like a fine evening to him. After he downed a burger or two along with several beers he was sitting by the pool enjoying the night air and another beer, or two. He picked up his cell. Turning it on he began to scroll through his pictures. He came across the one of Samantha in her black robe. He stopped.

He seemed mesmerized by the picture until he finished his beer and grabbed another one from the ice chest sitting beside him. He took a selfie of his own legs in his black swim trunks, thought about it momentarily and then sent the picture to Sam in a text message. Within minutes she text back:

"Wow sexy legs! What are you doing?"

He responded: "Oh just sitting out by the pool all by my lonesome self, thinking about a gorgeous green eyed devil woman. Having a few beers too many."

Sam instantly became worried. One that he was at the pool alone, drinking too many beers apparently. And too that he might fall asleep before clearing his phone of their text and Jan might see them. It was not like him to text her on the weekend, or at night. She was beside herself trying to figure out what on earth to do.

She text back: "Are you swimming alone, it is kind of cool tonight isn't it? Where is Jan?"

He replied: "No not actually in the pool I was earlier but all dried off now and yes a little too cool for a swim. Well unless some green eyed beauty devil woman was with me in a red, no wait to skinny dip, I might be able to stand it then."

Looking at her phone reading the text that put her mind to some ease. At least he was not swimming. Now, to worry about him erasing this conversation and picture... Oh geeeze...she thought as she contemplated what to say to him next. She didn't want to treat him like a child but knew he had consumed too many beers and was concerned he might just forget to clean up his phone.

She finally text:

"TC please be careful. Don't fall asleep without clearing you phone! You worry me. And don't fall asleep by the pool, the mosquitos may carry you off and I would miss you!" She was trying to add some humor to ease the command. She waited... no response. After twenty minutes and looking at her phone for what seemed like a hundred times she laid it down.

Shit! I sure hope he cleared it. Nothing I can do. I can't very well go over there. I can't call anyone to go check on him. That would be unexplainable. So, guess I will have to hope for the best at least I know he wasn't in the pool. So all I have to be worried with is Jan finding the text on his phone. Oh gezzz, rolling her eyes she headed for bed herself, it was late.

Sam was apprehensive all day Sunday, but didn't dare send a text to TC. She figured he would be in church Sunday morning with Jan and Jacob. Sunday was family time. She couldn't chance it. She would just have to wait until Monday morning.

Monday could not come fast enough to suit her. By seven a.m. she was texting TC. She waited. No response. That was not like him, at least not often, every once in a while it might be hours even the next day on a very rare occasion. Fine she thought angrily. I will wait till I get to the office and call his office that is innocent enough. Sharply at nine a.m. she was on the phone to Susie. "Susie, Hi this is Samantha at River House, how are you this morning?'

"I am fine Ms. Samantha how are you? What can I do for you?"

"I am fine too Susie, thank you for asking. I was wondering if TC might be available this morning."

"Oh, Samantha I am sorry." Before she can finish Sam's heart skips a beat fearing something terrible has happened.

"TC took the day off today, thought he would have let you know." Sam's heart quickened.

"Oh, well I am sure he probably mentioned it and I neglected to note it on my calendar. Will he be in tomorrow?"

"Yes, ma'am he is picking Jan and Jacob up at the airport at nine in the morning and will be in shortly after."

Confused, Sam replies with a thank you and hangs up. Looking at the phone thinking about what Susie has just told her she becomes angry. What! He has the entire weekend to himself and doesn't call me or try to plan a visit! She is angry and hurt at the same time. Why would he not try to see me while Jan is gone? A perfect time! No fear of getting caught! No lies to be told! I don't understand. She looks at his smiling face in her cell phone photos, and she can't help it, the anger dissipates and is replaced with crushed and hurt feelings. Even with that she could not stay angry at him. I can't cause him pain, she thought, still starring at his photo. That is Jan's job, not mine. Was that a devil woman thought? No, just simply that she loved him too much to cause him upset. Hopefully he would call her tomorrow or text once he sees her missed texts to him. She would just have to be patient a little longer.

Tuesday morning TC picks up Jan and Jacob. They are both excited to be home and share their stories with him over breakfast at the local I Hop. Jan with stories of Annalisa and Davis and Jacob with stories of the base all the military things he was in awe of. TC listened and told them he was glad they were home. By noon he was at the office going over a mass amount of messages Susie had left on his desk. One of which read simply. "Samantha called." He starred at the note in his hand, hesitating for a few moments. He figured he best make that call.   He called River House. "Deidra is Sam available, this is TC'

"Yes I know TC good grief if I didn't recognize your voice after all these years then I'd be in trouble!' Laughingly adding that she would connect him with Sam.

"This is Samantha how may I assist you?' Her voice is so lovely it takes him aback for a moment. "Hello?"

He hears her say again.

"Oh, hey Sam! How are you?"

I am great TC how about yourself?" Her reply was stern and not with any of her usual cute comebacks. Hum she is not making this call easy he thought.

"I am good Sam, say listen about the other night I sort of fell asleep before I could answer your last text. I am sorry if I worried you."

"Well you did TC. I was very worried."

"I am truly sorry, is there a possibility that I could make it up to you this evening, at the office? Say about five thirty?"

Sam thought for a moment.

"I will look forward to it TC, see you then."

"Great." He replied and they ended their call.

TC arrived at her office prompt as usual. She unlocked the door to let him in. He smiles sheepishly at her, she sort of avoids his eyes.

"Come on back TC would you like a drink?"

"Um, no I am good Sam, thank you."

They sit in their respective usual spots and it is a moment

before either of them speaks.

"So, TC I understand Jan was gone for the weekend? I can't believe you didn't call me. We could have planned a night together."

"I know Samantha, I know. I should have. I just had a lot on my mind lately. I needed some time alone." He doesn't look at her, except for quick glances.

"I see." Sam is not looking at him now and fidgets with the pen on her desk, her mind crazy with worry that he was about to break it off with her.

"So how are you now? What brings you to see me?' He gets up and goes to her pulling her up to stand.

"I missed you Sam! Oh God how I missed you!" Sam gave in. The passion between them was explosive to say the least. TC swoops her desk clear with one sweep of his arm, the other one gently guiding her down to the top of it. Pulling his shirt off, he then reaches for hers. Making a quick assessment that it is a stretch top, no buttons, so easy off, over her head. He tosses hers to the side with his. No time to worry about shoes the passion won't wait. He raises her skirt removing her silk red panties, feeling her as he does. She is so moist, so ready for him. He drops his own pants, he is more than ready, throbbing for her. All the while they are sharing feverish kisses, neither letting the other one go. Finally he is in her tight little box, so tight he moans in pleasure. He pounds her hard and fast making her gasp in delight. Sam calls out his name begging for more. He has never wanted her as badly as he does at this moment. He wants her, all of her! They both explode in fireworks! TC's body shivers in pleasure, he moans insatiably. Sam is breathless and shaking in sensual overload. TC leans up against her body staying inside her for as long as he possibly can, trying to catch his own breath and not wanting the moment to end. Finally having no choice he removes himself from her taking her hand and guiding her to the floor to lay beside him. He just needed to hold her for a moment longer. They were both exhausted. They lay there beside each other arms entwined, listening to each other's labored breaths in silence until their breaths are back to normal.

Sam looks up at TC, her eyes wide and vivid green. TC's steel blue eyes penetrating back to her. TC reaches over and gently removes a lock of her hair that is partially covering one eye.

"TC remember what you said we couldn't do?' TC frowns but only for a moment. He smiles and squeezes her tighter.

"Yes, Samantha I remember."

"Well TC I am sorry but I broke the rule. I am in love with you."

Before he could respond and afraid of what he might or might not say she hurriedly continues. "How could a woman not fall in love with you TC? You are caring, handsome, sexy a fantastic lover, giving of yourself to others in need without a selfish thought in your head. ..."

TC puts his finger over her lips to quite her. Smiling he says. "You love me!" His strong arms engulf her even more. "I can't give you want you need Sam. Or rather what you want."

He quickly closes his eyes. But not before Sam sees them fill with mist.

"It's complicated, Samantha. It's complicated." He quietly whispers in her ear.

Chapter 22

Sam's insecurities continued to be running rampant this week. She woke from another dream about TC; it was not a pleasant dream, not at all. She got her pen and journal out to jot it down. It always helped her to remember it, if she wrote it.

The dream: TC and I were at some kind of a meeting or class and the instructor was pairing people up two to a table. I had been paired up with some stranger. "

Oh great! The message symbol yet again! I will have to figure out what this one is trying to tell me. She said to herself as she paused for a moment remembering more of the dream she continues to write it in her journal

The stranger was a very handsome bald man. Upon taking my seat at the tall table I secretly hoped TC would get a little jealous, but it did not seem to affect him. When I sat at the table I looked at the man and told him I was sorry he got stuck with her when the room was filled with so many other gorgeous women. He smiled at me and said "He was starting from the top" It confused me a little at first, but then I realized he meant it as a compliment, to mean the top of the gorgeous women.

Hum, maybe my self-esteem needed a boost? Keep on writing Sam, don't get sidetracked now. Think now! What else happened? Oh! Yes!"

TC was kissing Jan! He seemed to have a contented look on his face. He had just walked by me and asked me what my plans were for the day and just kept on walking without waiting on me to answer. That! Is when he kissed Jan!

Oh dear! I don't like the sound of this! Does this mean TC is going to walk out of my life? To Jan!" Tears start streaming down her cheeks. She continues on blinking through the tears.

The dream then switched to something about being on a street in traffic and a young girl was beside her on a bicycle and she herself was pushing a grocery cart.

I swear my dreams are so crazy sometimes. She thinks s she continues to write.

A police officer was in the middle of the street directing traffic, he put up his hand for us to stop. She and the girl look at each other, neither saying a word.

And, and...what else? Oh shit! I can't remember anymore! This dream is going to be a difficult one to figure out, it jumps around too much, making absolutely no sense at all. Hum, I think the police officer was dressed in an old time uniform with one of those funny hats, like back in the thirty's or even earlier perhaps? Geezzzz even my damn dreams are complicated! Disgusted at the dream, she climbs out of bed. At least I know I am insecure especially after telling TC I loved him and his comment afterward.

"Well duh Sam it doesn't take a rocket scientist to figure that part out!" Belittling herself verbally.

She showers, dresses and leaves for work. To hell with coffee this morning, I will stop on the way in as she passes through the kitchen to the garage door slamming it shut behind her.

Sam arrives at work with a large coffee in hand and one for Deidra along with a couple of boxes of donuts for the rest of her workers. Deidra is pleased. She smiles at Samantha taking the boxes and her cup of coffee to the kitchen.

"Would you like me to bring you a couple and a napkin?"

"No, thank you Deidra. I am not very hungry this morning, I may have one for an afternoon snack, if one should be left.

"Ok" Deidra replied.

"I will take these on to the kitchen." Once there she grabs a plate taking a sprinkle cake and a cherry filled one for herself. She places a chocolate covered cake on a separate plate using a bowl for the lid and tucks it away in a corner cabinet. She gets another plate and took a pineapple filled for John, she knew those were his favorite and that he would only have one. Pleased with her planning ahead she goes back to her desk and sends an email to everyone letting them know donuts are in the kitchen. John isn't in yet so she just places his on his desk. Going back to her own desk happily anticipating the sweet bliss she is about to partake in.

Maybe, fifteen minutes go by and Deidra is at Sam's office door. Sam senses her and looks up from her desk.

"Yes, Deidra what is it?" Deidra looking rather forlorn at Sam asks.

"Are you ok this morning? You aren't getting sick are you?" Sam takes a deep breath.

"No Deidra I am not getting sick and yes, I am fine. Thank you for your concern, I simply didn't sleep very well last night."

"Oh. Okay, well if you need anything just let me know." Smiling she turns to go back to her desk.

"Thank you Deidra, I appreciate it." Sam focuses on her computer again.

"I just got to get through today, then I will have the weekend to myself."

It was a pretty Saturday morning TC is home. Jan has gone shopping and Jacob off with some friends. He had told Jan he would spend the day getting her honey do lists done around the house. Not one of his favorite chores. But since he did try to be a man of his word, well except for maybe where Samantha was concerned. He thought warily. He was in the process of dragging the power washer around to the back of the house. He couldn't seem to keep his mind focused. His RTP was driving him insane. Every thought seemed to somehow bring his mind back around to Samantha, causing him to be in a state of dejection.

Samantha, she was the dilemma! The complication, the devil woman that was his angel. The woman that made his heart skip a beat at every encounter. The woman with whom his soul felt connected.

I don't know what to do about Sam and my feelings for her. About Jan and my feelings for her. I made a promise to Jan before God and I have not honored that promise, well not since Samantha has stepped into my life.

"Damn it!" He said aloud between gritted teeth.

His face turning red in anger. Tossing the power washer to the side. He had lost the desire to clean the house.

Screw the honey do list. She should be here helping me instead of off spending money on nonsense! Then he remembered a conversation last spring with Samantha about him power washing the house. He was in her office one day and she had asked what he had done the prior weekend. He mentioned he had power washed the house and that was pretty much his boring weekend. She had commented had she been there it would not have been a boring task. That she would have drenched his body until sopping wet with the hose and he would have chased her and done the same to her until their exhausted and wet bodies lay laughing and clinging together in the grass. He smiled at the memory. She sure knows how to paint a pretty picture. And she sure knows how to make me smile. He mused over those thoughts for a few moments.

Then there were his kids, what kind of example, has he set for them? Would they ever forgive him? It would seem his choice is to either break many hearts, or only break two. His own and Samantha's. She had promised him once that she would never do anything to hurt him. He knew she meant emotionally and actually, like spilling the beans of their affair to Jan. He trusted her and appreciated her candor. He also knew she would be true to her word no matter what. He couldn't explain the unsurmountable amount of trust he had in her. Or why it was there even, just something about her.

Shaking his head trying to collect his thoughts to just one thing. "Impossible!" he yelled up at the heavens as he walked back to the garage putting the power washer back into its rightful place. "Another day." He said looking at it.

Going back to the back deck he goes inside to the kitchen, looking in the fridge he grabs a cold beer then his cell phone. Going back outside as he dials Gunny's number.

"Gunny! Hey man you busy today?" Gunny did have plans but he knew he could change them and from the sound of TC's voice he had best do it.

"No, TC no I don't have anything too pressing, what do you need son?"

TC pauses before replying.

"Yeah, well I thought maybe you might come over for a while and just hang. Uh, you know maybe share a few beers or something." Gunny was really worried now, TC sound very strange, very strange indeed.

"Sure thing TC I would love to I can be there in thirty. Is that okay?"

"Yeah, yeah Gunny that would be good."

"Ok, son see you then."

"Gunny!' He hears TC say anxiously just as he is about to hang up.

"Yeah TC?" Gunny replies trying not to let TC hear his concern in his voice.

Damn! I hope he is not suicidal! He has sure been acting strange lately! He thought as he waited on TC to reply.

"Thanks Gunny! See you soon."

Gunny hangs up with TC and tells Estelle he has to cancel lunch TC is in some trouble. He assures her not to worry though. She sends him off with a kiss on the check and a sympathetic smile. Silently trusting that Gunny can help TC through whatever the issue may be.

Twenty minutes later Gunny is pulling in TC's driveway just as TC opened the front door.

"Hey Gunny, come on in I got us some beer in the ice chest on back deck. We've got the place to ourselves for a change." Giving him a half smile while directing him inside.

Settled comfortably on the deck, their chairs side by side and beers in hand, they are facing the pool. Gunny sips his beer, waiting on TC to start talking. He knew with experience that it was better this way. In his own time he would get around to it. After thirty minutes or so TC finally spoke.

"Gunny, man I got a real issue. I've got to make a decision. A tough decision to either go left or go right."

Pausing for a moment to shake his head as his body slightly slumped downward.

"If it were only that simple. Don't ask me to explain what it is, just know I have to choose. Choose to do the right thing. It is ripping me apart inside Gunny."

A tear rolls down TC's cheek. Gunny sees it out of the corner of his eye but does not turn to make eye contact with him, knowing that would keep TC from confiding and he didn't want that. "Okay TC, okay. What else son, what else?"

"Well, I. I don't know. I don't know Gunny. Isn't it okay to let the past be the past sometimes Gunny? A man can't be faulted for wanting to better his life, now can he?"

TC takes another drink of his beer. It made a loud gulping sound as it went down his throat, taking tears along with it, he still just looked straight ahead. His hands were shaking now.

"Well, Son." Gunny thinks for a minute being cautious with his words of choice.

"That would depend I suppose on the consequences of that choice. Weighing the best with the worst, I mean. After all is said and done, well, a man has to do what he feels in his heart is the right thing to do. You have a strong heart Son. And a damn good sense of using that gut instinct of yours."

Stopping again to give TC a chance to interact if he needed to. After a few minutes Gunny started again.

"Then of course there is sacrifice, well that too can be difficult. Who's to say that is even the right thing to do? Gal Damn it! It is a tough one for sure, making the right decision."

He again cuts an eye over at TC but he still doesn't appear to be ready to make a comment, so Gunny continues again.

"Somebody will be hurt, with a tough decision like that. Question is how many will hurt? Who will hurt the most? And who will heal the quickest?"

It was at this point that TC realized that Gunny knew about Sam. He just kept looking ahead as the tears fell more frequently. He tried wiping them but they came faster than he was able to wipe them from his face, so he just let the waterworks run. Dropping quietly between his feet onto the deck. His hand trembled, as he placed the beer bottle to his lips attempting to take another drink, turning the bottle to the side and wiping his mouth with the back of his hand.

'Then you have your own feelings to contend with. Does a man no good to make a decision just out of obligation, if he is just going to be miserable the rest of his life. Tends to make those around him miserable too." Gunny stops again to take a drink and see if TC has anything to add. And again he does not speak.

"On the other side of that coin TC is the fact that things do change, people change, situations change. Everything happens for a reason. Figuring out the reason seems to be the biggest issue.

Sometimes we come to a stalemate, I suppose. Perhaps remembering the beginning and all the happy years will suffice that stalemate. There are a million clichés out there son, but the only one that matters is the one in your heart. You got to go with what's in your heart. That, my son, is your only real and true answer." Gunny leans back in his chair and chugs the last of his beer sitting it on the table and going for another. TC does the same. They sit in silence for a long while.

"You are right Gunny. You always know what is right."

Chapter 23

Sunday afternoon Sam gets TC's chime on her phone. She is surprised and has a horrible gut feeling.

She looked at the text: "I need to see you can you get away and meet me at your office in about an hour?"

Still looking at the phone, her first instinct is to say no. But she knows that would not solve what she fears she is about to hear. "Sure TC see you in an hour."

Luckily, Ash is out of town and won't be back until Monday. She drives methodically to her office dreading every minute of it. She beats TC there, going on in to wait for him to arrive.

He is late. She looks at her watch. It has been an hour and a half! What is keeping him? She waits fifteen more minutes and is about to text him when she hears a knock on the door. She goes and lets him in and without either of them looking each other in the eye until they reach her office.

TC walks over to her Water's Edge painting. His hands in his pockets. His shoulders start to shake uncontrollably and his chin drops to his chest. Sam immediately goes to him, wrapping her arms around him while he still has his back to her. She knows. Oh God!

er tears start to flow insuppressibly. He turns

his face filled with agony. They cling to each other

both crying tears of torment.

oks at Sam. Seeing the tears in her gorgeous eyes,

onsible for.

It broke his heart into a million pieces.

He takes his hands and places one on each cheek lifting her face up to his. They look into each other's eyes, tears still flowing from both of them nonstop. He kisses her cheeks as though to catch each tear as it streamed down them, mumbling between kisses.

"I am, so sorry Samantha! I am so sorry! I….Jan….the kids."

He breaks down in sobs and is unable to finish. Sam takes her hand and places it gently over his mouth.

"Shhh, TC, Shhh, it is okay." Her own tears streamed down her face. Her voice distraught.

"I knew it would happen someday. God I love you TC! Oh god how I do love you!"

She is now sobbing uncontrollably and goes limp in his arms. He supports her and as he is about to kiss her one last time, but she stops him.

"Go!' He looks at her somewhat shocked.

"Go TC please go! I can't! I can't! She is sobbing horribly now.

"Please just go now."

Tears were still flowing down TC's cheeks as he left her office. He got in his truck he headed for home.

Sam locked the door behind him and went back to her office. She collapsed on her desk and sobbed, until she had no more tears within her. Having cried herself to sleep, she woke several hours later. She checks her phone and there is a text from TC, he sent it after he left her according to the time.

It read. I am sorry. Never meant to hurt you, Samantha. Ple don't hate me.

She cried again. Catching her breath she searches for pen and paper in her desk. Jotting a note for Deidra.

"Deidra I will not be in the office next week, taking an unexpected vacation. John is aware. Thank you. Sam."

She decides she will call her Uncle from home or send him a text. It was a slow week next week so she knew they would be fine. She would also text Dakota. She knew Dakota would want to talk but she was in no condition to do so. No condition at all. She needed solitude. Complete solitude.

Upon arriving home she sent the texts to John and Dakota. She packed a suitcase and left Ash a note that she had to go to Florida for a week to close up some of her Uncle John's rental property there and would return the following Sunday. She would call him when she could. She left the note on the kitchen counter where he usually left his keys each night.

Chapter 24

Sam awoke sprawled across the bed on her tummy. Her naked body tangled in the covers from a spasmodic night of sleep. The covers were in such disarray that she had to untangle herself just to get up. She sat on the edge of the bed. Looking out at the ocean through the sliding glass doors next to her bed. She had hoped the ordeal with TC had all been only a nightmare. She thought that each and every morning that she woke up. It was a nightmare alright, but not an imaginary one.

She had been there for five days already. She had to make peace with it, somehow. Just to be able to function she had to make peace. Eventually she had to go home and be able to pretend all was good. Because she would have no explanation, that she could share, for her tears.

She had finally spoken with Dakota who had vehemently insisted that she fly up to be with her, but Sam told her no. That she needed time to sort things out. Dakota understood but made her promise to at least text her every day and to call her if she changed her mind. Tony had also sent a text to check on her. Saying he wasn't real sure what was going on with her, but Dakota had mentioned to him that she was in Florida trying to work things out. Saying if she needed him, he would be there in a flash. He text her everyday thereafter as well. Of course Dakota had not shared the real reason for her being there and she was sure. She did reply telling him she was grateful to have him care so much about her.

Ash had called to check with her on the third day and she made up some believable excuses to him. Her Uncle John and Aunt Estelle also called and she told them she was fine and would be back at work on Monday. They respected her need for privacy and assured her they were only a phone call away.

Every day the hurt it, was still there, she wondered if it would ever leave her. Deep within her, she knew it would not. It hurt way too much.

Oh God how it did hurt. Sam had never felt such pain in her entire life. She ached down to her soul.

She worried and wondered how TC was doing, she knew he was hurting too. She so wanted to know, but she would not make contact. He had made his decision, she must respect it. Besides, you can't make someone love you if they do not, or love you enough anyway. She learned that at the end of her first marriage. A simple but true fact.

All of her dreams that she had for her and TC shattered, along with her heart, which ached so very much.

It was just before sunset and Sam decide to go for a walk on the beach. She would be leaving in a couple of days. She knew she needed to soak up as much of the comfort that the beach afforded her, as she would definitely have to rely on it once she returned home.

She walked and walked the water's edge. The waves gently slapped against her ankles with each step. The ever changing waves of life. The sound of a lonely seagull calling out every now and again bounced off the sound of the waves splashing to shore. Sam loved that sound. It was indeed a beautiful night. Stopping now and again to turn and face the ocean, to take in its beauty, wishing she could stay here forever. But she knew that was only wishful thinking.

As she continued walking the wind had picked up a little more causing her hair to swirl over her shoulders and back again. The moon was full and shinned brightly upon the water, the stars were twinkling adding their own light to the sky. It had been a beautiful sunset, a perfect sunset. She thought about the past few years with TC. They had been the best years of her life. The tears began to emerge again gently cascading down her cheeks. Not tormented bawling as she had experienced the first days she had arrived there. Just gentle little streams of tears, some falling to hit her bare toes as she walked in the sand and some of which to be caught by a wave, affording the ocean ownership and therefore taken back out to sea. A part of her to ever remain with the vast sea, much like her heart to belong to TC's.

She has stopped again to pick up a seashell as she faced the ocean. Gazing at the shell, lost in thought wondering if she would ever be able to face the world again. She had walked farther out into the water, the waves slapping up to her knees at times. Suddenly she feels a hand upon her shoulder and another hand clamp around her waist holding her body tightly. By all rights she should have been scared out of her wits, but his touch alone gave her a feeling of security, even though she had no idea who this mysterious person was, that came from nowhere in the darkness.

She attempted to get a look at the mystery man, but before she could get a view of his facial features he lowered his head to her right shoulder, she could feel his warm breath on the lower part of her neck where it meets the shoulder, as the chill bumps started to form, she felt the tingle of his beard against her supple skin. Then came the warm soft, yet firm touch of his lips to the lower part of her neck, she could feel his lips move slightly as his tongue touched her skin with a light caress, and the light pull of her skin as his lips released their hold.

Slowly and methodically his soft tender kisses were easing up her neck, with what felt like an eternity between each move as he worked his way up to her earlobe. The chill bumps across her soft skin resembled a field of clover waving in the breeze. His breath upon her skin, his lips teasing her ear, the passionate feeling was overwhelming, where did this person come from?

She realized that while the sensual overload was taking place on her shoulder and neck, his hands were working their magic elsewhere. He had grasped her sides with a light but meaningful touch, and slowly eased his hands down the sides of her body slowly and methodically, like a well-trained masseuse. As they reached the area of her thigh, his hands changed position from the side to the front of her thigh, favoring the inner portion, as he slowly changed direction and started the return upward, like they were on a special mission. She felt the hem of her dress sliding up with the movement of his hands, letting soft ocean spray dance upon her legs like a thousand ballerinas floating across the stage. As the fantasy continued, the seashell that just a few moments before had her full attention now slipped from her hands and fell back to the water's edge. The moment his hands reached the level of her hips he lightened his touch and her dress cascaded down her legs like the curtain after a Broadway show. He gently turned her around to face him. Sam became hysterical at the site of him, the mystery man now revealed.

"Samantha, I couldn't stick with it. I made the wrong choice. I realized it the minute Dakota told me you were gone! I shouldn't stay with a woman I don't love and lose one that holds not only my heart buy my soul."

Samantha is crying, barely able to breathe not saying a word just looking at TC as though she didn't even know him.

"Samantha, I know I don't have the right to ask you this."

At this point TC's own tears start to fall.

"But, Samantha do you think you could find it in your heart to forgive me? You are the other half of my soul, you are what has always beaconed me to the water's edge. Forgive me and be my wife. I love you more than every drop of water in this vast sea! Samantha, I will always love you!"

Samantha has no words she is able to speak. Tears are streaming uncontrollably down both cheeks. She leaps into his arms, smothering him in passionate kisses.

Acknowledgements

Special thanks to fellow authors J.L. Davis, Liv Moore, and the multitude of others on Facebook who were kind, considerate, encouraging and welcoming throughout this process.

Special thanks to Madeline Martin, front cover design.

Liv's Lovely Designs, back and spine design.

Irish Ink, formatting.

And last and most appreciatively Cast a SPELL Editing, by Gina.

About the Author

Having discovered my love for writing and my crazy imagination many years ago, I put it aside for a long and successful career in the corporate world in an unrelated field.

I decided it was time to finally follow my dream of being a published author.

I live with my husband and our three fur babies. Both of my sisters refer to at least two of them as devil dogs. Unrightfully so! I have one daughter and one granddaughter.

I also enjoy photography, gardening and various DIY projects around the home. I love sunshine, the beach and making people laugh.

I currently reside in Arkansas, however I am a Native Texan, mind, body, soul and heart.

More to Come...

Please join me:

www. facebook.com/ewbrentauthor

www.ewbrentauthor.com

Twitter and Instagram

Reviews would be greatly appreciate on Amazon and Goodreads.

God bless you all.

Made in the USA
Columbia, SC
23 July 2018